Zahrah *the* Windseeker

by Nnedi Okorafor-Mbachu

Houghton Mifflin Company
Boston 2005

Illustrations by Stephanie Cooper.
The text of this book was set in Cochin.

Library of Congress Cataloging-in-Publication Data

Okorafor-Mbachu, Nnedi.
  Zahrah the Windseeker / Nnedi Okorafor-Mbachu.
    p. cm.
  Summary: Zahrah, a timid thirteen-year-old girl, undertakes a dangerous quest into the Forbidden Greeny Jungle to seek the antidote for her best friend after he is bitten by a snake, and finds knowledge, courage, and hidden powers along the way.
  ISBN 0-618-34090-4
  [1. Adventure and adventurers—Fiction. 2. Coming of age—Fiction. 3. Flight—Fiction. 4. Best friends—Fiction. 5. Jungles—Fiction. 6. Fantasy.] I. Title.
  PZ7.O4157Zah 2005
  [Fic]—dc22   2004015783

ISBN-13: 978-0618-34090-3
Manufactured in the United States of America
MP 10 9 8 7 6 5 4 3 2 1

To the late Virginia Hamilton,
who showed me that people could fly,
and my father and mother, who gave me the means to soar

The eyes of eagles see far

Zahrah the Windseeker

Dear Reader,

My name is Zahrah Tsami. This is my story. As many of you may know (and some of you may not, for who knows how far this book has come), I decided to write this book because of the stupid photos published in the Ooni Inquirer. *Anyone who would stalk two* innocent *teenagers, hide in a tree, and take pictures of them really needs to question his or her job. That's* not *journalism. Yes, it was Dari and me in those photos. Yes, I can fly. No, I am* not *a witch, a jinni, or a ghost posing as my living self. I am a* Windseeker. *My story will tell you what* really *happened. And no matter where you're from, I want you to understand it well.*

Sincerely,

Zahrah Tsami

MY WORLD

When I was born, my mother took one look at me and laughed.

"She's . . . dada," said the doctor, looking surprised.

"I can see that," my mother replied with a smile. She took me in her arms and gently touched one of the thick clumps of hair growing from my little head. I had dadalocks, and woven inside each one of those clumps was a skinny, light green vine. Contrary to what a lot of people think, these vines didn't sprout directly from my head. Instead, they were more like plants that had attached themselves to my hair as I grew inside my mother's womb. Imagine that! To be born with vines growing in your hair! But that's the nature of dada people, like myself.

"Look, she's smiling," my father said. "As if she already knows she's dada."

To many, to be dada meant you were born with strange powers. That you could walk into a room and a mysterious wind would knock things over or clocks would automatically stop; that your mere presence would cause flowers to grow underneath the soil instead of above. That you caused things to rebel or that you would grow up to be rebellious yourself! And what made things even worse was that I was a girl, and only boys and men were supposed to be rebellious. Girls were supposed to be soft, quiet, and pleasant.

Thankfully, when I was born, my parents were open-minded, well educated, and familiar with some of the older stories about dada people. These stories said that the dada-born were destined to be wise beings, not necessarily rebels. As a result, my parents didn't cut my hair, and they weren't scared by it either. Instead they let it grow and, as I got older, made sure I understood that being dada was not a curse. In fact, it was a blessing, because it was a part of me, they said. Of course I didn't feel this way when I was old enough to go to school and my classmates called me names.

Now I'm fourteen and my dada hair has grown way down my back. Also, the vines inside are thicker and dark green. Sometimes all this hair is heavy, but I'm used to it. My mother says it forces me to hold my head up higher.

❧❧❧

A large part of the culture in the northern Ooni Kingdom where I live is to look "civilized." That's northern slang for stylish. There's no way the typical northerner would go outside without wearing his or her most civilized clothes and looking clean and nice. Not even for a second.

We all carry mirrors in our pockets, and we take them out every so often to inspect our reflection and make sure we look good. On top of that, our clothes click with tiny style mirrors embedded into the collars and hems. They're really lovely. I have a dress with style mirrors sewn all over it. Sometimes when I'm alone I like to put it on and dance in the sunlight. The reflections from the little mirrors look like white insects dancing along with me.

My people love to use mirrors everywhere, actually. If you go to the downtown area of the great city of Ile-Ife, you'll understand what I'm talking about. Downtown, many giant plant towers reach high into the sky. In my history class, I learned that every year, the ten tallest plant towers grow ten inches higher and five inches wider and that they're thousands of years old.

At one time, long ago, they weren't even inhabited by human beings, as they are now. There were no elevators or computer networks or offices or living spaces inside. They were just big big plants! The Ooni Palace Tower is the tallest (standing 4,188 feet high) and oldest of them all. That's where the chief of Ooni and his council reside.

The top of the building blooms into a giant blue flower with purple petals. My father told me that this flower serves as a netevision transmitter for most of the Ooni Kingdom. Even this far north in Kirki, it's a beautiful sight, especially at night.

Anyway, from up in any of the plant towers, you can see the north with all its mirrors shining like a giant galaxy, especially on sunny days. Our homes and buildings are encrusted with thousands of mirrors, inside and out. And there's always sand in the streets from those messy trucks transporting the grains to the factories to make even more mirrors.

Some like to say that northerners are arrogant and vain. But it's just our culture. And look at the four other ethnic groups of the Ooni Kingdom. They have unique customs, too. I just find them interesting, as opposed to wrong.

The northwesterners cook all day and most of the night! Over there you can practically eat the air, and everyone is gloriously fat! The people of the southwest are as obsessed with beads as we northerners are with mirrors. People wear them everywhere: around their ankles, arms, necks, on their clothes. The people of the southeast make all things metal. I've never been there, but I hear that the people always have soot on their faces and the air is not fresh because of all the metalwork.

And northeasterners are masters of architecture and

botany, the study of plants. All the best books about plants are written by northeasterners, be they about pruning your office building or growing and maintaining the perfect personal computer from CPU seed to adult PC.

But despite all our diverse knowledge and progress here in Ooni, my dada nature and hair will never be truly accepted, not here in the north or anywhere else in Ooni. During the past two weeks, I've been doing some research, and now I'm starting to understand the reason for this prejudiced attitude.

It's not just the northern culture that made people react badly to my dada hair. It's a general fear of the unknown that plagues the entire society of the Ooni Kingdom, a discomfort with things that may have been forgotten. And maybe my hair gives people a glimpse of memories they can't quite remember. Have you ever tried to recall something but couldn't and it was right on the tip of your tongue? It's not a good feeling, is it? It's irritating, and sometimes you'd rather not remember anything at all. That's how it is here in Ooni, with the past, I think.

Our planet, Ginen, is a world of vegetation; there isn't one part of it that's not touched by plants, trees, vines, grasses, or bushes. At least this is what explorers who claim to have traveled all the way around the world say. Cutting down trees or attempting to clear plots of land is a waste of energy. Within days, things will creep back in. But the people of Ooni don't bother to fight nature. Instead, they try to team up with it. This is one of the old ways that the people of Ooni have not forgotten.

However, there are times when people avoid nature at all costs. My small town of Kirki is right on the border of the Forbidden Greeny Jungle, a vast untamed wilderness that covers thousands of miles. No one ever *thinks* of venturing there. It's full of the most savage madness. As the old saying goes, "You go into the forbidden jungle and even your ghost won't come out."

In Kirki, where fear of the unknown was strong and where so much of the past had been pushed aside and forgotten, my dada hair was like a big red badge on my forehead that said, "I don't fit in and never will." It kind of made me like the forbidden jungle.

Several months ago, I'd given up on being accepted and just wanted to be left alone. I wanted to blend in so I wouldn't be noticed. But my hair wouldn't let me. Little did I know that there was so much more in store for me. It might have started with my hair, but it certainly didn't end there.

Papa *G*rip

"Blend in?! Bah, you should never wish for things you'll never have!" Papa Grip told me not long before it all started. Papa Grip was the village chief and my grandfather's best friend. And since the day Grandfather died, he vowed to keep an eye on his best friend's family.

My parents had both tried to talk to me, and their words did help like always, but I was still upset at all the kids' teasing and taunting. When Papa Grip stopped by to invite my mother to speak at the next city council meeting (my mother was the head of the Kirki chapter of the Market Women's Association), my father called me down to say hello.

When I refused to come out of my room, my parents

explained to Papa Grip that a bad day at school was currently making me a little . . . antisocial. Papa Grip, always nosy, insisted on coming to my room to speak with me.

"Ah, how people have forgotten the old ways," he said, his voice growing dreamy and soft. "Some of our old ways are better forgotten, but not *all* of them."

I sat on my bed, refusing to remove the covers from my head. I was pretty upset and just wanted to hide. I hadn't moved since he came in.

That day, I'd finally had enough and walked out of school before classes were over. My parents had come home to several netmessages from my teachers only to find me still in my room sulking under the covers. *Why do they always have to single me out?* I thought. *Especially that ignorant Ciwanke girl. Ugh, why does she have to be so mean?*

Ciwanke, who had the roundest Afro and the greatest number of friends in my entire grade, would gather many of those friends at least twice a week, track me down in the hallway, and lead a chant. "Vine head, vine head, how long will it grooo-oooow!" That day Ciwanke had laughed loudly after their little song and shouted, "Go live in the trees, since your hair grows like their leaves, all wild and dirty! Hee-hee! That way, you won't be around us, causing all that bad luck!"

All the other girls burst out laughing, and Ciwanke slapped hands with each of them. Then they walked away, leaving me humiliated. Of course, through the whole thing I was silent. What could I say without sounding silly and pathetic? I wasn't good at hurling insults, even to defend myself.

"Vine head," "snake lady," "swamp witch," and "freak" were names I heard almost every day. Though I knew I shouldn't have cared, the words still hurt like pinches. And pinches can be very painful when done in the same place many times in a row. The classmates who didn't make fun of me didn't defend me, either. Except my best friend, Dari. My only friend.

"Why can't they just leave me alone?" I whispered from under the covers.

"Why should it matter?" Papa Grip asked. *Good question,* I thought. *It shouldn't, but it does.* I heard him stand up. "Let me take those sheets off your head, so we can talk face to face."

I sighed but let him. I loved Papa Grip. Everyone did. Aside from being like a grandfather to me, he was the reason Kirki didn't have any armed robbers, murderers, or untidy streets. Papa Grip knew how to mediate between groups. He knew how to organize and make sure everyone was happy. He wove peace and understanding with his bare hands.

"Look at these things," Papa Grip said, taking one of my locks in his hand. "Look strange, no?"

I nodded.

"Like the vines that grow in the trees. Like dangerous serpents! Wild and *rebellious*," he shouted, dramatically flinging his hands in the air. He took a deep breath and smiled broadly at me, his wrinkly dark brown skin bunching around his cheeks. "Look, child, they're a part of you. Accept them. Mark my words: there's nothing wrong with being different."

He stood up.

"Look at me, I am the chief of Kirki, but I like to wear hot pink caftans!" he exclaimed, dancing over to the large mirror that spanned my bedroom wall. He danced in a circle, his bright pink clothing billowing out as he twirled.

I giggled despite my sadness. Papa Grip was funny. He was the only man I or anyone knew who loved to wear hot pink. And Papa Grip was a great dancer. Even though he was old, he was the one at the party who never left the dance floor until the night was over. I envied him because I was too shy to go out there and dance for even five minutes.

"You were born dada. Embrace it," he said. "There aren't many of you in Ooni. You're the first ever born in this town! Be proud. Didn't your parents tell you that anyone born dada is destined to be a wise man or woman?"

"People say that I make things go wrong."

"Nonsense!" he said. "Silly superstition. There's nothing wrong with you. Wisdom is sprouting in your heart. That's obvious. You have lots to look forward to, young woman."

I didn't feel wise at all. And I definitely wasn't a woman. I was only thirteen years old. And regardless of what Papa Grip said, my hair would still make me the laughingstock at school.

"Look at yourself in that mirror," Papa Grip said. "What does your mind tell you?"

I glanced at my image in the large mirror on my bedroom wall. I looked away, focusing on the brown-green wall, and pouted. "I dunno. I see . . . me."

Just looking at myself made me think of all the horrible names.

"You barely looked," said Papa Grip. "Get up, come stand next to me, and *really* look."

I slowly got up and stood next to Papa Grip.

"Do you look like this so-called monster so many of your classmates seem to think you are?"

I stared at the long coarse ropes of hair on my head that I'd had since I was born. The hair that made my mother smile the day I was born. The hair that was so different from everyone else's. I looked at my feet and shrugged.

"I look OK, I guess," I mumbled. "I just don't understand why other people think I don't."

"Come on, dada girl, you want to cut your hair? Because we can arrange that if you like," Papa Grip said with a smirk.

"No!" I exclaimed before I could stop myself. It was a knee-jerk response. I didn't quite know why, but the idea of cutting my hair always bothered me. "I mean . . . I . . ."

"You don't have to explain." Papa Grip chuckled. "It's OK to care about what other people think, but you should give a little more weight to what you, yourself, think."

I sat considering this as Papa Grip got up to leave.

"The habit of thinking is the habit of gaining strength," he said as he closed the door behind him. "You're stronger than you believe."

When I was sure he was gone, I put the cover back over my head and sighed. *If only life were really so easy and made that kind of sense,* I thought. Under the cover I batted one of my locks out of my face.

$\mathcal{D}$ARI

"That Ciwanke girl can kiss my backside," my friend Dari said. "Want me to tell her that?"

I smiled, looking straight ahead.

"No," I said, though I wasn't quite sure. I knew Dari would do it.

Dari was a joker and one of the more popular kids at school. But he was also my guardian in some ways. If other students made fun of me when he was around, he always jumped to my side to defend me. I really appreciated that.

In general, I was a pretty quiet girl. I preferred to sit and think about things rather than talk to people about them. Except when it came to Dari.

Dari and I had met on the playground when we were

both seven years old. I was sitting by myself on a bench looking at the Forbidden Greeny Jungle in the distance. From where I sat, I could see the last building of Kirki and then the looming dense wall of palm, iroko, mahogany, and eke trees and goodness knew what others.

I was pondering over what lay inside the jungle. *How come no one ever goes too far into it?* I wondered. Hunters and explorers went in every once in a while, but they rarely came back, and when they did, they were usually crazy. I knew I wasn't supposed to think about the forbidden jungle, but I couldn't help being curious.

Then Dari walked up to me in that bold way of his and loudly asked, "Why do you sit there?"

I looked up, my thoughts broken.

"What?" I said, straightening out the hem of my dress. I pushed one of my thick dadalocks out of my face. The piece of palm fiber I was using to tie my hair back had broken earlier in the day.

"Why do you sit there?" he repeated.

I only shrugged and looked away, hoping he would just ignore me like the other children always did. He didn't go away.

"Why is your hair like that?" he asked.

I sighed and rolled my eyes. Even at the age of seven, that question was not new to me. I shrugged again and continued hoping he'd go away. Instead he put his hands on his narrow hips and kept talking.

"My mother said that *my* hair could cut steel, that's why she shaves it so close," he said, running his hand over his practically bald head. It was such a funny thing to say. When I smiled and looked him in the eye, in that moment, we became friends.

"Dari?" We were almost at school now.

"Mmm?"

I paused. I knew I could trust him. But the things on my mind were *very* personal. And I didn't quite understand it all myself. All I knew was that something was happening to me. For days, things had been . . . moving around me. Or so it seemed. Everywhere I went there was a breeze. Even when I was inside, it was like there was a window open nearby. My homework would get blown around, or I'd step out of the shower and a cool breeze would send me scrabbling for a towel. I was scared that maybe all the bad rumors about being dada were coming true!

I stopped walking. I knew I wouldn't say a word once we got to school.

"Dari, can you keep a secret?" I asked, my heart beating fast.

"Always," he said, checking himself out in his mirror. Then he looked me in the eye. I knew I could trust him. I could always trust Dari. "What is it, Zahrah?"

I held my breath, trying to urge the words out of my mouth. Then I shrugged and looked away, deciding not to tell him. I needed to think about it some more first.

"Nothing," I said. "I was just . . . thinking, that's all."

Dari looked at me for a long time. Then he opened his mouth as if to say something. He closed it. Dari knew me too well. If he tried to talk me into telling him, I'd only re-treat more. He knew it was better to wait for me to talk.

"OK," he said. "Thinking is good."

I sighed and hiked my backpack higher up my shoul-ders. I didn't really know what was going on; all I knew was that whatever was going on was extremely strange. And then something even stranger had happened.

I'll tell him when I figure it out, I thought. *Yeah, that's what I'll do.*

CHAPTER 3

OLD *W*AYS

If I only knew then what I know now.

The reason I didn't understand what was going on was that such a thing had never happened to anyone in the history of my entire town! Kirki was only four hundred years old, but that's still a long time to me. I was experiencing one of the "old ways." Something people thousands of years ago used to experience quite often. Something that was once normal but was now quite strange. Stranger than my dadalocks!

Few people remembered such old ways. My hometown was not a place where people liked to look too closely or deeply at what had happened centuries or millennia ago. When people wanted answers, they looked up their question on the network and got an answer. People didn't really care where the answer came from. As long as it was "correct," which really meant as long as things made some sort of sense and weren't too complicated. We liked to focus on how we could get ahead, further into the future, and we ignored the past. So I had no point of reference for what was happening to me.

It all started after my mother left my room that night. Well, maybe it really started before that with the breeze that had followed me around since the morning. Still, when I got home from school, I temporarily forgot about the strange breeze because when I went to the bathroom, I discovered that I was bleeding!

It didn't hurt, but still I was afraid and ran to tell my mother. I remembered the things we had been taught in school about menstruation. But things are always different when they actually happen to you. After my mother explained, I realized all was well and normal. Then I realized that because I had gotten my menses, my mother would prepare a delicious feast, and everything was fine. No, actually, it was great! I stuffed myself with candied plantain, mango slices, rice and red stew with big chunks of goat meat, all my favorites. Afterward, my father gave me his gift, which he had run out to the market to buy as I was eating: the latest installment of the Cosmic Chukwu Crusader Series. He also gave me a whole blue petri flower! That's ten petals! Enough to buy several style mirrors and some sweet treats and still have some money left over!

I squealed and threw my arms around my father.

"Thank you, Papa! I didn't even know it was out yet!" I said.

I couldn't wait to pop the disk into my computer and read about my favorite superhero's next adventure. Rumor had it that the Cosmic Chukwu Crusader would meet his greatest challenge yet, the Wild and Crazy Universoul Lady.

Later that night, I shut my door and climbed into bed. I had a slight bellyache, but I had too much to think about to really care. Plus my mother said that such a thing was normal. I closed my eyes, smelling the sweet scent of the blue burstflower that grew up my windowsill.

It was my first night of physically being a woman. It was like being in a new body and in a new bed. I fidgeted for a while, trying to get comfortable. My eyes were closed, and I was almost asleep when things suddenly became strange.

At first, it was just that annoyingly mysterious soft breeze blowing about my room. Then my skin began to feel tingly and itchy, the way a scab feels right before it falls off to reveal new skin. I scratched my arms and legs but still felt irritated. Then I, *myself*, felt light and breezy, like a feather swept high into the air by the wind. Then slowly, I began to rise off the bed!!

At first I thought I was dreaming.

I was terrified of heights. As a matter of fact, just the

thought of the great city made me nauseous. The buildings and towers were so tall, and the idea of being inside them, way up in the sky, made me want to sink to the floor with my hands over my head.

Nevertheless, when I slept I often dreamed of the very thing I feared. Being in the sky. But in my dream, I flew about, circling the great city towers, even as high as the Ooni Palace. I woke from these dreams with my heart beating fast, feeling horrified but exhilarated. It didn't make sense.

However, what happened that night was different. I was awake, wide awake.

"What . . . ?"

I felt for the bed but reached several inches below me before I found it. Slowly, I looked around. My room was dark, lit only by the moonlight, but I could see myself in the large mirror next to my bed. It was the most eerie sight. My hair and bed sheets were hanging down as I floated above my bed. Immediately, I dropped down onto it with a thud.

"Oof!" I said, rolling onto my side and then jumping to my feet. "What the . . . ?!"

I stood there in the middle of my room, my legs slightly bent, prepared to run away from whatever was coming after me. I don't know why I thought something was after me. There were no noises in my room, other than the sound of flapping paper as the breeze continued to blow about. But still, I had this feeling. When I think about it now, I wonder if it was a premonition of the near future.

I slowly climbed back into bed. Maybe it was just a really vivid dream.

Yes, a dream, I thought drowsily. I was extremely tired from all the excitement of the day, and my eyes quickly grew heavy. I lay back down and tried to get comfortable. The minute my body relaxed, the breeze started again. This time, I was sure I was awake. I looked around but didn't move. I held my breath.

And then I felt it, right through my covers: a soft current of air circulating around me. Then I started to rise! I rose about two inches from my bed. The current of air lightly blew underneath my long yellow nightgown.

"Oh my," I whispered breathlessly. I tried to wiggle my toes, and I dropped down again. I frowned. I wasn't one to kid myself when something was obvious. This was really happening. *But why?* I wondered. *And . . . can I make it happen? If so, how?*

I considered calling my mother. But instead I licked my lips and took a deep breath. Then I concentrated on the air current.

I imagined the breeze to be a light blue friendly mist surrounding me and slowly lifting me off the bed. Nothing happened. Even the breeze died down.

I just lay there for several minutes, confused. Then I

15

tried again. Still nothing happened. By the third try, I was slightly disillusioned, and I visualized the blue mist with little hope of anything happening. I was relaxed and nonchalant. Suddenly, the breeze quickly returned as did the circulating air.

Easily, I floated a little higher. I urged myself to go higher and higher until I realized that I didn't know how to stop or get down! Nothing was supporting me, and there was nothing to grab on to. The moment panic set in, I plopped back onto my bed.

I blinked and looked around. *What's happening to me?* I thought. I looked around my small bedroom again. I had several potted leafy green plants growing in the windowsill and another leafy green plant growing out of the wall around my large mirror. I could see my desk weighed down with my schoolbooks. Everything looked normal. I concentrated and tried again. Nothing.

Then I just lay thinking and thinking and thinking. I didn't sleep much that night. And when I did, I dreamed of flying.

THE DARK MARKET

A few days later, I stopped just outside the market.

I leaned against a large tree and pulled off the piece of twine holding my hair together. I wanted to scratch my scalp, but I knew there were people already staring at my freed dadalocks. If they only knew that my hair was far from the most peculiar thing about me. Since that first night, the floating thing had happened several times. Actually, I'd *made* it happen.

The night before I even did it on the first try, and I managed to float halfway to the ceiling! I was too scared to go much higher. Always, the minute I lost concentration or got nervous, I'd plop down. I can't convey to you what it felt like to be able to do something so odd and impossible.

But at the time, all I could think of was my dry itchy scalp and the fact that it wasn't polite to scratch it. The day before, I'd washed it before I realized I'd run out of the rose oil I always used afterward. By lunchtime at school, my hair had finally dried, but boy was my scalp itchy!

"Just scratch your head if you want to!" Dari had exclaimed at school. "Why do you torture yourself?" Then he'd dug his hands into my hair and scratched until I was crying with laughter. Dari usually came with me to visit my mother at the market, but that day he'd had too many chores to do.

I shook out my hair, and that gave me a little relief. Then I retied the twine, brought out my mirror from my backpack, and made sure I looked OK. My hair was neat, and my long green dress was spotless and unwrinkled. I smiled at myself in my mirror. I avoided looking at my dadalocks. Even if they were neatly tied back, they were only a blemish to my appearance. Still, I looked nice and civilized.

The oldest tree in Kirki, a tall, tall iroko tree whose top was seen only by the birds and the army of leaf-cutter branch hoppers that took care of it marked the entrance of the market. I tapped its trunk as I passed. To do so brought good luck.

The market was busy as always, and I was glad to quickly be swallowed into it. My mother's fruit stand was on the far left side, which gave me plenty of time to listen to arguments and discussions along the way. The market was always full of life. Tomatoes, videophones, both hydrogen and flora-powered cars, netevisions, clothes, crude leather, digi-books, leaf-clipping and -mending beetles, paper books, all species of CPU seeds, from the most expensive to the cheap—one could find anything at the market if one knew where to look. I walked slowly, as I always did, taking in all that was around me.

A man wearing a long white caftan was standing in his market space, looking miserable. He was selling every kind of music one could think of on flash disk: Highlife, Hip-Pocalypso, Tree Rhythm, Spice Soul, Hip-Hop, Ju Ju Funk, Jungle, and everything in between. At that moment, he was blasting Highlife on his flash disk player to attract customers. Normally one would be happy to work around such music, but this man looked as if his dog had just died. I found myself smiling and walking to the beat as I passed him. I giggled to myself, trying not to look him in the eye.

The reason he was miserable was that his music had attracted a swarm of rhythm beetles, and an insect party was going on above the man's head. Several landed on his arms and in his thick Afro. He swatted at them in annoyance as a customer handed him a flash disk she wanted to purchase.

Most of the beetles were crowded on his umbrella; they were raising their shiny black wings and shaking their behinds to the beat of the music. Some of them had even landed on the flash disk player to dance. *He must be used to them,* I thought. Though rhythm beetles were more active at night, they were attracted to music like moths to bright lights.

I moved on, inhaling the smells around me, and for the moment I forgot about the strangeness of the last few days. Perfume, sweat, cooked meat, leaves, soil, fruit — there was a bit of everything. I loved the hustle and bustle that went on whether I was there or not. I smiled when I saw my mother sitting among her pyramids of oranges, mangoes, and lychee fruits. The lychee fruits were my favorite.

The small round fruits had thin brown skins that were easily peeled to reveal the sweet white fruit. I could never get enough of sucking the soft fruit from the brown smooth seed in the middle. My mother bought all her fruit from a family connection at the farms on the fringes of the Forbidden Greeny Jungle. So it was always the best. Sometimes I'd pop one in my mouth and peel the fruit with my tongue! My mother would always yell at me when she saw me doing it. She said it was unladylike the way I spat out the fruit skin. Of course I did this only at home, never in public.

"Good afternoon, Mama," I said, walking around the fruits and setting down my backpack. I sat on the small wooden stool.

"Good afternoon," said my mother. "How was school?"

I shrugged. "The usual."

"Are you feeling fine?" she asked. I had been feeling slightly queasy and crampy since the day before. In the morning, my mother had me eat a mango and drink some warmed goat milk sweetened with honey. It helped.

I nodded. The coming of my menses was not as much of an ordeal as I thought it would be. Once my mother showed me what to do and I realized it was just a part of life, it really was no big deal at all. What *was* a big deal was the fact that I could float in the air when I chose to. And sometimes when I didn't.

A breeze picked up around me and I felt my stomach rise. I could feel myself lifting slightly. Luckily my mother's back was turned.

"I have a lot of homework," I said, grabbing the stool and pulling myself back down.

"Nothing you cannot handle?" my mother asked.

The breeze continued, but I was able to keep myself on the ground.

I smiled and said, "No. Nothing I can't handle."

"Good. Now, go buy me a bag of cashew fruit and some light bulbs," my mother said, handing me two petri

21

flowers. The red flowers were about the size of my hand. They each had five petals. "That should be more than enough."

"OK."

"Be quick. I need you to sort this fresh batch of lychee fruit."

I got up and said, "Is it OK if I buy some rose oil, assuming I use some of my gift money?"

"Just be quick."

I nodded.

"I hope I can find it," I said. "The lady who sells it is always moving her stand around."

"That's bad for business," my mother said, turning to a new customer. She smiled at the woman and asked, "Can I help you?"

"I'll be back, Mama," I said, stepping into the milling crowd.

I loved being by myself in the market with money in my pocket. Everything I could afford suddenly looked brighter. And I loved the feeling of being on a mission. It was almost like being someone else, someone who was capable of anything. My mother could always rely on me. It didn't take long to get the cashew fruits and the light bulbs. Like my mother, both sellers had kept their stands in the same place for years.

"You look nice, Zahrah," the woman who sold light bulbs said. Her daughter was the annoying Ciwanke

Mairiga from school, my worst harasser. Nevertheless, unlike her daughter, she was quite nice.

"Thank you, madam," I said. "So do you."

"How is your father? Your mother?" Mrs. Mairiga asked.

"They're fine, madam," I said, taking the potted light bulbs. The light bulbs were buried in the cups of soil, though I could still see their glow. My mother was the best at coaxing the light-producing plants into the walls at home. "Do you know where the oil lady is today?"

"I think she's in the Dark Market," Mrs. Mairiga said apologetically. "Sorry. You'll probably find her elsewhere tomorrow."

I frowned, my shoulders drooping. The Dark Market was where the strangest market items were sold, like stockfish teeth, six-legged dogs, and juju magic potions. You could even buy dream ticks, insects that bit you and injected an opiate into your blood that was fifty times stronger than the one used in hospitals . . . among other darker items. My parents always warned me not to go there, and I never had. Dari, on the other hand, had sneaked into the Dark Market several times.

"I don't just blindly believe everything I hear," he would say. "I need a good reason. And no one could give me one when it came to the Dark Market, except, 'Oh, it's a bad place.' Why?! That's not good enough," he'd said after the first time. "I needed to see for myself." He crept closer to me with a mischievous grin on his face, a small brown sack in his hands. "And you know what, Zahrah? It was great! Look at these!"

He held the sack up to my face and I peered in. The smell that came from it made me sneeze. Then I gasped.

"Personal pepper seeds!? Dari!"

He laughed with glee and I frowned with disapproval. Not only had he gone to a place that every parent told his or her child not to go, but he'd also *bought* something there!

"Hey, I had to have something to prove that I went," he said, still grinning. "Plus I didn't go very far. I just bought the first thing I could afford."

"Well, you certainly don't need those," I said.

If you grew and ate your own personal pepper, you became socially spicy; people laughed more at your jokes, found you more attractive, wanted to be around you more. Basically, you cultivated more popularity. But you had to beware of eating *someone else's* personal pepper. That could be fatal! Thus the seeds were sold only in places like the Dark Market. Still, personal peppers were a favorite among politicians, pop stars, and car salesmen. Oddly enough, when Dari planted his personal pepper seeds, they never grew. I guess Dari already had enough personal spice. I suspected that the results would have been different if I tried to grow them.

After buying the cashew fruits for my mother, I stood thinking about what I should do. I'd never been in the Dark Market, so, like Dari said, how did I really know it was so awful? But Mama and Papa had forbidden me to go there. Still, I wanted that hair oil *today*. I couldn't bear another day of school with this itching. Why did the oil lady have to move around like this? And Dari *had* been there many times and come out just fine. In that moment, I concluded that the Dark Market couldn't be that bad. Or it couldn't be as bad as my desperately itchy scalp. *I'll run in, get the oil, and be out so quickly that it will be as if I haven't been there at all,* I thought.

The way to the Dark Market was known by word of mouth, but with parents guarding their children's ears, it wasn't likely that any child would even know the way, let alone go there. But Dari had overheard his uncle and father talking about it one day.

"My uncle Osundu lives in the southwest and owns an auto parts business," Dari told me. "But that morning I learned that he sold other, more exotic things too. He'd come to the north to buy some kind of potion ingredient at the Dark Market. I happened to be coming down the stairs when my father was telling him how to get there."

I knew I shouldn't have encouraged Dari to continue talking, but I couldn't help myself. I was curious.

"So . . . how *do* you get there?" I asked.

He'd grinned, and I knew the damage was done. Dari now knew that some part of me envied him for going.

"Well," he said. "It's simple, really. It's at the center of the market."

I frowned.

"No," I said. "The meat section is."

Dari shook his head with a sly grin.

"That's what parents tell their kids," he said. "If you go to the meat section, you'll see that behind all the sellers is a thick green tarp. Well, it's not space that's behind that tarp."

He laughed as my eyebrows went up with understanding. All this time the Dark Market had been that easy to find. That available.

"Uh-huh," he said. "And there's only one entrance, on the side where they sell live fowl. A dark green veil covers it. When you lift it aside, you'll see that the veil is really soft, like expensive silk!"

So there I stood in the market with my itchy scalp. I looked around, hoping no one had noticed me standing there. I quickly reached into my pocket and touched the money. I looked around again. There were a lot of people, but no one was paying any attention to me. I started walking toward the center of the market.

Though I wasn't facing the sun, I wished I had sunglasses. It wasn't the worst time of the day to be in the section where mirrors were sold, but it wasn't the best either.

The best time was dusk. The mirror section was the only area of the market that was allowed to stay open past five p.m. As I walked, I passed many baskets full of tiny style mirrors of all shapes and sizes. There were even more rows of mirrors with organic backs designed specifically to grow into house walls.

Soon, the air became heavy with flies as I came upon the part of the market where meat was sold. This was the first time I stopped there. Usually, I walked past it as fast as I could. My father usually bought the meat, so I had no reason to go there. My father didn't mind the flies, and he loved the variety he could choose from. My mother, who did most of the other shopping, didn't complain and neither did I.

All around me were chopping blocks. Slabs of red, pink, yellow, and purple meat were draped from vines, cracked clams and filleted fish were piled on ice, and there were bowls of meat spices like curry and bitter leaf sauce. The air smelled coppery from all the blood, and I felt nauseous. As I walked, I thought about where I was heading. *What will the Dark Market be like?* I wondered with a chill of excitement. *Will it look like the rest of the market, except for the items sold? Or will there be a magical overcast of clouds hovering above it? And what will the people there be like? They can't be much different from the other people in the rest of the market.*

Though I slowed my pace, I kept walking.

I finally approached the place where live fowl were

sold. I stopped and looked around. One man sold bush fowl and chickens of all sizes, from tiny enough to fit in the palm of my hand to the size of a large dog. Next to him, a woman sold rare Gunson birds, disheveled-looking brown and black birds with long legs. But she had to keep them in a special pen because though they were tall, they were scrawny and weak and other birds liked to peck at their legs. A man was selling candy birds, large, red, chickenlike fowl fed only caramel squares and sugar toast. Behind all of them, I could see the mysterious green tarp that I'd never thought twice about.

I softly gasped. This was it. Between a woman selling smoked owl meat and the man selling candy birds, there was a break in the tarp. An entrance covered by a veil that fluttered in the soft breeze. I slowly walked toward the Dark Market entrance.

I gazed up at the ten-foot-high entrance and looked behind me and then at the woman selling owl meat. I wrinkled my nose. The meat she was selling didn't smell very tasty at all. She wasn't paying any attention to me. *Good*, I thought, *no one's watching*. I reached out and touched the veil. Dari was right. It did feel as if it were made of the finest silk. Hundreds of people must have pushed it aside every day, and there wasn't an oil stain or tear on any part of it. I went in.

The market that I had known all my life was open-air;

everything was out and under the sun. But this part of the market, the Dark Market, was surrounded by a group of high trees. The large blackish green tarp hung from the trees, blocking out the sun. Circles had even been cut in it to let the trees grow through. I stopped for a moment, waiting for my eyes to adjust to the dimness of the shade. Now I knew where the Dark Market got its name.

Did I want the hair oil *this* much? I thought and considered turning back. But . . . I was curious. I thought about what Dari had said about seeing for yourself if it was so bad, and I had to agree with him.

I blinked and looked around, hearing my mother's voice in my head: "The Dark Market is where thieves, con artists, evil magicians, and shady people do business. There are things there that you can't explain; some are fascinating but most are dangerous. Keep your distance from that place, Zahrah." That was what my mother had told me years ago, when she first brought me to the market.

A lot of good her advice had done. I knew the Dark Market was not safe, but yet there I stood. I was scared and already felt guilty, but my legs began to move. Feathers of different shapes and sizes from the bird section blew around me as I took my first steps into the Dark Market.

Once I was under the tarp, the air grew stuffy. *The Dark Market must have a lot to hide,* I thought with a shiver of anticipation. The air seemed to grow clearer as I moved farther in. That was when I understood; the Dark Market was only for those who wished to enter. Not for cowardly outsiders.

I stopped and looked around, taking it all in. I crossed my arms around my chest as if to protect myself. I felt shivers of rebellious excitement. Above me, the green tarp billowed with the gentle breeze. There was a small nest of green toucans in one of the trees' lower dead branches. They whistled and chattered loudly, but no one seemed to notice them . . . except me.

Like the rest of the market, the red dirt path before me was narrow, with booths and tables set close to one another on both sides. To my left, a man with a patch over his left eye and tightly braided cornrows stood behind a table selling live vultures! Some of the vultures stood miserably on the table, their talons clacking whenever they took a step, and others were perched on thick black sticks.

What do people do with live vultures? I wondered, looking at the birds' oily black wings, vulnerably bald necks, and red heads. They can't possibly *eat* them! Ugh! I rubbed my arms, frowning with disgust. Vultures lived off the dead and decaying! The man grinned at me as I passed, and I saw that all his teeth were stained green. I bit my lip. In school, we'd learned about drugs and how terrible they were. But never had I met or even seen anyone who actually *did* drugs. Until then. This man was probably addicted to mystic moss. I politely smiled back, hoping I didn't look as scared as I felt.

Next to him, a root woman waited to tell fortunes. Now root workers, I had seen before. This one was dressed in a wide bright orange billowing dress with hundreds of tiny style mirrors embedded all over it. She clicked with every move. It was quite a lovely and civilized dress and probably very expensive. I was glad she was in the process of telling someone's fortune. Root workers have a reputation for harassing passersby by shouting out one's most embarrassing problems until one gave in to having his or her fortune told. Plus the preoccupation with her customer gave me a chance to get a good look at the dress.

I passed a man who illustrated ghosts. "Update that portrait of your beloved passed-on relative! You bring 'em, I see and draw 'em! Only one blue petri flower," he announced. Two women were selling different-colored dung-scented inks. Pew! A man claimed he could exorcise haunted computers. And of course I saw several people selling the worst kinds of poisons: poisons that caused a slow death, instant death, amnesia, comas, terrible pain, a loss of one's mind, a loss of physical control, and the most horrible hallucinations. I didn't pass too many booths selling antidotes to poisons though.

The heavy air must have changed scents with every ten steps I took. From camel dung to scented oil to incense to flowers to garbage. It was all very exotic. Though I was still afraid, I was beginning to understand why Dari would go there despite all the warnings. Imagine what you could buy with a few tiny petri flowers!

Still, I didn't see the oil lady anywhere. So I walked farther in.

The people shopping in the Dark Market were of every type: men, women, young, old, tall, short, happy and sad looking, nervous like me, and bold as if they went there every day. The only thing they all had in common was that no one made eye contact and everyone walked quickly with a strong look of purpose. It seemed that everyone wanted to be there but not for longer than he or she had to.

I crept along, trying to stay as far from each stand as possible. The merchants seemed to be selling stranger and stranger items the farther into the market I got, and I was quickly losing my courage. A man selling brown toads the size of dogs didn't even make a move when one of his toads flicked its tongue at a fly zooming by an inch from my face! Such toads were used for ridding homes of flies, ants, and spiders and were employed for only the worst infestations. Dari had heard terrible stories about these toads eating small children.

I sneezed as I walked past three men selling personal pepper seeds. I paused, contemplating buying some. *It would be nice to have more friends,* I thought. *Or at least have people be nicer to me.* Then I shook my head. *What am I thinking? I shouldn't even be here! And how bad it would be to buy them with the gift money from Papa for becoming a woman!*

Before I could ask someone where the oil lady was stationed, I was cursed at by a caged wood gripe, solicited by a computer with a large flowering monitor that claimed to channel another world through the network, and then hit by a spout of water from a singing fish swimming in a large green half pod filled with water. The seller next to the pod laughed loudly, and the pink fish lifted its mouth out of the water to sing a tune that, despite my shock, I had to admit was very pretty. My hands were shaking as I walked up to the first person that I got a good feeling about.

"E-e-excuse me, madam, can you tell me where the oil lady might be today?" I asked, stepping up to a tall, tall woman with dark brown skin. She leaned against a tree smoking a cigarette. Her head was shaved so close that she looked bald. She had a strange, elaborate symbol tattooed just below her neck. Behind her were several peaceful-looking large baboons, sitting cross-legged on the ground.

They were scratching complex symbols in the dirt and on pieces of paper. I stared at them, forgetting my question. I had never seen baboons in real life. I'd heard that baboons, gorillas, and all other types of monkeys were as intelligent as human beings or more so. These seemed like the latter. The symbols they drew were so pretty. Loops, swirls, lines; they were little artists!

The woman blew smoke in my face and I coughed.

"Where are your parents, dada girl?" the woman asked in a smooth voice that reminded me of thick orange mango juice.

"Um . . . well . . ." I said, my eye still on the amazing baboons. "My mother works back in the fruit section—"

"If I tell you where the oil lady is, will you go to your mother right afterward?"

I vigorously nodded my head. I was more than ready to leave the Dark Market. I had already spent more time there than I planned and was starting to wonder if I was going to get in trouble. And I was sure that I had come farther than Dari had on his first visit.

The woman pointed to my left.

"Go that way," she said. "She's stationed next to Deloris, the woman selling the dried and live bush hoppers."

"Thank you," I said.

"Oil for your hair?"

I nodded.

The woman smiled.

"You can always do what I did. Especially when it gets too long," she said, rubbing her close-to-bald head. My jaw dropped.

"You . . . cut your dada hair?"

"My mother and father are still angry," she said with a smirk.

"Why did you do it?" I asked. I couldn't believe it. Couldn't imagine it.

"Why not?"

"Was it because people . . . gave you a bad time?" I asked.

She laughed.

"Do people give you a bad time?"

I nodded.

"People will always be difficult when it comes to being dada," she said. "We're more connected to the trees and plants." She smiled, looking up at the Dark Market's green tarp. "And the sky. We're born with memories of long ago."

I didn't really understand what she was saying. And she seemed to notice the confusion on my face.

"Hey, if you're lucky, your greatest problem will be people making fun of you," she said. "Most likely that's all you'll have to overcome, and that's no big deal, really."

"Yeah, I guess," I said with a weak smile.

We stood looking at each other for a moment. One of the baboons made a clicking sound behind the woman and handed her a piece of paper. She looked at what the baboon had scribbled.

"No, I don't think so," she said. All of the baboons waved their sticks and pens in the air. But the woman shook her head again and said, "Not likely."

Then she turned back to me.

"What's your name?"

"Zahrah."

"My name is Nsibidi," she said. "Come and see me sometime, if you're not too scared to return. The idiok seem to like you. Now, go find your oil."

CHAPTER 5

THE $\mathcal{S}$OFT PARADE

I pushed open my window and took a deep breath. It was one of those warm nights when the wind makes music in the treetops. I turned and looked at myself in my bedroom mirror and smiled at my long white dress. The nightgown was old, but it was my favorite. The material was silky like water. Such clothes were never uncivilized.

I sat on the floor facing the window with my flora computer in my lap. My father had given me the CPU seed when I was seven years old, and I had planted and taken care of it all by myself. It was my first responsibility. My flora computer had grown nicely because of my care. Its light green pod body was slightly yielding, and the large traceboard leaf fit on my lap like a part of my own body. The screen was large and oval, a shape that I had always found soothing. The computer would pull energy from my body heat, and I'd link a vine around my ear so that it could read my brain waves. It would grow in size and complexity, as I grew.

"Music," I said as I looked out the window and touched the traceboard. "The Soft Parade."

I shut my eyes as my computer started to play "Reedy Bells," the Soft Parade's best song. It was an instrumental tune with gentle drumbeats and three birdlike flutes. I always liked to listen to this particular song on windy days. Not surprisingly, a rhythm beetle flew in to enjoy the music. I didn't bother trying to shoo it out. As long as it was only *one* beetle, I was fine.

I could hear my parents chatting away downstairs. There had been a town meeting about this year's yam festival, and once again Papa Grip gave a wonderful speech. Or so I heard my parents saying. I hadn't gone because it was a school night.

"Dari," I said to my computer. The screen turned a light purple, and a few moments later, Dari's face appeared in a small box on the upper right-hand corner of my screen.

"Good evening," he said, straightening his long blue nightshirt and pants. He glanced at himself in the mirror behind him to make sure he looked good. Then he said,

"Just a minute. I'm cleaning my room. Almost done. Gimme two minutes."

"OK."

When I saw him turn around and walk to his closet to hang up his clothes, I set my computer on the floor and went to my dresser. I opened the pink slender bottle of rose oil, squirted some onto my palm, and massaged it into my hair.

"You won't believe where I went today," I said proudly. My door was closed and my parents were talking, so I wasn't worried about them hearing.

"Where?"

"The Dark Market!"

There was silence, and then I heard scrambling as Dari ran back to his computer and sat on his bed. The picture shook as he put it on his lap.

"What? You're kidding! Forget your hair! Get over here and talk!"

I laughed, running back to my computer and setting it on my lap. I turned my music down a bit and maximized Dari's face to the size of my entire screen.

"Dari, it *is* a magical place," I whispered, looking out the window at the blowing trees. I had been terrified when I was there, but after I got home and was able to sit and think about it, I realized that the Dark Market was wonderful. There was strange magic and even stranger people. And because I wasn't supposed to be there, well, underneath the guilt, I was excited.

"See? How many times have I told you," Dari said, grinning widely.

"I know. But I was so scared."

"Of course you were scared," Dari said. "It's a scary place! Why'd you go, anyway?"

I laughed and shook my head. "I needed oil for my hair, and the oil lady was stationed there today."

"How far in did you go?"

"Far, kind of. I dunno. What's far?"

Dari paused to think. "Did you see the man selling mirrors that show jinn if you look into them?"

My eyebrows rose.

"No! Thank goodness."

"I didn't think so. It would have been the first thing you told me about. He's near the middle," Dari said. "He likes to trick people into looking at his mirrors by telling them they have something on their face."

"Oh how cruel!"

"Did you see the lady selling the bush hoppers?"

"Yes," I said grinning. "She was next to the oil lady today."

"Wow, you went much farther than I did my first time!"

"I thought about buying one of them. I've never seen them before."

"Don't bother," Dari said. "Bush hoppers are neat, but they're just like grasshoppers; the first chance they get they escape. And since those things can jump over two thousand feet in the air, you won't be able to recapture them."

"Wow!" I said, fascinated. "I wish I had bought one anyway."

"You can buy one the next time we go," he said.

I grinned but didn't say anything. I wasn't sure if I wanted to go there again.

"So what else did you see?"

"There was a fish who spat water at me and sang like a rainbow spirit," I said, leaning back. "The man selling it laughed so hard, he almost fell out of his seat. And I saw where they sell the personal peppers, and . . . oh! How could I forget, there was a woman with many baboons! She was beautiful but not in the usual way."

"I've seen her," said Dari.

I frowned and bit my lip. "You have? Are you sure?"

Dari nodded. "She has really short hair, and some marking just below her neck."

"Yeah, that's her," I said. "I stopped and asked her if she knew where the oil lady was, and then she talked to me a bit . . . did you know she is dada?"

Saying the word made me think about my ability to float. I hadn't thought about it since I'd gone into the Dark Market. All the strangeness there made my own strangeness seem normal, almost forgettable. But now it bothered me again.

"Really? No, that can't be right, she doesn't—"

I said, "She cut hers."

"No," Dari said.

"Yes."

Dari ran his hand over his rough hair.

"Her hair is shorter than *mine*," said Dari.

"Yeah."

"That's sad," he said. He paused and then shrugged. "Maybe she just wanted to be normal. No. She still stood out, from what I remember."

We both sat there for a moment, quiet.

"Dari?" I said.

"Mmm."

I was going to tell him.

When I'd gotten home and gone to the backyard to water the plants, a strong breeze blew by, and my feet completely left the ground! I thought that I'd be swept away! Thankfully the breeze died down and I landed on shaky legs a few feet away between my mother's favorite disk flowers. No one saw me. What if it happened again when I was walking to school or just out in public? Imagine the talk that would spread.

Dari was very observant and he picked up on my new anxiousness. I stared at his face on my screen; his thick lips were slightly smirking like usual, and his dark brown eyes were looking into mine. He seemed to be looking right into my eyes, his mind perfectly understanding mine. I could tell him anything, and he would know what to say and do. But I was still scared and confused, not ready to talk about it. Instead I shook my head.

"Nothing," I said.

Dari rolled his eyes. "OK, Zahrah. Anyway, have you finished your Ginen history homework yet? I'm way ahead! All that stuff about all those southwesterners who migrated south during the Carro Wars and were never seen again, that was so amazingly interesting. Did you know that some people speculate that they actually *walked* into another world called Earth? But there's no proof that Earth exists. No one who has supposedly gone has ever returned and . . ."

I settled back, glad to let Dari talk about one of his favorite subjects. I hadn't done my history homework yet. I knew that I probably wouldn't have to after listening to Dari.

CHAPTER 6

THE $\mathcal{P}$EARL

I was like a tree clam rolling a pebble under its tongue until it made a pearl. I was meticulous, thorough. I liked to gain some sort of comfort with things that bothered me before I discussed them with others. That was just me, I guess. And so it was a while before I spoke my secret aloud. Three weeks, to be exact.

Whatever had started happening to me that day was still very much happening. The only difference was that my control of it increased. I could truly levitate. I began to relax and even enjoy it at times. It was nice to sleep an inch off the bed. The air was more comfortable than my mattress! And I could water the delicate green flowers that grew near my ceiling much more easily.

As I grew a little more used to being able to float, I realized that I didn't feel as bad at school when Ciwanke and her entourage of friends gathered around me in the hallway and talked their nonsense. Their words sounded sillier, more childish. Still, I wished they'd quit it, though. Why did they have to be so cruel? Sometimes I thought about levitating right in front of them and watching them all run away screaming. They often called me "swamp witch," so why not do something witchlike? Just the thought was enough. Of course, I'd never *do* such a thing.

Telling my mother or my father was a laughable idea. I was sure that they'd just make a big fuss and then, before I knew it, they'd decide that I should be taken to the hospital where doctors would stick me with needles or make me swallow pills. Or equally horrible, they'd take me to the witch doctor, who'd make me drink some foul-smelling concoction.

I considered asking Papa Grip if he knew anything about what was happening to me. He certainly wouldn't laugh at me, plus he was old, and old people tend to have a wide range of knowledge about a wide range of things. But I knew Papa Grip would tell my parents after I spoke to him. Or if he didn't, he'd say that it was only right that I tell them, and then I'd either have to tell my parents or lie to Papa Grip. No, I'd just have to keep it to myself.

I thought about going back to the Dark Market and asking Nsibidi, the dada woman. But what would Nsibidi know? She'd cut her dadalocks off. And what if being dada had nothing to do with my ability? And even if Nsibidi knew something, I wasn't about to go back to the Dark Market without Dari.

I had to tell him first.

We were sitting in the baobab tree behind my house, studying for our organic mathematics class. The baobab tree was our favorite because it grew wide and low and had sturdy thick branches from the bottom all the way to the top. Of course, I stayed on the low thick branch due to my fear of heights, and Dari was on the one above it. Whenever we studied in it, I brought my potted glow lily, which provided a soft pink light. The light was easy on our eyes. We'd been silently engulfed in equations, numbers, cells, and patterns when I said, "Dari?"

I was tired of thinking about it. Doing so wasn't yielding any answers.

Dari smiled. I think he knew his patience had finally paid off.

"Yeah?"

I hesitated, picking a bit of tree bark from my orange dress and looking at myself through one of the small mirrors sewn into the sleeves. Then I chewed on my pencil. Dari continued trying to memorize the cellular patterns of the four subphyla of CPU seeds and magnetic diatoms as he waited for me to continue speaking.

"What is it, Zahrah?" he said closing his book.

I paused again, the words stuck in my throat. *What if*

Dari thinks I'm weird after I tell him? I wondered. The thought of losing his friendship made me feel sick.

"Just tell me. Goodness." He looked down and then back at me. "Your parents won't hear."

"You promise you won't think I'm weird?"

"I already think you're weird."

I frowned.

"Just tell me. How long have we known each other? Have you no faith in me? I'm insulted!" Dari said with a laugh. "You think me monstrous, like . . . like an elgort!? Vicious and simple-minded? Shallow? Unthinking? Ignorant? Insensitive?"

I laughed.

And then carefully, hesitantly, slowly, I told Dari about the breeze, the coming of my menses, and that night.

"Show me," he whispered.

And right there in the tree, hidden among the leaves, I showed him. Dari gasped as I quietly lifted a few inches off the tree branch. When I finished, I looked at him, waiting to hear the words he'd speak. It was a rare moment. Dari was at a complete loss for words.

When he finally found some, all he could say was "Do it again! Do it again!"

CHAPTER 7

THE $\mathcal{L}$IBRARY

Dari liked me for several reasons.

"I like how you always think before you speak," he'd said once. He probably admired this because it was something he had a hard time doing. He usually ran his mouth, rarely considering before he spoke. Of course, Dari was very clever, so this wasn't much of a problem.

When he was in a good mood, which was most of the time, he couldn't help but spread the joy by telling jokes, overblown stories, and just talking. At school even his teachers let him ramble on and on during class for longer than they should. People just loved to listen to him.

These same people said I was creepy with my "strange" hair and quietness. But Dari didn't care either way, and that day, when we were seven years old, I had caught his interest.

"You were frowning and staring at the jungle," he said. "I've seen you on the playground before. I just thought it was odd that no one was saying a word to you and you weren't saying a word to anyone either. I was curious."

Dari said his father once asked him why he'd befriended "that dada girl." Dari shrugged and said, "She's thoughtful and nice." His father nodded and said, "That's true. And she's sharp too." Both of his parents thought I was nice, bright, very polite, and dressed civilized, even if I was born with that strange hair. When Dari told me this, I was very pleased.

Dari loved me in the way only a best friend could love a best friend. It was as if I were his other half. We completed each other. But Dari had a lot of friends and knew girls who wanted to date him.

I sought him only before and after school and once in a while during midday break. But most of the time, I preferred to keep to myself, finding a nice spot under a palm tree to be alone with whatever it was I was thinking about. Our classmates didn't even know that Dari and I were so close.

I liked the silence and didn't really care to bask in Dari's sunshine at school. I didn't need him to vindicate me. And anyway, there was often a crooning, purple-beaked dove in that palm tree I sat under that would sing the loveliest songs, but only when it was quiet. If Dari were around, he'd make too much noise with all his talk and chatter. Dari and I understood each other.

That Friday, Ciwanke and one of her friends slowly walked past me as I waited for Dari at our usual spot a little ways down the road from school. I rolled my eyes at the sound of her voice and looked away.

"Whoo, look at that ugly monster on her head. Who knows what's growing in it," Ciwanke said, stopping. With my peripheral vision I could see the wooden pick she always wore in her large Afro. A wooden pick that would break if I tried to comb my hair with it.

Her friend, Amber, dramatically grabbed Ciwanke's arm with a grin and said, "Don't get too close to her. Who knows what bad luck will rub off on you."

I only looked at my hands. The thought of looking up and speaking to them made me nervous. To speak to them would keep them there longer. Plus my mother always said that silence was the best answer to a fool.

"Ugh, pathetic and disgusting. I don't know why you're allowed to attend this school," Ciwanke said, walking away and patting her soft halo of black hair.

Some steps away, I could see Dari saying goodbye to a few people. Ciwanke glanced back as he began to walk over.

When he got to me, he dropped his backpack on the ground, put his hands on his hips, and looked at me.

"Was she —"

I shook my head, a signal that I didn't want to talk about it.

"Doesn't matter," I said. "Nothing unusual."

"Hmm," he said frowning. But he left it at that, knowing that I didn't like talking about Ciwanke and her harassment. The less I talked about it, the less of a role she played in my life, which was fine with me.

"I don't have much homework today, do you?" I asked.

"Nah."

"So you want to come over or something?"

"How about . . . we go to the library?" he asked.

I shrugged. "I don't have anything I need from there. Do you?"

"Well," he said slowly, "we could go to look up stuff about, you know, your ability, if you want."

I paused, biting my lip.

"I don't think there's anything in the library about . . . it," I said. But I wasn't sure. Actually, my instincts were telling me that we might find something, but I was not one to follow my instincts. I didn't trust them, plus the idea was so sudden.

"Well, we'll never know unless we look."

❧❧❧

The Kirki Public Library was a huge five-story building with a cluster of impersonally grown computers on each floor. The traceboard leaves, monitors, and technological sophistication were all cultivated to suit the "average user." Dari and I both hated using them because the traceboards—large, moist, sensitive leaves that you traced commands on—were not made for our long, skinny fingers, the monitors were too big, and they functioned way too slowly. But at least the computers did what they had to do.

I hoped with all my heart that we would not have to venture to the fifth floor. We learned a lot about the Kirki library in history class. It was grown and nurtured forty years ago by an artist turned architect named Cana. Cana was obsessed with the beauty of glass and thus began his greatest masterpiece, a building made entirely of glassva, a transparent plant! It took Cana years to turn his idea into reality because the glassva plant was very fickle.

After years of failure, Cana threw down his hoe and watering pod and gave up. Still, he couldn't help visiting the plot of land where he'd planted the glassva plant every day and wallowing in his failure. A month later, as he was walking to his place of barren neglect, a strange blue lightning bolt struck the plot of land. The next day, when he returned, he was shocked to find that his plant had begun to grow.

From that point on, the plant flourished and Cana was able to cultivate it as he pleased. To this day, no one has been able to repeat the floral miracle. The building is one of a kind. Well-known authors from all over Ooni often give their readings at the Glass House of Knowledge, the name Cana gave his library masterpiece. Once, I even got to meet the author of the Cosmic Chukwu Crusader Series there! And tourists still travel to Kirki just to see the library. It's one of the most beautiful places in the world during sunset.

But because the library looked as if it were made entirely of glass, it made me *very* aware of how high up I was at all times. Especially on the fifth floor. The ceilings of all the floors were very, very high. Many say that Cana made them this way so that women wearing dresses and skirts wouldn't have to worry about people looking up from the floor below. In all my years of going to the library, I had never gone past the fourth floor. It was simply too high. If I needed a book from the fifth floor, I asked one of the librarians to get it.

"Just relax," Dari said. "Don't think about it until you have to. What are the chances, anyway?"

We browsed through the catalog on the computer and found books about birds, the history of the Ooni Palace, a field guide to the flies of Ginen, but nothing about human beings who could levitate at will or even fly. Nothing even close. We sat at a study table and slouched in our seats, exhausted from typing and thinking. This was when it popped into Dari's head.

"Ah, I've got it!" he exclaimed. "Why didn't we think of this before?!"

We had been looking up *facts*. But what if what we sought wasn't believed to *be* a fact? What if people thought it was only a myth or legend?

Still, Dari's inspiration proved far less fruitful than we expected. Only one book popped up which dealt with the myth of dadalocks. It was called *Ooni Fashion Magazine's Best of the Year*. Dari frowned. "What could this have to do with the dada myth?"

I shrugged, scribbling down the call number. I froze when I saw where the book was located. Dari laughed.

"Oh come now. We are *not* calling the librarian! You're a big girl. It's about time you got over your fear of heights, anyway."

I didn't agree with him, but I didn't say so. I knew my fear was childish and embarrassing, but that didn't change the fact that I was afraid. Instead of begging Dari to just get the librarian, I followed him up the stairs.

I did anything but get over it. By the time we stepped onto the fifth floor, I was sweating rivers, my legs were shaking, and my heart felt as if it were ready to jump out of my chest. The walls, the floors, the stairs, were all transparent. Only in the bathrooms were the walls and floors opaque.

Once I started moving, I was determined to make it. The sooner I made it up there, the sooner I could pretend I was on the ground by not looking down. And I was curious about what information we could find. All Papa Grip really told me about being dada was that I would grow up wise. Because of all the mystery around my hair, I, too, was sure that my strange ability was connected to my being dada. If there was more to it, I wanted to know.

When we were between the rows of books, I wiped the sweat from my brow and relaxed a tiny bit, making sure not to look at the transparent floor. There were a couple of hours of sunlight left, and it lit up the entire library. The dusty books stacked on the bookcases, however, were not transparent, and Dari and I stood in their shadow. The cluster of computers was in the center of the floor, surrounded by several desks where people did homework, read books, or whispered softly. It was very quiet. So quiet that I could hear people's footsteps perfectly.

"You OK?" Dari asked, looking at me with a smirk.

"Why'd you make me do this?" I grumbled, wiping a tear away and sniffing.

"It's good for you. You won't die, Zahrah," said Dari.

I only "humphed."

"OK, the call number is HR2763, page fourteen," he said, turning to the bookshelves.

We walked for a while, looking at book spines.

"Here it is," he said, pulling out the slim book.

We stood close together, flipping through it. It was a book on fashion. We turned to the right page. There was a small picture of a woman with dadalocks, wearing a lot of face powder and coloring, grinning with all her teeth. I frowned. The woman's locks looked too shiny and perfect, each one the same length, not one hair out of place.

"Hers are fake, aren't they?" Dari asked. "At least they look nothing like yours."

"Yeah, hers look like they're made of pliable plant byproduct. And look at the vines! They're pink!"

"How can she have byproduct hair?" Dari asked.

I laughed. A lot of women had byproduct hair.

Dari and I read the few paragraphs next to the picture.

TUNDE OLATUNDE'S JANUARY FASHION PREDICTION:

Do you want to know what's hot? What's chic? What's most civilized? What'll make people who see you stand on their feet? Well, you don't have to go to the north to find out. I, Tunde Olatunde, am the man to ask.

For the New Year, comes an old style! Few of us have ever seen a real person born with dadalocks. Oh, they're born here and there, northeast, northwest, southwest, southeast, and north of the great city, goodness knows exactly where. Most of them choose to lop off their strange locks in order to live a normal life. The ones who keep their hair are quiet people who somehow grow into wise men and women, excelling in whatever career they choose. Or so legend says. But then again, another legend says that those born with dadalocks are rebels whose only cause is to make things go wrong.

This year, anyone can take part in the myth and get the chic look of a wise (or strange) woman or man. Dada extensions! The chunks of hand-rolled oil-plant byproduct, fresh from a mature pliable plant, are melted onto the hair to give *anyone* this wonderful look that only a few are born with. Dada extensions are this year's hottest look! Vines braided into the locks come in all colors, not just green! Many celebrities are even sporting the fab style in digi-movies and on netevision.

My old old grandmother once told me that a few of these dada-born folks were born with the ability to fly. Windseekers, she used to call them. But she also told me that there were little blue men three apples high who lived in the mushrooms that grew in our backyard. I know a friend of a friend who knows two dada-born folks. He said neither of these individuals has ever left the ground without any help. So maybe my grandmother is not so reliable, but you can trust me when I say that this year's most stylish will be wearing dada extensions.

The next article was titled "New Line of Palm-Fiber Dresses Now Available from Palm Tree Bandit Women's Wear!"

Dari and I finished reading and then looked at each other with wide eyes. Then we read it again. It wasn't the kind of thing we were looking for, but in a way it was. I would never have guessed that I'd learn such a key thing about myself in a fashion book!

"Windseeker," I said. "So I'm a . . . Windseeker?"

Just saying the word made me feel like leaving the ground. I could feel the air around me begin to shift.

"I guess so," Dari said. "I like the name."

I wanted to go home and read the article again and sit and think about it. Now that I had a name for what I was, it felt all the more real. It meant that there were others like me. The man who wrote the article hadn't spoken of Windseekers as something bad, even if he didn't believe we were real.

"You know, the Ooni Kingdom is a great place, but it's not *every* place," Dari said. "It's just a small patch of land on Ginen that we've grown a civilization on. We don't know *everything*."

"What do you mean?" I asked.

Dari was always talking philosophy. He would read books and even search the network for philosophy nodes where he'd discuss his ideas with people three times his age. I was rarely able to follow his train of thought when he started talking philosophy.

"I mean that all we know about is a few hundred miles of city, towns, and villages. The Ooni Kingdom. But what do we really know about the rest of Ginen? You're a Windseeker and that may be strange here, but what about everywhere else?"

"There *are* no humans living anywhere else in Ginen," I said.

Once in a while an explorer or two would venture out of the Ooni Kingdom into the wilderness, but there were no human cities or towns. If there were cities or towns, they were populated by other beasts and creatures.

"How do we know?"

I shrugged.

"And what about places like Earth?"

"Oh, Earth is a myth, Dari. Come on."

"So are Windseekers," he said, smiling and looking me in the eye.

We made a copy of the page, and then Dari wanted to look up one more book. It turned out to be an electronic one. When we found it, Dari was very pleased. The black digi-book looked well used and old, with scratches on the oil-leaf cover. Oil leaves were cheap and ugly, but they lasted forever. The digi-book was small, about the size of his hand, and very light.

"Oh, I hate digi-books," I said. "They always have more information than they need."

The last digi-book I'd read was by my favorite author, Periwinkle Okeke, the author of the Cosmic Chukwu Crusader comic series. The book was called *The Bravest Girl in the North*. It was about a loud-mouthed girl who went to a spooky place called Bush Town to save her little sister. I'd read it four times. But not once did I read the rambling thoughts of the author—on how to cook the perfect holiday fowl—that came stored in the digi-book along with the story. Of course, as I read the book, every ten pages a little window would pop up on the bottom, saying, "Hey, why don't you read a bit about my thoughts on glazed bush fowl? As you can see, I write brilliantly. I cook even better!"

"This book would be thousands of pages long if it were in regular book form," Dari said. He laughed to himself as he looked at it with big, glassy eyes.

He pressed the digi-book's "on" button and the screen lit up, showing a lush green jungle. The title at the top read *"The Forbidden Greeny Jungle Field Guide* by the Great Explorers of Knowledge and Adventure Organization." Then it started listing over a hundred names of men and women.

"That book is about the forbidden jungle?!" I exclaimed. "Are you going to borrow that?!"

"Yep."

"If your parents see it, they'll go mad!"

Dari shrugged. "Who says they'll see it? And how mad could they get?" He grinned. "It's just a book from the library."

I frowned, not knowing what else to say. How could the library carry such a book? I didn't even know such a book existed. How did they get all the information for the book? It was probably more fiction than fact.

"Why do you want that anyway?" I asked. Dari's pace was brisk as we walked to the checkout desk.

"Because *this* book is revolutionary," he said. "It's great that they carry it here! I *love* the library! It's the most unbiased place on Ginen!"

At that time I wasn't aware of this, but *The Forbidden Greeny Jungle Field Guide* was a very significant book. It was the only book of its kind that addressed northern Ooni's most taboo topic: the Forbidden Greeny Jungle. But though the book was controversial, it wasn't hard to find. The information was out there. There were copies, both electronic and paper, in several libraries and bookstores. However, these copies always tended to be covered with dust because people preferred to avoid the subject.

Dari gave the librarian his library card. She chuckled, wiping the dust off the digi-book with a tissue.

"You're the first person to borrow this digi-book in twenty-six years," she said with a smile.

Dari looked embarrassed.

"I guess not many people want to read about the Forbidden Greeny Jungle," he said. Then he grumbled low enough for only me to hear, "Or any other place outside the Ooni Kingdom."

"I don't even want to *think* about that place," the librarian said with a shiver as she scanned the book.

"But it's where we grow much of our cocoa beans and fruits," Dari said. "You like chocolate and lychee fruit, don't you?"

"Those farms are on the *outskirts*," the librarian said. "This book, I believe, talks about the places far into the jungle, hundreds of miles in."

Dari took the book from her.

"OK, *The Forbidden Greeny Jungle Field Guide* is due in eight weeks," the librarian said with a pleasant smile. "Happy reading."

"Thank you," Dari said, taking the book.

As we walked out, my mind went back to the info on the folded sheet in my hand. I was a Windseeker! I giggled. Then it dawned on me, and once it did, I couldn't have felt surer. I had to go back to the Dark Market and talk to Nsibidi. And I had no doubt that Dari would gladly accompany me.

CHAPTER 8

Two Heads Are Better Than One

I followed Dari because he knew the way better than I did.

It was four o'clock on Monday, the busiest day and hour of the week at the market. This would work to our advantage. The fact that it was also the day that both of our mothers left their stands to do the week's food shopping wouldn't. We walked swiftly, zipping around milling customers.

Yes, it was my idea.

I immediately began to sweat when we stepped underneath and through the veil. Slowly, we walked down the dirt path between the stands. All around us were shady activities. To my left I noticed two men standing close, exchanging a large handful of bright yellow petri flowers. I looked away and my eyes fell on three women standing on a red platform. Another woman stood next to them talking loudly to the surrounding crowd of men. The women on the platform weren't wearing a lot of clothing. I quickly moved my eyes to the back of Dari's head.

"You OK?" Dari said, glancing back at me.

I nodded. I could still see those women in my mind, however, and it didn't make me feel good. My father always said, "You can buy anything at the market if you know where to look." I guess that included human beings.

Nsibidi wasn't hard to find. I could see her shiny, almost bald head hovering higher than those around her, and her bright marigold dress was eye-catching. Nsibidi smiled when she saw me emerge from the crowd. This made me want to talk to her more.

"I'm surprised to see you here," she said. The necklaces she was selling were draped on her arms. Each had glass luck charms of various shapes and colors hanging from them.

The soft-furred golden-eyed baboons that Nsibidi had called the idiok were seated in a circle in their booth space behind Nsibidi. They sat on olive green pillows with pads of paper and pens, scribbling on the pads and then showing them to each other. Once in a while they'd laugh at what they saw.

"I'm surprised to be here myself," I said.

Nsibidi turned her eyes to Dari with a soft chuckle.

"And look at this one. I've seen you before," Nsibidi said to Dari. "You're the boy who's always asking questions."

Dari shrugged shyly.

"*This* is my closest and dearest friend, Dari," I said, elbowing him. "He comes here all the time. Though he knows he shouldn't."

"A curious mind must be properly fed," Dari said.

"True," Nsibidi said with a nod.

"Wow," I said, looking past Nsibidi. "I thought people were lying when they said *those* existed."

Two-headed parrots, about twenty of them, were either squawking to themselves or to someone nearby. "Two heads are better than one," the man selling them shouted to passing potential customers. Some were bright green, others were blue. One of them was speckled with every color of the rainbow. This one's heads were fighting with each other. The seller poked at the parrot with a stick to make them stop.

"He's only here once in a while, thank goodness," Nsibidi said. "We won't get much business today. No one likes to have the idiok read them when there's so much noise."

"Read? What do you mean?" I asked.

"Yeah," Dari said, staring at the large baboons with fascination. He stepped closer. "And where are they from? Are they your friends? Do they work for you or do you work for them? They're obviously superintelligent."

"Hmm, always so many questions," Nsibidi said. "They can hear people's personal spirits, Dari. Everyone has spirits that have taken an interest in him or her. These spirits know the past, present, and future. Some people have more spirits than others. The idiok can hear and speak to them. They write down what they say. I'm the only one who knows how to read the idiok's written language, and I translate it for customers. The idiok taught me when I was young. When I mastered it, they tattooed this on me." She raised her chin so we could see it more clearly, just below her neck. It was a circle with what looked like a shouting woman in the center. There were tiny *x*'s all around the woman.

"It means storyteller," she said. "It's what they call masters of the language. Anyway, people pay a lot of money to be told what their personal spirits have to tell them. It's not always good news, though."

Dari and I looked at the furry brown baboons, who were paying no attention to us. They were too absorbed in scribbling on their pads and looking at each other's pads.

"What are they doing now?" Dari asked.

"Why don't you ask them? This one here is their spokesperson, Obax," Nsibidi said, pointing to the one closest to Dari. "He's named after one of the great gorilla chiefs."

Obax looked at Dari, got up, and moved over, sharing a cushion with one of the other baboons. Then he held out his hand and made a clicking sound.

"Go on," Nsibidi said. "Sit down."

Dari sat down on the green cushion, closing the circle again. Obax started scribbling something on his pad, and the baboon on his other side stood up and laid a cool hand on Dari's cheek. Dari smiled as the baboon brought its face close to his, sniffing his skin.

"So Zahrah, what brings you back here?" Nsibidi asked. "By the look on your face last time, I didn't think you'd ever come back."

"Well," I said. "I sort of . . . had a question."

I glanced at the charm necklaces wrapped around her arms.

"I have a weird question," I said. "About a weird subject."

Nsibidi put her arms around her chest. "You came right from school to ask this?"

"Yes. It's important. I think you're the only person who might know the answer."

I noticed Nsibidi's clothes for the first time. Her long yellow dress had shells sewn into the hem. The dress of a northern woman, except for the shells and the lack of mirrors. "Oh," I said quietly to myself.

It hadn't crossed my mind till then. I was so flustered

by the Dark Market that I hadn't realized it. Nsibidi was not from the north. Aside from the lack of mirrors, she shaved her head close, probably to keep the dadalocks and vines from re-forming, and wore three large gold hoops in each ear. She wore no assortment of beads like southwesterners. She wasn't fat like the northwesterners. She wore no bracelets made from vines like a northeastern women. And she didn't smell of molten metal as the southwestern women did. *Where* is *she from then?* I wondered.

I looked at the ground and then stepped back. *Maybe I shouldn't talk to her after all,* I thought. My instincts were telling me that I should, but, as I said before, I wasn't one to really trust my instincts. I wrung my hands and nervously grabbed one of my locks, my eyes trying to look anywhere but at Nsibidi's shaved head.

"Zahrah, just *ask,*" Dari said, turning from the idiok for a moment. "We're in the Dark Market. Nothing you say here is shocking."

Good point, I thought.

"OK," I said. "You . . . you're dada . . . well, have you ever had anything . . . strange happen to you?"

She frowned.

"Like what?" Nsibidi asked.

I shrugged, looking at the ground. I glanced at Dari. He was looking back and forth between something one of the idiok had written for him and the idiok next to him, who was wildly gesturing what it meant. Obax was still scribbling something else on his pad of paper.

"Why did you cut your dada hair?" I asked.

"Why don't you cut yours?" Nsibidi replied.

"No!" I said. "I would never . . . you didn't answer my question."

"You haven't asked your real question," she said. "I can tell."

"But I—"

"I cut it because it grew too heavy to bear," Nsibidi finally said, her voice lowering. "The funny thing was that, for me, it wasn't really about being dada. The hair was just a symptom."

"S-s-symptom of what?" I asked.

Nsibidi looked away.

"What is your question, Zahrah? What is it you came back here to find out?" Nsibidi suddenly snapped, looking me right in the eye. Normally, I'd have clammed up in that moment.

The caged parrots all stopped chattering, looking at Nsibidi. And the man selling them spoke more loudly to keep the attention of an interested customer. He'd found someone willing to buy a multicolored parrot, and he didn't want to lose his chance to be rid of the belligerent bird.

I unconsciously stood up straighter at the sound of

Nsibidi's commanding voice. Suddenly Nsibidi looked ten feet tall, tall as a tree.

"I . . . I . . . oh." I glanced at Dari, who nodded for me to continue. I took a deep breath, and then my words came like water through a bursting dam. "I think I can fly or something, I can float, it happened when I got my menses, I was near the ceiling, oh I am *terrified* of heights. Am I a Windseeker? I think I am. Do you know the word? We read about it in the library. What do I do? What do I *do*?"

I stood there, tears in my eyes, terribly embarrassed at my babbling. My hands were shaking and my heart was pounding hard. I wanted answers so badly, but I was so nervous.

"Practice. Nothing good comes easy," Nsibidi whispered, her eyes wide with shock. Then she nodded, looked up at the tarp, and smiled. "Learn to love the place up there. The rest will come when you want it to." She paused, her dark eyes burrowing into mine. "You understand?"

I just stared at her. It was all too much information to process so fast.

"You *understand*," Nsibidi said more loudly and sternly.

I blinked and then nodded slowly. Nsibidi and I stared at each other for several moments. It was the strangest feeling. She knew what I was talking about. She must have lived it all, and she had answers. I felt stunned, speechless. All I could do was just stand there. I wanted to remember her face clearly for when I was home thinking about all she said.

"Can your parents fly, too?" Nsibidi finally asked.

"No," I said. "Just me."

"Both my mother and father are Windseekers, as I and my brother. I've *never* met any others. And you have no idea just how much I have traveled. It's funny. You're afraid of heights," Nsibidi said with a laugh. "How ironic."

She paused for a moment.

"I first cut my hair when I was sixteen because I didn't understand what it was to be a Windseeker," Nsibidi said. "Didn't change what I was, thank goodness. It was just hair and vines. Zahrah, there are things about being a Windseeker that are tough to handle, but that's for when you're a little older. For now, just know that you shouldn't bother resisting the urges you'll have. Now that you know what you are, be ready for things to start."

Obax tapped Nsibidi on the shoulder and handed her a piece of paper on which he'd written many symbols. Then the baboon pointed at the necklaces around her arm. Nsibidi read the paper.

She frowned. Then she plucked one of the necklaces from her arm. It had a green leaf pendant. She looked from me to Dari and back to me. She then reread the paper.

"Great Joukoujou," she whispered, placing her hand on her forehead.

"What?" I asked.

She only shook her head.

"It's best that you don't know," she said. "You two . . . hmm . . . Obax wants you to have this charm, Dari. You'll need it."

I wanted to ask why again but decided against it. I didn't think she'd answer me anyway.

"Um, OK," Dari said with an uncertain smile. He looked at the charm as it twinkled in the dim light. It was very pretty. "Thank you very much!"

"You're welcome."

I felt a shiver in that moment as I watched Dari put the necklace on. *Why would Dari need a luck charm?* I wondered. That piece of paper Obax had given her . . . Obax must have "read" Dari. Oh the questions I had in that moment but was too shy to ask. If only I had been more assertive. And if only we'd had a little longer to talk.

"Zahrah," Nsibidi suddenly said. She paused and looked at the idiok with frantic eyes. I could have sworn many of them were frowning as they waved their hands in the air. She turned back to me with a pained look and said, "Listen to me . . . I can't *not* tell you this. I just can't. It would be . . . irresponsible. You're going to —"

"Dari!!!"

Dari and I both yelped. It was the voice of Dari's mother. What a horrible moment. Dari and I quickly turned around, shocked at hearing Dari's mother's voice there. Dari jumped up. We could both see his mother's head peeking behind the milling crowd.

"We've gotta go," Dari said quickly.

"Come back when you can," Nsibidi quickly said, taking my hand. "In the meantime, *practice*. Please be careful. Both of you."

It was a strange thing to say. Be careful of what? And what had she been about to tell me? But we had more urgent things to deal with. We held our breaths as we moved toward Dari's mother. It would have been wrong to try to run away. Dari's mother obviously knew we were somewhere in the Dark Market.

When we got close enough, she smacked Dari upside the head.

"For over a *year* Mrs. Ogbu's been telling me she's seen you coming here," she shouted at Dari. I cringed. Mrs. Ogbu sold Ginen fowl sometimes, so at some point she must have been stationed near the Dark Market.

"I didn't believe her! I called her a liar!" his mother continued. "But for some reason, when she told me today she'd seen you, I decided to see for myself. And here you are! I should have taken her more seriously! And you've brought Zahrah, this time?! What in Joukoujou's name are you two doing here!?"

"We were just . . . looking around," Dari said, rubbing the side of his head.

His mother was so angry that she didn't say another word. Instead she turned around and began walking. Dari and I quietly followed. She drove me home, and the short trip was silent and very tense. To make things worse, both my parents were home. I knew Dari's mother would go inside with me and tell them. As I got out of the car, I didn't dare speak to or even look at Dari.

"*Chey!* Zahrah, how could you be so stupid?!" my mother shouted the minute Dari's mother was gone. She sucked her teeth with annoyance and put her arms around her chest and just stared at me with amazement. "You and Dari are so bright, I wouldn't expect this of you two."

"I'm sor—"

"What do you have to say for yourself?" my father said.

"I just—"

"Forget it," he interrupted. "You don't have the privilege of defense tonight. Just sit there and be ashamed. Be glad you came out of there without some sort of strange disease. It's not a place for people who don't know what they're doing."

"Remember what happened to the Ekois' son?" my mother said, looking at my father.

"Of course," my father replied. He turned to me and looked me right in the eye. "He wasn't seen for fifteen days! They found him chained to seven other children at the Ile-Ife Underground Market! That's a two-hour drive away! Some sick evil man was selling them as child slaves. This man had met the Ekois' son in the Dark Market and promised him free personal pepper seeds if he drank a special drink, a drink that put him to sleep. He woke up in chains. You can guess the rest."

I frowned. Did such bad people lurk in the Dark Market? I knew the answer. Who could forget those miserable-looking women standing on the platforms or the many types of poisons for sale or those men exchanging all that money? But even with this knowledge, I hadn't *really* thought that I was in any danger. I would never accept anything from a stranger. Did my parents think I was that stupid?

"I'm sorry," I said, my chin to my chest. And I was. I hated worrying, disappointing, or angering my parents.

"You should be," my mother said, lowering her voice. "Now go take a bath and sit in your room and do some thinking."

That night, Dari and I weren't allowed to talk to each other on our computers; nor was I allowed to use my computer for anything but schoolwork. Nonetheless, when I closed my bedroom door, my mind immediately went back to Nsibidi. She was a Windseeker, too. She could fly and she'd traveled far.

I flopped onto my bed and breathed a giggle. I'd never felt so energized in my life.

"Practice," she'd said. I could do that. But where?

$\mathcal{W}$ELCOME TO THE JUNGLE

"I must be crazy to let you talk me into this," I said as we walked down the road. I nervously glanced behind us. "Crazy!"

"Oh relax," Dari said. "I know what I'm doing."

But I knew Dari. I could hear a little fear in his voice.

"No you don't," I whined. "Someone will *see* us . . . or something! What am I *doing*! Oh this is so crazy!"

Only a few days ago, we'd gotten caught in the Dark Market, and what we were doing now was far more forbidden.

"Some risks are worth taking," Dari said.

We'd had to lie this time, telling our parents that we were going to the library. As punishment, we couldn't go anywhere except the library. But we were really going into the Forbidden Greeny Jungle, and we had only a half mile to go as we passed the last building. There was no wall between the outskirts of Kirki and the jungle. For decades, the people of Kirki had tried to build one. The forbidden jungle simply wouldn't allow it.

"This stuff isn't in our school history books. It's really interesting," Dari said as we walked, always a wealth of historical information. "Our government, a long time ago, announced this grand project to build a nine-foot-tall cement wall to shield Kirki from the jungle. But the roots of nearby trees grew under it, and eventually the whole thing just fell apart!"

I shivered as Dari told me about the failed project he'd read about on the net.

He said that when they rebuilt the wall, this time using wood, voracious termites gnawed at it until it fell down. When they rebuilt the wall using metal, insects that had no scientific name dissolved it with acid produced in their thoraxes! These insects glowed a bright orange during the night, and for days, the wall kept nearby residents awake with its light. Eventually the metal wall melted. The wall looked as if it were on fire. It was Papa Grip who put a stop to all the wall-building efforts.

"It's not the Ooni way to do battle with nature," he said that year during his annual address to the town. "If the jungle doesn't want us to put up a wall, then we must *listen* to it, for it's our neighbor and one must respect his or her neighbor."

And so there was no protective wall. The buildings just ended, the grass began to grow higher, then the trees started. A road led to the cocoa bean, palm kernel, and lychee fruit farms located in the jungle's outskirts. The cocoa bean was used mostly for making chocolate. The palm kernels, red clusters of fat seeds chopped from the tops of palm trees, were pressed for oil and then used for cooking and in body lotions and moisturizers. The road went a mile or so into the jungle, and then it quickly tapered off into a very narrow path.

"And who made that path?" Dari asked. "I mean, if no one goes into the jungle, who made it! And why haven't the plants and trees grown over it by now?"

I only shrugged. Who could explain the ways of the forbidden jungle?

"It's as if the jungle wants people to go into it," Dari said.

There were no guards stationed on the road. For what purpose? No one in his or her right mind would go in. This was the road Dari and I would walk down.

Going into the jungle was Dari's idea.

"I've been reading a lot in the field guide. The jungle's 'forbidden' only because we don't understand it. It's all politics really," Dari had said the night before as we talked on our computers. It was the first time we'd talked through the net since getting caught in the Dark Market. Our parents said we had only fifteen minutes a night for a week. "Nsibidi said you should practice. What better place to practice?"

Though Kirki was a pleasant town, it also, like any other town, had a bush radio. "Bush radio" is Ooni slang for "gossip." News travels fast in Kirki because it's such a small town. The bush radio would have been hard at work if I had gone with Dari to my backyard to practice.

Mama Ogbuji, my neighbor, would have peeked over the fence while she was gardening and seen me floating in the air. She'd exclaim, "Great Joukoujou!" in that annoying way she does when she sees something that would make good gossip. Then she'd immediately run to her net-phone and call her best friend, Ama, and say, "You won't *believe* what I saw the Tsamis' daughter doing! She was zooming about the yard like a witch!"

Ama would call his friends—let's say they were named Ngozi and Bola—and tell them, "You know that dada girl, Zahrah? A friend of mine just told me she saw her turn into a bat and fly around her backyard! And that boy she likes to hang around with, well he was growing hair like a bush beast!"

Bola would then call her sister and say, "I hear there is a witch in town! Keep your eyes open when you go to the market! She probably does her business in the Dark

Market." And so the bush radio would continue growing and dropping seeds of nonsense from person to person. Dari was right to seek out such a quiet, unused place.

Nevertheless, I also suspected that Dari just wanted to go into the jungle to see it for himself. He'd been reading that field guide a lot, absorbing its every detail. All our lives we'd been told not to set foot in the forbidden jungle. Few children ever asked why, and the ones who did were told, "It's just not the right thing to do. It's a place of madness." And we accepted this.

"Zahrah, this book is *amazing*," Dari had said the night before. We went offline after agreeing to meet after school. Then Dari sneaked a quick call back a half-hour later, utterly energized by the field guide.

"Did you know that there's a tree that changes the color and shape of its leaves every year? The Forbidden Greeny Jungle is the rest of the world! We live in isolation with our eyes closed!"

I rolled my eyes and said, "Sure, Dari," and quickly got offline. The Forbidden Greeny Jungle was insanity. Its outskirts, as the librarian had said, were the only useful place. Once one went a few miles in, everything grew ragingly wild. And anyone who ventured in was not likely to come out.

But the book had charmed Dari since the day he'd borrowed it from the library. He'd even started wearing green, as the writers of the book had, and pumping his fist in the air and chanting the Great Explorer's slogan "Down with ignorance!" He also lectured his friends at school about how they lived in an isolated world because they were afraid to explore the places just outside their home. People listened as always because it was Dari talking and he could make anything sound wonderful. Still, no one was so moved that they started to believe him.

"This book tells you everything," Dari said as we passed a path to the palm tree farm.

"Hey?" someone shouted behind us. "Where are you kids goin'?"

We both whirled around and then froze. We'd been caught!

"Dari," I hissed with panic. "I thought you said we wouldn't meet any —"

"I thought we'd have heard someone coming," he said, looking frantic.

Oh, we were in trouble. There was no point in running. If we ran, they would catch us. And even if they didn't, they'd certainly report us. *Oh my goodness*, I thought, *our parents are going to go crazy.*

"Stay fresh," Dari whispered.

But I didn't feel fresh at all. I felt trapped and terrified. We were caught, and all we had in the future was punishment. A minute ago we'd been OK; then things had suddenly changed. We didn't move as the three men approached us.

They were obviously workers from the farms. They wore the light but tough tan jump suits made of palm fibers that protected them from tree branches and the heat. We'd learned about the farmers in school. Though they wore plain and often dirty clothing, we saw them as courageous heroes. They worked right next to the jungle, risking their lives daily. And so, as Dari and I stood there and they approached us, we were also struck by a sense of awe.

Their faces were dark like the midnight sky. My mother is very dark and so am I. But these men spent all their time in the very top of the oil-palm trees being baked by the sun as they watered and preened delicate oil sprouts. They were black like shadows. And not surprisingly, their skin glistened and their jump suits were damp with tree oil. They each carried around their shoulders a sling made from hundreds of enriched palm fibers that they used for climbing trees. And a machete hung from their waists. They also had tags with their names and work numbers sewn on their jump suits.

"We're . . . just walking," Dari said.

The men laughed, looking both of us up and down. How silly we must have seemed to them. Silly and childish and disobedient.

"You know where you are? You lost your mind? Eh?!" the tallest one, named Tabansi, said with narrowed eyes.

"Methinks they have, yes," said the one named Kwenu.

He carried a large lunch pod. He addressed us directly. "Tabansi, let's just report 'em and be on our ways, *o*." He rubbed his oily meaty arms with his hands and swatted at a fly. "We don't have much time for our break!"

Tabansi reached into his jump-suit pocket and pulled out a net phone. The one named Iwene looked at us both as he brought a chewing stick out of his pocket.

"Never seen such stupid children," he grumbled, putting the stick between his teeth.

"Now wait a second," Dari said quickly. "OK, we know where we are."

I stared at him, but he didn't look at me. He just kept talking. Really fast.

"We're just curious. We've heard so much about the Greeny Jungle and we wanted to see for ourselves. Is that so wrong? I mean, really? We don't plan to go that far. We just want to see it. How many people do you see here? None, right? Other than you farmers who know this place like the back of your hands. So why report two kids who are curious? We won't be long. We just want to see for ourselves. Surely you must understand. I mean, you get to see the jungle every day. At least from close up in the farms. Please don't report us. If you like, we'll turn around and leave right now."

The three men just stared at Dari. In confusion, with humor, or impatience—I don't know. But something sparked their attention.

"Tell me your name," Iwene asked, his chewing stick hanging from the side of his mouth. He brought it out, looked at its chewed frayed end, and then rubbed his teeth with it as if it were a toothbrush.

Dari hesitated. I could feel his indecisiveness.

Iwene snapped his fingers. "Ah, ah, come on. We don't have all day. Speak up."

"D-Dari," he said finally.

Iwene looked at Dari for a moment longer, then he smiled and nodded.

"You, dada girl?"

"Zahrah," I said, following Dari's choice to tell the truth. I figured since he gave his real name, I might as well, too. We would both get in trouble.

"A mile from here is your death, you know," Iwene said.

"Iwene!" Tabansi said. "Don't—"

"Don' scare 'em?" Iwene asked. "And why not? Might as well know what they getting into."

"True, true," Kwenu said. "If they not scared now, they going to be once they get in there."

Iwene stepped up to us and cocked his head. Dari only flared his nostrils, maintaining eye contact with the man.

"We can tell you stories that will keep you awake at night. And these aren't made-up stories. No, no. These really happen. Look at me. I been working in the oil-palm farms since seventeen. Over twenty years of being right next to them green, green crazy trees and such. We seen things, children. And trust us, you don' want to go in there. You won't come out."

"What have you seen?" Dari asked. His eyes were wide in the way they get when something has 100 percent of his attention.

Iwene squatted down in front of us and rubbed his oily chin with his oily hands. His skin was black and smooth, like polished onyx. He turned to his friends.

"Should I tell him 'bout Yabu?" he asked.

They both nodded. He threw his chewing stick into the bushes.

"Yabu worked in the palm kernel farms. Palm kernel trees are the closest to the cursed forest. They run right next to the forest. None of us knew him in body, but we know a friend who knew his best friend. All us farmers know 'bout Yabu. His story reminds us to be careful, that we work in a place that can eat us alive, leave not a trace of us behind. You listenin'?"

We both nodded. I didn't want to hear anymore. This was all I needed to hear to turn back. I didn't want to listen to the rest of the story at all.

"Yabu was a hard-workin' man, but he was like you two—his eye was always wandering. To the sky, the dirt, and to that cursed jungle."

"And he was always asking questions," said Kwenu.

Iwene nodded.

"He was curious. And one day, curiosity changed his life forever," Iwene continued.

"No," corrected Kwenu. "Curiosity ended his life."

"It was the day that it rained," said Iwene. "And as Yabu leaned back on his sling, machete in hand, chopping at the palm kernel cluster, red palm oil on his face and hands, something must a caught his eye. The first thing that one who works this close to the jungle is told to never do is look directly into the jungle. Even if you see a glimmer with your side vision, hear a noise that sounds like a crying baby, a smell that reminds you of your mother's tastiest dish.

"Never ever look into the jungle. You too close. You too vulnerable. Just focus on your tree and your job. But this day, something caught his eye. Must have caught and held it because he climbed down from his tree and walked right up to the forest border.

"I tell you, his fellow farmers all yelled at him to look away! 'What are you doing, Yabu,' they shouted. Some of them started to climb down from their trees, but it was like Yabu couldn't hear them. Like he was in a trance!

"When a bunch of farmers made it down, they could see what caught his eye. And that's why none of them was able to stop him. No one would go near him. No one wanted to get infected by the jungle. We all got families, husbands, wives to love, children to feed, responsibilities.

"You want to know what it was that he saw, eh? You

want to know what caused this man to do the insane and stand right on the border of the forbidden cursed jungle and stare into its innards? You all know what masquerades are, no? See them dancing during festivals. People dressed up in layers and layers of colorful clothes and raffia and grass. Some got heads with three or four faces, all with different expressions. Some stand ten feet tall. Supposed to be the spirits of the dead who come up from the anthills to frolic with humans during celebrations.

"Well, this was like no masquerade anyone had ever seen, and the other farmers quickly moved as far from the forest as they could, without a look back.

"But poor Yabu . . . was it curiosity or fascination, or was it the glam of the jungle? Coulda been all three. But he just stood there staring at that thing. Folks described what they had glimpsed as being over twenty feet in height! That it had a great big head made of smooth wood with at least seven angry faces. The ones facing Yabu all looked at him.

"Its body was wider than two cars and made of layers of hanging green vines and dried grass and ribbons of blue cloth. And something else was dripping off of it. Something green and smokelike. Could have been any substance!

"Anyway, something did something to Yabu. Made him lose his mind. Who knows what went through his head in those last moments. His sanity was sapped away.

Just that fast. Gone. Because he started walking. He crossed that border, the place where the dry grassy ground turned to tangled vines, gnarled tree roots, and Joukoujou knows what else.

"And he kept walking. He walked right up to that horrible monster. And as he walked, it was like something was pullin' him in a direction that he didn't want to be pulled. He moved stiffly and jerkily, as if he was fightin' whatever had a hold on him. He walk right up to that horrible monster and *phhoooippp!* Green thick vines shot out from the masquerade! So many vines, *o!* Wrapped him up like a yam fest present. You could hear him scream as it happened. And those vines must have had barbs in them because some people who saw it happen from their trees said they saw blood ooze from between the vines.

"The screams stopped and he fell. Without a glance in the farmer's direction, the monster dragged Yabu between the trees and was gone. Just . . . like . . . that.

"Yabu was never seen again," Iwene said.

Oh, I felt so sick. I could see that horrible masquerade. An evil ghost just waiting for its chance. And when it had it, it would have no mercy. You could scream and thrash, but it would never let go. It would suck the life from you and then return to where it came from, having fed on your blood and spirit. I wanted to flee from that road that was so close to where this beast probably lived. We were heading into certain death, I was sure. Our schoolbooks had not lied. Why would they lie? They were just looking out for us, teaching us to look out for ourselves.

I looked at Dari, knowing I'd see the same look of fear and agitation. Dari was a proud boy. It would be hard for him to admit he'd been wrong. It would sting him. But a little sting was better than being torn apart by some evil masquerades' otherworldly vines! And evil masquerades definitely weren't the only things in the forest that could kill us. Of course not.

I bit my lip hard when I saw the look on Dari's face. And then I felt my heart flip with horror as he opened his mouth and laughed out loud.

"Nonsense!" he said. "You speak as if you were right next to the man! You weren't. You didn't even *know* him."

Iwene looked at Dari as if Dari had grown ten years older and punched him in the face.

"You don't believe me?" he exclaimed with shock. He looked at Kwenu and Tabansi. Kwenu sucked his teeth loudly, looking angry.

"Enough of this," Kwenu said. He waved a dismissive hand at Dari. "The child is just vomiting trash. The minute we leave, they'll run back home. Look at the girl."

They all took a moment to look at my terrified face. That seemed to be enough to satisfy them.

There was a loud siren sound, and all three men stood up very straight.

"Ah, ah! What is the time?" Iwene exclaimed.

"Noon! We won't make it now."

"Oh Joukoujou! We'll be fired this time for sure," Tabansi shouted.

It was as if they had forgotten we were even there. They hoisted their things onto their backs and scrambled toward the place where they'd come from. And within seconds they were gone.

"Cursed forest indeed," Dari said. Then he did something that made me almost faint with shock. In that moment, I felt deathly ill. Nauseated with terror. My legs felt weak, like overboiled sweet bean sprouts. He looked back to make sure the men were gone, and then he turned and started heading down the road again. He was still intent on going in.

"Dari! You still want to—"

"Of course!" he said. "I didn't come all this way to be scared off by some old farmers' legend. We're both smarter than *that*!"

I followed him, trying to think of ways to get him to stop and go back with me. As we walked, I looked around, more aware of my surroundings than ever. The trees were evenly spaced and grew tall and slender. A warm breeze ruffled their tops. From far away, I could hear the chopping sound. *Were they chopping palm kernels?* I wondered. And if we could hear them, that meant we weren't far from the jungle's border.

"I don't know why they don't make us read the field guide in school. Oh yeah, because it's too taboo for our school's curriculum. They say the field guide corrupts children. It's just information, *accurate* information, unlike some stupid farmers' legend."

"Well, look at what we're doing," I said. By this time, I was so scared that my voice was shaking. "Because of that book, we've lied to our parents and are now on our way to the jungle. I think the school board might be right."

Dari frowned. "If you don't want to do this, then you can just turn around and go home."

"If I went home, you'd keep going," I said, whining.

"Yes, I would," Dari said firmly.

I stopped walking and stamped my foot in frustration. Always so hardheaded.

"Well, I can't leave you to go alone," I said, wiping the tears from my eyes. I couldn't help it. Whenever I felt cornered, I cried.

"Then don't," he said, continuing on his way without looking back.

He was my best friend. And best friends always watched each other's backs. If he was going to get eaten by masquerades, then I would, too. I hung my head, resigned to my fate, my heart twittering in my chest like a caged bird. *Oh I hope he knows what he's doing*, I thought as I followed him.

We walked in annoyed silence for a while. An owl hooted from far away and another owl answered. Day owls. I had heard of them but never *heard* them. They lived on the farms, eating field mice and sunbathing lizards. Unlike all other owls, these were diurnal; they slept at night and were active during the day. They were large birds with small yellow eyes, known to make their nests on the tops of palm trees.

"Don't you want to see the jungle?" Dari asked after a while.

"No," I said. "It's d-dangerous. We shouldn't go in there. We shouldn't. I don't know why I'm still here walking with you. You're a lunatic and you're leading me to more lunacy."

"You sound like a malfunctioning mechanical man," Dari said. "You didn't even think before you spoke."

I said nothing. I didn't know what to say. I had initially agreed because Dari's excitement was contagious. As I've said before, Dari has a way with words. Maybe a tiny part of me wanted to go so that I could practice without worrying about being seen. Anxiety affected my concentration, and my concentration affected my ability to lift from the ground. And I did want to see for myself, too. But after the warning from the farmers, I just wanted to turn back.

"Let's turn back," I pleaded. "What if we meet more farmers? They'll surely report us."

Dari shook his head.

"That loud noise was calling them back to work, I'll bet," he said. He looked straight ahead and said more to himself than me, "Noon is probably when they take their breaks. I'll remember that."

"Well, let's turn back anyway," I said. "If they're all back at the farms, then at least we can be sure not to get caught on the way home."

The farms were ending, and the Greeny Jungle spread before us, turning the open dirt road into a tunnel through dense trees. The trees already looked wild, gnarled, incredibly healthy, and relentless. I saw a glint of something gray and furry near the top of a tree. Then it blinked out of sight. A green bird sew from one of the trees, squawking as it went on its way. Dari shook his head.

"Come on, Zahrah," he whispered. "Let's just do it. Let's just go *in*!"

I let Dari take my hand and we walked into the Forbidden Greeny Jungle.

CHAPTER 10

ℬORDERLANDS

"T-t-this must be the border," I said, staring at the ground where the soil turned from dusty red to a deep rich brown, soil that looked like any seed planted in it would grow wild. I held Dari's hand tightly. I was shaking so badly that if I let go, I would have probably fallen over.

Dari glanced at me with a worried look. He was afraid too, maybe even wondering if it was time to turn back. But instead, he used his other hand to bring out the field guide from his pocket. He flipped the digi-book open, pressed a button, and frowned. He slapped it on the side.

"This thing is so screwed up," he said. "Sometimes I have to really smack it to get it to work."

"M-m-m-maybe it's just old," I said.

"Yeah," he said as he smacked it again and shook it.

There was a peeping sound and he smiled. "There. OK, it's working." He pressed a few more buttons. For a moment, he stood reading. Then he looked at the soil and at the book.

"Hmm," he said, rubbing his chin.

"What is it?" I whispered. Something made a deep, long cooing sound followed by three hollow-sounding clicks. It came from the tree to my right.

"In the book it describes the soil as red . . . not brown."

"Well, m-m-maybe it's a trick of the light? Or l-l-lack of. It sure is d-d-dark in there," I whispered.

Still Dari continued frowning. Then he shrugged.

"Maybe," he said. He looked at me. "Are you all right?"

"N-n-no," I said. Who knew what would happen if we stepped over that border onto the brown rich soil. Would the road behind us, the way out, disappear? Or maybe we just wouldn't be able to find it. Or maybe the moment our feet touched that tainted soil, we'd sprout branches and stems and be turned into trees ourselves!

"Zahrah, stop being so scared and think for a moment," he said. "Let your brain do some work. You were born with dadalocks, something that most people view as an annoying curse. Funny how all things people don't understand seem to be 'cursed.' It's known all over Ooni that those born dada cause things to go wrong. Has this ever happened to you?"

"No," I said very quietly.

"And has anyone said anything about being able to fly? Have you, in all your life, ever heard of a Windseeker before we went to the library and came across the name in a fashion magazine?"

I shook my head.

"And what about the Dark Market? Has either of us come out of there with some strange magical disease or a curse upon our head? Were we kidnapped? It wasn't what it was rumored to be, was it? We both found that out once we saw it with our own eyes. And what of Nsibidi? She's like you! And now we have this book that tells us so much about the things in this jungle, written by people who went in and spent lots of time in there! Put that against what we've been taught all our lives by people who have never gone near the jungle and by three farmers who may work near it but have also never gone in it. Whom would you believe?"

"Well . . . I . . ."

"And this place is the perfect place for you to practice," he continued. He was out of breath with excitement, all signs of fear and apprehension gone. He'd worked up his confidence with his own speech. Convinced himself. And quite frankly, though I was still scared, my knees had stopped shaking. He made a lot of sense. "You want to practice, right?" he said.

I nodded slowly. I did, sort of. I wanted to explore my

ability without the fear of someone seeing me. See what I could do and what I couldn't. Just let it all hang out.

"Well, let's kill two birds with one stone!"

I looked at the dark tunnel of trees and hanging vines. The sky was clear and the sun was close to its highest point, yet the jungle of foliage was so thick that most of the sunshine was blocked out. To the left and right of the trail was solid foliage. On both sides, there were several places where tree branches and leaves shook as some creature moved behind them.

A slight breeze blew, and I felt my feet wanting to leave the ground. I grasped Dari's hand more tightly, and he grinned.

"Look at you," he said. "You're just as strange and misunderstood as the jungle. It'll welcome you, I'm sure of it."

And with that, he started walking . . . and so did I.

I remember the exact moment that I stepped over the border. It wasn't as if there were any real feeling of change. The air didn't feel warmer. There was no overpowering smell of evil. And the trees did not crowd behind us to block our exit, as I thought they would. Nothing really happened—nothing outside of myself, at least. Inside me, however, I felt something shift. Something change. At the time it reminded me of what a snake must feel like after it has shed its first skin—wet, new, strong, and vulnerable. Different.

Dari and I looked behind us at the road and then looked at each other with raised eyebrows.

"I want to make sure," I said.

So I walked back over the border of the jungle into the sunlight. There was no barrier, no tree or monster to stop me. The sun felt good on my face. Then I stepped over the border again into the darkness of the jungle.

"See?" Dari said triumphantly. "They were wrong."

"Maybe," I said. I needed to think about it more.

We walked slowly down the road, looking around at every sound. We looked around a lot. One thing that did change the moment we entered the Greeny Jungle was the amount of sound. Everything suddenly grew louder. Creatures clicked, chirped, squawked, screeched, howled, grunted, and croaked. The jungle seemed packed with creatures behind every leaf and under and above every branch.

We stopped and just stood there for a moment.

"Wow," Dari whispered.

I whimpered and he looked at me.

"Zahrah, relax. We're still alive and nothing's tried to—"

Something dropped on my shoulder. Whatever it was felt cool and wet through the cloth of my dress. And it was still moving.

My eyes grew wide as I twisted my head to see what it

was. I was too horrified to scream. Instead I made a peeping sound and scrambled closer to Dari.

"G-g-g-get it off me," I whispered, pointing to it. My father had always told me that one should stay calm in terrifying situations and focus on getting out of the situation safely. Only after reaching safety could you scream with panic and shock. My father would have been proud of how I handled the giant slug that had dropped onto my shoulder, even if he'd have been ashamed of where I was. "Get it—"

Dari spotted the slug quickly as it clung and slowly moved down my shoulder.

"Wait," he said. "Don't move, so I can—"

He quickly picked it off and threw it on the ground, where the slug continued on its way as if nothing had happened. It was gray and about the size of my hand, its two fleshy gray antennae round on the tips and bobbing as they sensed its surroundings.

"Ugh! Eww!!! Blah!" I shouted, absent-mindedly running over to a tree and grabbing a leaf to wipe the large amount of slug mucus coating my shoulder. Dari only laughed.

"It was just a slug," he said.

"Only the biggest slug I've *ever* seen!" I said, looking up into the trees. In my experience with the small slugs in my mother's garden, where there was one there were always more. "Yech! Disgusting! Look at this nasty stuff it left on my dress! My outfit's ruined."

Dari stepped over for a closer look.

"Sorry, Zahrah," he said, using his hand to wipe my shoulder. "It'll dry. And we're in the jungle; no one's going to see you. We'll go straight to your house when we leave so you can change."

The slug tainting my outfit lessened the focus on my fear. As we walked, I couldn't help but wonder who was going to see me with that large dark patch of wetness on my dress. The slug mucus dried but still remained dark and tacky looking.

"You feel as if something is watching us?" Dari asked a few minutes later.

I shrugged. I was still holding his hand, but I wasn't as huddled next to him as before the slug had dropped on me.

"I'm willing to bet there are a thousand things watching us right now," I said. My words made me shiver a bit, but my panic seemed to have been pushed far away. I slapped at a mosquito on my neck.

"Yeah, but something's . . ." He stopped and looked around. "Oh, I dunno."

I didn't say anything, but I knew what he was talking about. Something specific was watching and following us. It was up in the trees, and I kept thinking I was going to catch it with my eye, but then just as I tried to focus, it was gone. It wasn't very big, whatever it was.

About twenty minutes later, after we'd walked about a mile, we stopped—for two reasons. The first was that the dirt road before us abruptly ended, becoming a narrow path that was barely a path at all. The second reason was that there was sunshine to our left. We were at a small clearing where the trees seemed to move aside, allowing sunlight to reach a patch of low-growing green plants. Both of us were struck by how beautiful the place was. A few flowers were budding in different places, lush vines draped the trees, and everything looked so alive and sweet. I'd much rather have gone into the clearing than down the creepy dark path.

Dari must have agreed.

"That looks like a good safe place," he said. "You can practice there."

"Fine," I said. "But not today. Let's go home. I've had enough of this place for one day."

I led the way back down the road. It didn't take us long to get home. But we were dusty and grimy with sweat. Thankfully, we saw none of our classmates along the way, and my parents were not home yet. After Dari left, I threw my soiled dress in my hamper and took a very long bath, making sure to scrub my left shoulder several times. And all I could think about as I washed the dirt off my skin was how I was still alive and how lovely the clearing was in the sunlight.

My feet tingled with excitement. Maybe I was living up to my dada expectations after all—with a little persistent pushing from my best friend, that is. I scooted down deeper in the hot water and giggled to myself.

It was crazy and stupid and dangerous, but it was true. Dari and I were going to go back into the forbidden jungle.

CHAPTER 11

THE WAR SNAKE

"What was that?" I asked, softly landing back on the ground. My legs were crossed and I opened my eyes. Dari sat against a tall mahogany tree, the digi-book he'd borrowed from the library in his hands. He'd become obsessed, reading it well into the night and even during class. It was still pretty faulty; sometimes it wouldn't turn on or it would conk out on him while he was reading, but he was usually able to get it to work.

The digi-book went well with the fact that we had been going to the Greeny Jungle every Wednesday, Friday, and Saturday for two weeks. It was Friday, and we had only one more day of school left before semester break. We planned to go even more often once school was out.

Our parents didn't suspect a thing, and they liked knowing that their children were spending so much time in the library. The library was much safer than the Dark Market. It's funny how once you tell one lie, you can always tell more.

Still, our trips to the jungle were starting to make me think. It was amazing how the people of Kirki pretended that the jungle wasn't there. I felt a little ashamed that I'd done the same only two weeks ago. Aside from the trucks that drove to the farms in the morning and left the farms at night and the groups of farmers who walked to and from the farmers' rest area during breaks, no one even so much as *looked* at the road that led into the jungle. It was easy for Dari and me to walk there unseen. We just had to make sure we weren't on the path at around nine, noon, and six p.m. Still, I wasn't sure if what we were doing was right.

"It's nothing," Dari said, playing with the charm he wore around his neck. "It's just the jungle. We're not the only ones here, you know."

"Yeah, that's what I'm afraid of," I said. Then I said what I'd been saying for two weeks. "We shouldn't be here."

"Well, do you have a better idea for a place to practice without being seen?" Dari asked.

I didn't. And I had to admit, coming to the forbidden jungle had turned out to be not such a bad idea.

Though there were certainly bizarre, even terrible,

creatures and beasts there and who-knew-what lived miles in, the Forbidden Greeny Jungle was just a jungle. With each visit, I relaxed more. And though I'd never admit it to Dari, I was beginning to look forward to our visits. The Greeny Jungle, even only a mile into it, had several creatures that I'd never seen before or heard of.

There were the turquoise-blue butterflies that sang a ghostly tune as they went from flower to flower. At first, I thought they *were* ghosts. Dari said that according to the field guide, the butterflies were fittingly called ghost flies. And, most important, they were harmless.

There were the red lizards with the hard golden feet that clacked when they scrabbled up a tree. Dari was still searching for their name. And I certainly couldn't forget the flies whose bites left orange circles on our skin until they healed. There weren't many of these flies, but all it took was one bite to be bothered for a few days. The bites itched a lot, especially during a hot shower. Bright orange circles on dark brown skin were easy to notice, so it took a lot of effort to hide them from our parents. My favorite creature was the giant dark-gray-colored, long-fingered dormouse.

"It's so cute!" I whispered.

"This one I've read about. It's very common," Dari said quietly the first time it let us see it. "Don't look straight at it or it'll run away."

I held my breath and tried not to move. We both could

smell it; it smelled of lemons and spice, the very things it fed on. The gray furry dormouse peeked around the trunk of the tree just above Dari. It had a wide round face with large red eyes, and each of its red, sticklike toes and fingers was over three inches long. It wrapped its fingers flat against the tree trunk as it leaned over to get a better look at us.

Since that first day, it had been spying on us whenever we went to the jungle. It was the creature we had both sensed was watching us that first time we came.

"It always seems to think that I don't see it," I whispered to Dari.

"It knows," Dari said. "It thinks it's smarter than we are."

Each time we went, this particular dormouse followed us. I knew it was the same dormouse because this one had a red spot on its left flank. Plus it grew more and more familiar with us. By the third visit, I was bringing it bits of mango and coaxing it from its hiding place for a snack.

That first week my ability greatly increased. The clearing turned out to be the perfect spot. The plants were cool and soft to sit on, and occasionally they blossomed into tiny turquoise flowers with green centers that the ghost flies liked to suck nectar from. It was a beautiful place. The open air seemed to allow me to unlock more of my ability. I could levitate several feet into the air, higher than my bedroom ceiling. It was beginning to worry me. I didn't want to lift up way into the air. I wanted to be able to fly, to zip around like a bird, a bird that liked to fly close to the *ground*. But for some reason, I couldn't do anything close to zipping around; I could only slowly levitate upward. I seemed to have reached a peak in my ability, and I hadn't improved since the week before.

"You can't have the ability to fly and never fly," Dari said. "Just keep trying."

I humphed. Maybe my ability wasn't that powerful. Maybe this was all I could do. Nsibidi's parents were both Windseekers, but neither of mine was. It wasn't strong in my blood. Still, I closed my eyes and concentrated. My brow was covered with sweat. It took effort to balance my mind and call up the wind. Especially when I was scared. But once I was floating, it was easier. I just didn't go *too* high.

As Dari sat on the soft green plants leaning against the tree, a creature slithered up to his hand.

When Dari and I followed the path past the palm kernel farms into the Forbidden Greeny Jungle that day, neither of us knew that a war snake was slumbering nearby. How could we have? We weren't psychic. War snakes were white with green splotches on their four-foot-long bodies. These splotches were shaped oddly, like badges and stars.

The females were slightly smaller than the males, but that didn't make them any less aggressive. If Dari had gotten far enough in his *Forbidden Greeny Jungle* digi-book at that time, he'd have read the whole ten pages dedicated to the many ongoing battles between the war snakes, battles that had been raging deep in the Greeny Jungle for so long that the snakes probably no longer knew or cared what they were fighting for! But Dari had read only a short definition of the war snake in the glossary. Still, he could never have guessed he'd encounter one only a mile into the Forbidden Greeny Jungle.

I like to imagine that this particular war snake was a first officer of her brigade (the book *did* say that war snakes moved in brigades) and had wandered ahead and lost her way.

She must have been wandering for days and was starting to grow angry. She'd never been without her people for that long. And she was so wrapped up in her scary situation that she didn't notice how close she was to the end of the Forbidden Greeny Jungle. According to the field guide, this snake would have been the first war snake to come this close to the forbidden jungle's boundaries in over a hundred years!

Nevertheless, the war snake was still a war snake, and when faced with something she didn't understand, she did what she'd been taught from the day she hatched: Go for the kill.

Dari didn't frown or shout at the snake. He didn't attempt to bash her. He didn't kick or throw his book at her. He didn't yelp and move away. Dari didn't even *see* the snake as she slid up beside him. But he certainly felt the sting of her bite and then the warmth as her venom seeped into his skin and deeper into his muscle.

Dari gasped and jumped up. "What the . . . ?!"

My eyes shot open and I dropped painfully to the ground.

"What is it?" I said, running over.

The snake quickly let go as Dari whipped her into a nearby bush. She probably slithered away yelling something like, "Retreat! Retreat!" in her snake language. Days later, when she finally found her brigade, she must have told them stories about a ferocious hairless brown beast that attacked her and how she bravely bit and fought back. Bravely indeed. Horrible creature! She attacked an innocent human being who didn't even know she was there!

"Does it hurt?" I asked, looking at his hand.

Dari nodded and I whimpered. Dari's face had suddenly gone from a healthy dark brown to a brownish ashy umber. And his eyes were barely open. I moved next to him.

"Put your arm around my shoulder," I said. It was the closest I'd ever stood to my best friend. He smelled nice, like soap, baby oil, and oranges. But I was more concerned with getting him to safety. He leaned heavily on me, and I wasn't very strong. But my fear and love for Dari gave me strength that day.

"OK, Dari, you'll be OK," I said as we started to walk.

"Feel so weak," he said. His face was slack as the war-snake venom sapped his energy. I was terrified that he would die right then and there.

"Just . . . um, f-focus on my voice," I said. I didn't know why, but I knew I could not let him give in to his tiredness. "Uh . . . what was it that bit you?"

Dari was breathing heavily and starting to sweat. He shook his head.

"Can't believe it," he said.

"Huh?"

Dari breathed a few breaths before he got the strength to speak. "I've been reading . . . the book."

I nodded.

"Wanted to know about . . . what was lurking in the jungle . . . since we would be spending time in there," he said. His walking was slowing, but we kept moving.

"Keep talking, Dari. . . . *Please,*" I said. I too was starting to lose my breath from holding him up.

"In . . . in the book," he said, "they list creatures and things that . . . explorers have documented . . . it's a good book, Zahrah."

"A good book," I repeated, not knowing what else to say. I was trying my best not to cry. I wanted to cry so much. To see Dari so weak was the worst thing in the world. Everything was happening so fast; I had no time to think!

"War snake," he said.

"A what?"

"They're poisonous . . . irrational, always . . . spoiling for a fight."

"How do you feel now?"

"Tired, dizzy."

"Concentrate on your feet," I said. "One step at a time."

Then I started counting out loud with each step. "One, two, three . . ."

Dari's eyes closed, but thankfully he seemed to concentrate on the numbers and moved his feet as I counted. We walked the long mile out of the jungle and emerged from the path onto the street. Then we stumbled down the street to Kirki's main road. Across the street were a few Kirki Farms office buildings.

"Help!" I shouted at the top of my lungs. Dari crumpled to the ground. I took another deep breath. "HELP! *Someone!*"

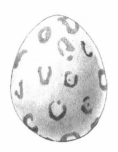

CHAPTER 12

ᗞECISION

"Your son is an extremely rare case," the doctor said hours later that night, clipboard in hand.

My parents stood pressed together, their faces still in shock. Dari's parents clutched each other, somehow hold-ing each other up. They were run down with stress. Dari's father rested his head in his wife's puffy Afro, his face wet with tears. Looking at him made me want to cry some more. The doctors had run a quick series of tests, and we all knew the news would be bad. Dari's mother's face was frozen in a sad grimace. The room smelled of baby oil, or-anges, and soap.

Dari had fallen into a deep, deep sleep even before one of the employees in the office building had finished calling the ambulance. I refused to leave Dari's side. I rode with him in the ambulance, and then sat next to him in the emergency room. When he was moved to a hospital room, I stationed myself in the chair next to his bed, holding his hand. Even though he couldn't communicate, I was sure he was aware of me, that he could hear every word being said. I sniffed and wiped my eyes.

"War-snake bite," the doctor said. She shook her head and looked at Dari's medical files. "I still can't believe it. You kids should *never* have gone into the forbidden jungle. You *know* that. It is called the forbidden jungle for a reason."

"I'm sorry," I whispered. I'd been saying that since Dari and I got to the hospital, and each time was like being stuck with a pin. We should have known. I explained how we had ventured into the jungle out of curiosity. I didn't tell them about my ability. What good would that have done? It would only have added more confusion and shock.

I wasn't asked much after that. At that moment, everyone was more concerned with Dari's condition than with why we were in the jungle in the first place.

"I'm sorry too, my dear," said the doctor. She looked at her clipboard. "Dari's condition has stabilized. He's not going to die from the bite . . . at least we don't think he will."

She paused and looked at Dari's parents.

"However, I have done some research and consulted

with other doctors. Let me present you with the situation. And I must warn you, it is not good," she said. Dari's mother sighed quietly. His father held her more tightly. My parents looked away.

"Your son was bitten by an incredibly rare snake from the forbidden jungle. Normally, it lives very deep in the jungle. How do we know this? Well, we don't. Not really. All the information we know about war snakes we got from this." The doctor held up a tattered green book. The edges were dog-eared, the pages yellowed and dusty. It was titled *The Forbidden Greeny Jungle Field Guide, Volume 439*. It was the same book that Dari had borrowed from the library, except this was part of the printed version. I took in a short breath and looked at my feet to hide my recognition.

"This is a field guide to the forbidden jungle," the doctor continued. "I'm embarrassed to say that the hospital owns a copy of it. We keep all the volumes in the basement . . . just in case. Most of what you find in here is nonsense. But we have no other way of knowing anything about the jungle. Anyway, the book says that the venom doesn't kill. War snakes eat small rodents. It is believed that they kill their prey by constriction. They bite only as an act of aggression. The venom affects all the victim's nerves. Lulls him into a deep sleep, a coma. One thing we know for sure after running tests on Dari is that he will not wake up."

Dari's mother gasped and began to weep. I rested my head on Dari's chest, all seven of my dadalocks spilling over his belly. I could still hear his heart beating through his hospital pajamas. He was still alive.

"The book, however, says there's a cure," the doctor continued with a soft chuckle. I held my breath. "But even if this were true, it's impossible to obtain. The yolk of an unfertilized elgort egg. Elgorts are raging with life, angry with it. The rage is transferred from mother to baby through the egg. For some reason, or so it says in this book, the extracted yolk reverses the effects of the venom."

"Elgort?" his father whispered. "But that's—"

"Yes, impossible," the doctor said. "And even if the book was right about the antidote and one could *get* an unfertilized elgort egg, Dari would have to be administered the elgort egg serum within about three to four weeks for it to work."

I glanced at Dari's parents. His father's eyes were shut, his eyebrows pressed together, his lips quivering. Is it not the worst pain to know there is a cure for your child's illness and then not be able to obtain it? *Oh it must be one of the worst types of pain in the world,* I thought. And it was my fault.

Dari's father must have wanted to tear himself away from his wife and run into the forbidden jungle and find an elgort, but even he knew that if he did so, the book's serum recipe might not work. And even if it did and he went in search of it, he'd never see his family again. One of the many mysteries of the forbidden jungle would certainly kill him before an elgort got the chance to do that. Most people of the Ooni Kingdom knew of the elgort, though very few had ever seen one. They were nightmarish monsters that populated the stories of children's books, adult horror novels, and gory digi-movies. The closest people came to elgorts was in the market, where hawkers sold false elgort teeth.

My cheek was warm from Dari's warmth, which radiated through his green pajamas. He still wore the glass luck charm Nsibidi had given him. It glowed a faint green. I looked at his serene face. I wasn't used to seeing him like that. He was usually smiling broadly, making jokes, telling stories based on history, and laughing loudly. Tears slowly dripped sideways down my face and onto his clothes. It was at that moment that I made my decision. It was like a seed sprouting, slowly growing and taking over my mind.

"But we have the best facilities to make sure he stays healthy," the doctor said. She paused and then softly said, "I'm sorry." Then she left the room.

I had things to do.

CHAPTER 13

THE CHOSEN PATH

I started my journey using the same path Dari and I had used only three days ago. I'd taken two days to think long and hard about my decision. I wanted to make sure I was doing the right thing. And in the end, I concluded that there was no other way.

I left Dari's side for the first time the morning before I went.

"You need to go home for a little while, Zahrah," my mother pleaded with me. I hadn't said a word to anyone while maintaining my vigil at Dari's side, and both sets of parents were growing worried.

"Take a bath, get some sleep," Dari's mother said.

I sighed and said, "OK. But can I have a few minutes with him in private?"

The moment the door shut, I leaned close to Dari's ear and whispered, "I'm planning something." I glanced behind me. "Don't worry. Maybe I'm too afraid to fly, but I'm brave enough to save your life."

My mother drove me home, and when I stepped into my room, I stared at my schoolbooks. It was Monday, and I hadn't even thought of the fact that I was missing the last day of school for the dry season. It didn't matter anyway. If I didn't do what I was going to do, Dari would miss more than the last day of school.

"Will you be all right?" my mother asked. "I have to go to work."

I only nodded, sitting on my bed.

"Take a bath," my mother said, and I took her advice. As I sat in the water, sponge in hand, I thought about my decision. I would pack my things that night and leave the next morning before my parents awoke.

So there I was, all alone, less than a mile from the forbidden jungle. I wished I'd had a chance to talk to Nsibidi before leaving, but there was no time. I stopped and looked at my digital compass. It was the size of a coin, and its face glowed a lime yellow. It pointed north. I pressed the button on its side and turned it on; it was showing the bright yellow rotating flower I had programmed it to show.

Then it said in its high-pitched whiny voice, "You are

heading north into the bowels of the Forbidden Greeny Jungle! I have no idea why you would do such a thing, but I am just a compass and you are just a thirteen-year-old girl. I must warn you, you are five hundred and forty yards north—"

I sighed and pressed another button on the side to shut the compass up. I wished there had been a built-in option to change its voice. And its attitude.

"Fine. You don't want to hear my words. It's your loss. Carry on then," the compass said.

I put it into my pocket, making sure that there was no way it could fall out. Of all the things I had, the compass was not something I could lose. It was the only thing that would lead me back home.

I carried a satchel on my shoulder and a bundled blanket strapped to my back. I'd considered bringing a carrying pod to hold the elgort egg in, but I had no idea how large elgort eggs were, and a pod would have been too heavy for me to carry as far as I had to travel. I figured I'd find a way to hold the egg when the time came. *If* the time came.

I held a paring knife that I'd taken from the kitchen in my left hand and a glow-lily hand lamp in my right. I had never gone camping, but I looked up tips the night before on the network. But even with that information, I felt like a fish out of water. I tried not to think about the fact that I really didn't know what I was doing.

I paused at the jungle border and bit my lip. On one side was the red soil, which was my home, all that I knew — safety and family — and on the other the dark brown soil, the unknown — danger, madness, and very possibly death. Fear landed on my shoulder like a heavy, bloodsucking masquerade. I pushed the story the farmers told Dari and me out of my head. It was just a story, I told myself. Maybe. I closed my eyes and stepped with a shaky leg across the line. This time I didn't look back.

I stopped at the tree where Dari was bitten. Of course the war snake was gone. But the digi-book Dari had dropped was still there. I brushed the spot with my foot to see if anything was skulking around the book. Then I flipped the book with my foot to make sure nothing was underneath. I slowly picked it up and pressed the "on" button. Nothing happened.

I pressed it again and still nothing happened. I jiggled the digi-book a bit, as I'd seen Dari do, and smacked it on the side. With the second smack, it made a peeping sound, and I quickly pressed the "on" button and up popped the title page. It showed the lush green jungle of palm, coconut, rubber, banyan, bush baobab, iroko, and mangrove trees, each of them labeled. The picture looked very much like the jungle around me.

The authors of the field guide were the Great Explorers of Knowledge and Adventure Organization, a group of radicals who had trekked into the Forbidden Greeny Jungle at different times over fifty years ago. Dari had read about these people. Just before he was bitten, these explorers had been his idols. Of course, the digi-book was packed with information about each of the many contributors to the book.

"They were a group of students from Ooni University who were determined to change the world," Dari had said during one of our days in the jungle. "Many of them didn't live past thirty! And even more of them emerged with odd afflictions. One came out of the jungle with strange green birds nesting in her hair and some even stranger disease that made her skin grow fish scales! But she also wrote three books about all that she saw!"

Dari said the digi-book offered not only lists and descriptions of creatures and plants of the jungle but also an extensive list of cures and precautions and even short stories and poems written by the authors while they were in the jungle.

Nevertheless, it wasn't until that moment that I became curious about the book. I guess I had been more absorbed with my ability, which I think was understandable. I clicked on the arrow, and the digi-book displayed the first page. I began to read.

Good morning, afternoon, or evening.

I'm glad you have chosen to enlighten yourself about the world around you. *Down with ignorance!* If there is one thing we, the Great Explorers of Knowledge and Adventure Organization, cannot stand, it is the fact that the people of Ooni choose to remain ignorant of the world around them! The Forbidden Greeny Jungle *is* the world. How can a whole sophisticated, matured civilization choose to live in a span of a few hundred miles? It is primitive! It is preposterous!

I had heard my father use this word, *preposterous*, when he was angry or thought something was ridiculous. I smiled and continued reading.

Now, we assume that you, reader, are sitting in your home, in front of your comfy computer, a cup of black tea or Ginen root soda in your hand, reading this for a good laugh. We, the Great Explorers of Knowledge and Adventure Organization, are not here for your amusement! This is real! Our travels are real and they were very difficult. Thus, we feel better pretending you are one of us, an explorer interested in venturing outside your little bubble, your silly comfort zone, and seeing the real world!

The first thing you need to travel there is a good, old-fashioned compass. We hear that there are digital

talking compasses out there on the market, but we
have yet to really see these pieces of science fiction.
So get a compass, any compass, as long as it works.

I closed the book, feeling better . . . a little. I felt a twit-
tery fear. But I had a compass. At least I'd done something right. Dari might have been reading this for fun, I
thought, but this book might save my life. Save his life. I
shivered, the weight of my task pressing down on my
shoulders. What I had to do was big. I was venturing
miles and miles into the forbidden jungle to get the egg of
a vicious mythical beast. If I didn't get it and get it within
a month, my best friend might die. I could feel my hair
heavy against my back.

I wished I'd found Nsibidi. She might have been able
to give me a little advice. I sighed. *Am I not a wise woman?* I
thought. *Or at least a wise girl? Whatever. It's supposed to be in
my blood . . . well, that's what I've been told, anyway. I do have a
lot of hair on my head. And birds would love to nest in it, I'll bet.* I
didn't check, but I hoped there were precautions listed to
keep birds away from my hair.

"Thank goodness for Dari's strange interests," I said,
putting the book in my satchel. A movement in the tree in
front of me caught my eye. I smiled. It was the dormouse.

"Sorry," I said sadly. "No fruit for you today."

The dormouse just stared at me, unsure of what to do
when it wasn't offered any food. I hiked my bundle higher

onto my back and wrapped a thin cloth around my glow
lily so I had just enough light to see where I was going. I
didn't want to attract too much attention.

I wasn't carrying a lot, just a small blanket, some food
and water, a lighter, my bottle of rose oil for my hair, my
daily vitamins, soap, two toothbrushes, and a few other
things. I wore green pants with a large mirror on the hip
and a caftan with mirrors around the collar that I'd taken
from the suitcase of clothes in Dari's hospital room. I
wanted something of his to bring along.

Sneaking out of the house that morning felt awful. It
wasn't that I risked getting caught. I was very quiet. It
was just that I was very afraid. It's a really strange feeling
to be starting a journey so dangerous that you could get
killed, to willingly leave the comfort of your home knowing this, while your mother and father slept.

I had thought about it all night, too. And the more I
thought about it, the more afraid I became. When I got
outside, my legs were shaking and I couldn't help crying a
little. My parents wouldn't have suspected my plan. To do
such a thing was so unlike me. But there I was, an hour
and a half later, in the dark. In the jungle. Terrified but
moving.

As I moved, I was sure something was watching me.
It wasn't the dormouse. The dormouse moved much more
quietly. I also knew that the dormouse didn't venture far
from its nest, which was around the spot Dari and I had

been spending our time in. I was well past that point. Whatever it was was probably more than one thing, too. The rustling leaves and snapping branches were coming from both my right and my left. I paused. Whatever they were, they grunted to each other and began moving away.

Fifteen minutes later, I was jumping at every little sound around me. I was farther in than Dari and I had ever gone. This fact looped around and around in my mind, and my face grew wet with helpless tears. Helpless because I knew I couldn't, wouldn't, turn back, and I knew that what lay ahead was so dreadful that I couldn't imagine it. Even with my bug repellant, tiny flies kept trying to land on my face to suck up the salt from my tears. I knew I had to stop crying but couldn't.

I felt faint whenever a bird flew from a tree, an insect buzzed by, a lizard crossed my path, or something snorted in the bushes. I walked slowly due to my shaky legs. And I kept my eyes cast to the ground for fear of seeing something in the trees or bushes that might hurt me.

Then came the group of spiders, each the size of a small child! There were about five of them, and they moved almost faster than my eye could follow. Their feet kicked up soil as they came at me. I'm humiliated to say that I was so scared that I froze and practically wet my pants! Not only were they huge, they were quite heavy. And when they got to me, they knocked me down and scuttled up and down my body and my satchel. Their many legs felt like stiff brushes scraping the exposed parts of my skin!

I screamed, instinctively curling myself up into a ball and bracing for the first sting. I was afraid they'd wrap me up in webbing and pull me up a tree to enjoy my blood and guts at their leisure. But after running up and down my body, they scrambled off and regrouped in front of me. They each made a huffing sound, blowing air at me from their mandibular mouths. It smelled like crushed bitter leaves and made me feel woozy. Then they ran off as fast as they had come! I remember reading somewhere that some insects and a few spiders taste with their feet. Maybe these thought I didn't taste very good.

I lay there sweating and shocked and relieved, blubbering like a baby, afraid to move for fear that they would come back. Eventually my heartbeat slowed down and I felt very tired, even drowsy. Whatever they blew at me must have been meant to keep me from going after them, as if I ever would.

I began to feel angry with myself. *How am I going to save Dari if I behave like a coward anytime something comes around?* I thought. I closed my eyes and asked myself a surprisingly difficult question. "Zahrah, do you really think you *can* save him? Can you *do* this?" I'm not one to lie to myself. The answer didn't come right away, and I lay in the soil turning it around in my head for several minutes.

Then I got up and brushed myself off. I stepped close

to a tree, for as much privacy as I could find, and urinated. Better not to take chances. I threw soil over the spot, stood up straight, and took a deep breath. Then I started back on the path. The next time something came after me, I would run.

Thirty minutes later, I was running from a large, squawking, brown, long-legged bird. I had accidentally crushed her nest of eggs when I stepped around a tree that had grown in the middle of the path. The bird was extremely distraught. I ran for about five minutes before she gave up the chase. When I was sure she was gone, I said a few words to Joukoujou about how sorry I was and to bless that bird with more eggs.

Two hours later, I was moving along the path, pushing branches and leaves out of the way. The path was getting narrower and narrower. Soon it would cease being a path at all and I would be moving around trees and bushes, checking my compass to make sure I was heading in the right direction.

Well, I knew the path would eventually end, I thought, wiping the tears from my face. I was surprised and thankful that it went this far.

"No more tears," I grumbled to myself. The flies were driving me crazy.

The more I walked the more I became aware of the noises around me and the more I couldn't believe I was doing what I was doing.

"I am in the Forbidden Greeny Jungle," I said out loud as I slapped at a mosquito. The repellant I had on was working (except for the flies that bothered my eyes), but no repellant was perfect. "Over two miles in. Alone. " I laughed to myself. "And goodness knows what is watching me right now."

I kept my eyes trained in front of me. I knew that if I looked to either side into the dense foliage, I'd lose my cool. Since the encounter with the spiders, I had been doing better. But I could feel panic rising with each step I took. Anything could burst through the trees and attack me at any moment. I heard the sound of thrashing leaves from far away and then several loud screeches and surprised clucks. My legs started shaking again, but I kept moving.

"As long as I don't bother things, then things won't bother me," I said quietly.

I imagined myself as just another creature whose home was the Greeny Jungle. I was just going about my business. *I belong here just like any dormouse or elgort,* I thought. And this was how I thought for the next several hours when the path deteriorated into nothing and the sun began to set. I'd stepped around some of the widest trees I'd ever seen and even come across a small pond of brackish water. It was teeming with wriggling mosquito larvae, and I quickly moved on.

By the time I slowed down, I was exhausted. But I was proud of myself. Since the spiders, I had not completely panicked; nor had I run screaming into the trees, not even when I'd seen the large black horse staring at me through the trees several yards away. The horse was trotting by and it froze, flaring its nostrils when it saw me. I froze too. It was probably deciding whether I was a threat or not.

Its coat was shiny, and it had a long mane that reached the ground and covered its eyes. When it decided I wasn't a problem, it trotted on its way. I let out a breath of relief and continued on my way, too.

It was time to find a place to sleep. A safe place. But in the Forbidden Greeny Jungle, there was no such thing. At least none that I knew of. As the sun set, the noise of the jungle grew louder. It was as if more things were waking up than going to sleep. My ears pricked at every sound. There were screeches, clicks, chirps, grunts, cheeps, growls, shrieks, hoots, and caws; twigs snapped, leaves rustled, branches bent, and somewhere a tree fell. It was terribly noisy. I walked tentatively, my shoulders hunched as I tried to make myself as small as possible.

"For you, Dari," I kept whispering to myself. "For you."

I scratched at a mosquito bite on my arm and looked at my dirty clothes. The cuffs of Dari's pants were caked with the soil, and they smelled strongly of dirty sweat. I reached into my satchel and brought out a small mirror. Small leaves and flower petals were stuck in my hair, and my face was greasy with sweat.

"Ugh, I'm repulsive," I said, quickly putting my mirror away.

Like any other northerner, I felt it was disgusting to wear dirty clothes and look so messy. But I had no choice. Itchy, dirty, and smelling of sweat and the outdoors, I needed to get over something more ingrained in my mind than my fear of heights.

"Where am I going to wash?" I whispered. "*How* am I going to wash?"

I hadn't thought of that when I left. But I knew the answer, and it made me shiver. I wasn't going to get to wash that night. I looked up at the patch of evening sky between the trees. I couldn't even wear perfume. Not that I'd brought any. Even I knew that wearing perfume attracted more mosquitoes. *At least there's no one here to see me looking like this*, I thought.

I stopped in front of a tall tree and then glanced around. I was alone. At least as alone as I could be in the jungle. I wiped a little sweat from my brow as I wondered what to do. *I must already be farther than anyone has been in years*, I thought.

Feeling very lonely, I sighed, set my bundle down, and stretched my back. I leaned against the tree and took out the digi-book. I pressed the "on" button and clicked to the table of contents. I clicked on the chapter called "The Fringes."

> The Fringes of the Greeny Jungle are the least dangerous. Rarely do you get any of the really good stuff there. If you've heard grumbling and shifting leaves, most likely you're being tracked by whistling bush cows, close relatives of the southern capybara.

Then the digi-book went into a long entry about these small but crafty furry mammals that liked to steal food from one's pack while one slept. They whistled when alarmed.

> Make sure you've zipped your bags securely when you go to sleep. And when we say securely, we mean securely. Zip it up, tie a rope around it, lock it if you can. Bush cows have been known to pick locks and even use sharp stones to cut through material if they smell something they particularly like.

I relaxed a bit. *Bush cows may be thieves, but at least they don't want to make a meal of me,* I thought. I skipped to the part of the chapter that talked about setting up camp. It was dark and I needed to find a place to sleep soon.

> The Forbidden Greeny Jungle is full of wonderful and often frightening beasts, as we all know. Once you enter the jungle, be ready to not see open land for a

while. Most of us traveled alone or in groups of two. But all of us did the same thing: We learned to climb trees. Most of us started doing this weeks after we ventured into the jungle, but our advice to you: Learn to climb and sleep in trees *now*.

There was more, but I was impatient. The fear was starting to set in again. I'd never spent a night really alone in all of my thirteen years. Someone had always been home.

I frowned as I felt the tears well up in my eyes. *I can't turn back now,* I thought. *It's night and I wouldn't make it out.* I frowned. It was time to stop crying. I looked around. I'd paused at a tall tree with plenty of space around it. I turned and looked up at it. A baobab tree, not unlike the one Dari and I liked to study in at home. At least something was familiar. I placed the digi-book back in my satchel and touched the tree's trunk.

Baobab trees had low branches, so I didn't have to climb too high. These fat trees with gnarled branches also tended to kill every plant around them so that they could spread themselves out. This one had the usual thick trunk, about as wide as a car. It reached high up, its many thick branches fanning out all around it. If I wanted to be safe, I had to go higher than the first branch.

I took a deep breath and whispered, "I have to do this," just as I had to learn how to be dirty. But instead I just stood there, my legs refusing to move. "I can't go up there," I said. I cried some more and sweat dripped from my forehead. "I can't go up there."

I was tired and something screeched close by. Then I thought of Dari lying motionless in his hospital bed. Forever. Never cracking his easy smile or laughing his loud laughs or voicing his philosophical thoughts again. If I didn't sleep and garner energy or if something attacked me because I was sleeping too close to the ground, how would I be able to save him? That was enough to get me moving.

At first I squinted my eyes so I couldn't see too much. Then I climbed without looking down.

"You're a big girl," I said as I ascended. My mother used to always say this when I complained about doing things I didn't like to do, like washing the dishes or cleaning my room. "And big girls are brave enough to do things they're afraid to do when they have to."

I let my mind focus on climbing, grasping the tree's branches and trunk, watching for strange insects and spiders and keeping my balance. This worked. Before I knew it, I had climbed as far as I could climb, which was just above the jungle's ceiling.

When I looked over all the trees, I gasped. I was very pleased, though my hands still shook. I looked over the treetops. It was a clear night and I could easily see the Ooni Palace lit up in the distance. I could even see my town at the edge of the jungle. But it looked very far away. *How far* have *I come?* I wondered. I could check my compass, but I didn't really want to know. It was better to look forward than backward.

When I accidentally looked down, I almost fell out of the tree. I was farther up than I imagined, and the sight made me dizzy. I could see the ground through a criss-cross of leaves and rough branches. I slowly sat down on the wide branch and closed my eyes until the dizziness went away. I inhaled deeply and opened my eyes.

"OK," I said, taking another deep breath. "It's not s-s-so bad."

It was bad but I was still alive and OK.

I'd always been a heavy sleeper, rarely changing positions when I slept. Sometimes I woke up in the exact same position I'd fallen asleep in, except for recently, when I awoke hovering above my bed. It would come in handy that night. But I needed more security. Vines were hanging from the tree's branches, and I pulled at one. It gave for a few feet, but then no matter how hard I pulled, no more would come. I yanked as hard as I could, and still the vine held. It was strong. Good.

I wrapped the feet of vine around my waist twice and tied it to itself. If I rolled off the branch, the vine would catch me. There was still a little give to it where I could move around.

"OK." I breathed. "This is good."

I nestled my things on the branch next to me, holding up my glow lily.

"Oh my!" I said as the light fell on a small flock of brown birds with short beaks. Sparrows. Most of them were hunkered down, their eyes closed. A few of them opened one yellow eye to see where the light was coming from.

"Sorry," I whispered, quickly wrapping a cloth around my glow lily. I didn't want to disturb them. The glowing-air flower would go out by the middle of the night, regenerating its light by the end of the next day.

For a while, I just sat there, listening to all the sounds around me, thinking about the fact that this was the longest I'd ever gone without a bath. I scratched at my skin and looked at the dirt that had gathered under my nails. I started getting scared. When I finally slept, due to mental and physical fatigue, it was hours later. I'd imagined over a hundred dreadful things that could happen to me up in the tree, all stemming from the many stories I'd heard over the years about the Forbidden Greeny Jungle.

A giant bird could come and carry me away in its gigantic beak. A swarm of invisible deadly mosquitoes could bite me as I slept until I had no blood left. The very tree I slept in could come to life and throw me from its branches. And many other things. In the end, my brain just got tired and I fell into a deep, dreamless sleep.

CHAPTER 14

Good Instincts

There was probably activity below as I slept.

I knew that bush cows had been following me for about an hour before I climbed into the tree. They were attracted to the food I carried. Nevertheless, as I snored away, there was nothing the dog-size creatures could do.

The field guide said that they had flat wide feet made for moving swiftly along the jungle's floor. They weren't made for climbing trees. I was fortunate, for I had no lock or rope to secure my satchel. If I'd slept on the ground, I'd have started my second day in the Greeny Jungle with nothing to eat. But there were stranger things than bush cows skulking about. Luckily, I didn't realize exactly what until the morning.

I woke with a start. I was lying on my back, and the

first thing I saw were trees, green leaves, and moss-covered branches. Then I heard the movement of something large below; it growled low and guttural. Instinctively, I didn't make a sound.

I quickly let my mind get ahold of where I was and why I was there. *I'm in the Forbidden Greeny Jungle,* I quickly thought. *I'm going north, in search of the most ferocious beast of all time: the elgort. I'm far from home. I walked many miles yesterday, and my muscles ache from all the walking.* But still, I didn't move. Instead I held on to the vine around my waist and listened, closing my eyes so that I could create a picture in my head of what was below by using the sound of its movement.

Mixed with my imagination, the sounds told me that whatever it was was big and had a large head and many big teeth. It wasn't an elgort. I wasn't far enough yet, and an elgort would move faster. I opened my eyes and slowly turned my head to the side. I didn't dare breathe.

It was directly below me, and it was hideous to my eyes: a giant lizard, about the length of a car. It didn't have the dry scaly skin of the lizards I had seen back home. This one had soft skin like a human being, except it was pale and pink like the inside of an unripe okonwe fruit. Its eyes glowed yellow, and its large mouth was filled with sharp, jagged teeth. The tip of its snout ended in what looked like the head of a shovel. It was using its strange snout to dig around the trunk of the tree.

I watched as it stopped and suddenly started digging with its claws. Then it leaned forward and bit into the dirt, pulling something out. The beast chewed on whatever it was and snarled with what I thought sounded like satisfaction. The sound made me feel less afraid. That such a frightening-looking beast could feel pleasure at eating something tasty made it seem less scary, made it seem normal. It walked into the bushes and went along its way. I sighed with relief and sat up. I stretched and waited a few minutes to make sure the giant lizard was gone. Then I untied the vine, gathered my things. The climb-down was nowhere near as scary as the climb up.

I stood before the tree feeling oddly good. I'd learned something that I didn't know before. Actually I'd learned four new things. The first was that I could spend the night in the Forbidden Greeny Jungle all by myself and live. The second was that I could be quiet in the face of danger. The third was that I wouldn't die or get sick if I slept with grimy skin and in dirty clothes. And last, I could trust my instincts. I'd awakened, and my instincts had immediately told me to be quiet and not move. I'd done this without my usual many minutes of pondering. Who knows what that strange lizard beast would have done to me if I'd screamed or gasped.

I smiled for the first time since Dari was bitten, embraced my newfound knowledge, and began walking, weaving my way around the trees, plants, and bushes. I walked for five hours before I decided to take a break. I brushed my foot in front of a tree to clear the leaves and mulch, laid my small blanket down, and sat on it. I ate a flour cake and brought out one of the five mangoes I'd picked from a wild mango tree along the way the day before. It was a small, strange-looking green one with blue splotches on the skin, but I figured a mango was a mango. I dug my nail into it and pulled the skin off. The flesh was a dull orange as opposed to the bright orange I was used to. Maybe it was a little overripe. I shrugged and took a bite.

"Ugh!" I exclaimed dropping it, wiping frantically at my mouth, and spitting out what I'd bitten. "Blah! Blah! Disgusting!"

The mango was horribly bitter. And the juice made my mouth cool, as if I'd eaten a very strong mint leaf.

"My mouth!" I exclaimed. "Numb! Numb! Ptooey!"

My tongue was going numb, and the roof of my mouth felt tingly. But I just sat there because something started happening to my perception of the things around me. Gradually everything grew odd. It was as if someone in my head were playing with my mental settings for color. The green leaves turned gold, and the brown tree bark looked purple. A grasshopper that hopped on my lap was every color of the rainbow. And a large squirrel in a nearby tree looked as if it were made of water!

"Oooh," I moaned, rubbing my temples. I smacked my

lips and chewed on my tongue. I tried spitting the bitter taste from my mouth some more. It helped a little. Aside from my mouth and my perception, I felt OK.

"OK, Zahrah," I said out loud. "Stay calm. You know what this is, and it's only temporary."

At least I hoped it was. When I was six, I'd experienced something similar to this. I'd accidentally eaten a chocolate-covered dimension cherry. My father's boss had given them to him as a New Yam Day gift. Dimension cherries were in season only once every seven years, and they're a delicacy among adults; these were potent ones. I thought the cherry was just a normal chocolate. I'd spent the rest of the day in my mother's arms as she told me over and over again that the house was not full of fuzzy green caterpillars and my skin was not blue.

So I knew a little about what was happening to me, that what I was seeing wasn't real and the effect would eventually wear off. Still, I was glad I'd taken only one bite of that strange mystic mango!

The mango's effect took about fifteen minutes to wear off. In that time, everything around me shrank to appear as if it could fit in my hands and then blew up to its normal size again; my legs grew long and lean, as if they were those of a woman, then they shrank back to normal; and I could have sworn I saw a large pink frog with gold speckles hop to my feet, humph arrogantly, and then hop away.

I would never eat a mango with blue splotches on it ever again!

When I was sure that I was OK, I stood up.

"Ridiculous," I grumbled, picking up my things. I opened my satchel and dumped out the rest of the mangoes. I took a moment to kick each one of them as far as I could.

Two hours later, I came across another mango tree. Almost all of the branches of this tree hung with plump red mangoes. *Normal* mangoes; mangoes that I was familiar with. I picked and sliced one open, and the flesh was bright orange. I sniffed it, poked it with my finger, and tentatively tasted it. Then I grinned with relief and took a big bite. It was the most delicious mango I'd ever had. I savored every bite and sucked the seed dry. I put my things down, sat in front of a tree, and ate two more. I put another four in my satchel.

I patted my belly and brought out my digi-book. I clicked to the book's encyclopedia and looked up "elgort." I quickly glanced around to make sure nothing was preparing to attack me, then I began to read.

"The elgort is a nasty, stupidly irrational beast. Mad as the Mad Hatter of the mythical *Alice in Wonderearth* tales. You don't want to follow one into any rabbit hole, trust us. Twenty-one of us explorers have been eaten by . . . *Source Page Error.*"

"Oh no!" I hissed, smacking the book on the side. "Not for this entry."

I turned it off and turned it on again with no problem, but when I went to the elgort entry, it said *"Source Page Error"* again. I tried one more time, but this time the digibook wouldn't even turn on. I sat thinking for a few minutes and then shook my head.

"Doesn't matter," I said.

I still had to get the egg. *Dari deserves a strong friend*, I thought. "Strong," I said. I nodded and then stood, packing up my blanket. "Strong," I said again. I was shaky but I was standing. Information or no information, I would move on. *If the elgort is not very smart, then I have an advantage over it*, I thought. I was dada, a person destined to be wise.

"And I'm a Windseeker," I said. Whatever that meant.

I kept hearing Dari's voice as I walked. "You should be flying," the voice told me. "It'll get you there faster and you'll be high above any elgorts if you see them." It was exactly what Dari would have said if he had been with me. I knew the imaginary voice was correct, but I was too afraid to try. *I'm a coward*, I thought. I bit my lip. *An elgort will have a field day with someone as scared as me.*

My mouth felt gummy. I hoped to come across a pond soon, though I wasn't sure if I would have the courage to wash in it. Who knew what kinds of things would be floating or swimming around in it. *I'll cross that bridge when I get to it*, I thought, not for the first or last time. I reached into my bundle, brought out my first bottle of water, and took a sip. I sloshed it around my mouth and then swallowed. Then I brushed my teeth.

The air was warm and humid but not too unbearable. Dari's pants and caftan felt comforting, though they were a little stiff from the dirt and didn't smell very good. I splashed some water on my face and reached into my bundle for another flour cake.

For the first time I thought of my parents. I had no idea just how bad things were back home in Kirki, but I could make some good guesses. Many miles south, my mother was probably sitting at the kitchen table wailing as my father paced the kitchen. I couldn't imagine either of them getting any sleep. Instead, the letter I had written would be on the kitchen table, a constant reminder of their only child's certain death.

This was what I wrote:

Dear Mama and Papa,

I've gone into the jungle. It's my fault that Dari is in a coma and it's up to me to make him better. I'll be back as soon as I get the elgort egg. I believe it will cure him. I'm sorry for leaving without your permission, but I know you wouldn't have let me go if I asked. And I must go. I love you and please tell Dari that I love him too.

Zahrah

Once they mentally collected themselves, my parents would probably call the authorities that very morning and maybe even alert the press or something. Regardless, because Kirki is such a small, tight-knit town, by afternoon, the news would spread fast.

"Don't look back," I told myself. "Not until you've succeeded." I focused on the plants around me. They grew progressively stranger as the hours crept by. The trees grew much taller, their trunks wider. I saw palm trees that grew so high that when I stood at their bases and looked up, their tops disappeared into the low-hanging clouds. Some of them dropped coconuts the size of large computer monitors. I made sure not to walk directly underneath these trees.

I saw seven long-armed, slow-moving furry black creatures with small heads sitting in some of the treetops. They looked down at me with curiosity, their large red eyes glowing like yam festival lanterns. Their heads could turn all the way around. I was afraid of them, but I had a feeling I could easily outrun them if I had to. They seemed more interested in eating the blue flowers in the trees, anyway.

Soon after that, as I was walking, I came across a very large pink frog with gold polka dots! The same frog I had seen while I was sick from the blue mango. It was real. The frog seemed to purposely stand in my way. Its skin was smooth and moist, and it had big golden eyes and stood in my path with no intention of budging. And if a frog's face was capable of frowning, this one was doing so. Then it spoke!

"What do you want?" it asked in a very annoyed voice, as if I were the one standing in *its* way and not the other way around.

"Uh, nothing . . . ma'am," I said, trying not to stare. It spoke with the voice of a tall, demanding woman, sort of like an older, less polite version of Nsibidi. I instantly went into the mode that I use with adults despite the fact that I was speaking to a frog.

"Yes, you do," she said. "You *allllll* do."

"N-no, ma'am," I insisted. "You must have the wrong—"

She sighed loudly and rolled her eyes.

"You can't remember?" she said. "Look at'cha! You shouldn't even be here. Your legs are too skinny, your arms aren't strong enough. You're food for trees, the bushes, the soil!"

Her words made my heart race with fear. She was right and we both knew it.

"Now wait just a minute," I said in a shaky voice.

"I don't have a *minute,*" she snapped. "I don't have a second. I don't acknowledge time. I'm too smart for that. I know everything already, *o.*"

"What do—"

"Annoying, annoying," she said, cutting me off and

hopping away. "Never know that you want what you want until you figure out that you want it, and by then you've just *got* to have it, but before that you don't know anything. Not my problem. Your loss and your hardship."

I watched her hop into a bush, still grumbling nonsense. When I was sure she was gone, I just stood there, my heartbeat slowing. Soon I was wondering why the frog so upset me. *Maybe,* I thought, *it gave off some substance that caused me to feel irrational fear. Like the spiders and their body-stunning breath.* I shrugged and continued on my way. Yet another peculiarity of the jungle.

Some time later, I passed a plant with a large green and orange striped pod that reached many feet high. It sat between two thick enormous waxy leaves. Once again, I listened to my instincts and walked a wide circle around it. And once again, my instincts proved correct. As I looked at the plant, a brown horse pranced directly in front of it.

In a flash, the plant snapped up the horse, its pod opening into a large, powerful mouth. The plant had no teeth, but judging from the crunching sound and the blood that dribbled from the pod, it didn't need any. I felt nauseated but quickly moved on, committing the deadly plant to memory and vowing to look it up in the field guide.

Each time I took a break, I practiced levitating. It was more out of respect for Dari than my actually wanting to. I'd sit, close my eyes, and concentrate. I didn't allow myself to float too high. Still, I had to admit I was getting better at it, feeling less shaky and slightly more at ease each time.

I also read a little from the digi-book, when I could get it to work. It helped keep panic at bay. Because I was being bombarded with so many strange, dangerous things, educating myself about the jungle helped calm my nerves some. But the elgort entry continued saying "error" whenever I tried to access it, and sometimes the digi-book simply wouldn't turn on. What if it never turned back on?

The farther I walked, the more I realized I needed it. "The Forbidden Greeny Jungle is so alive that you shouldn't be surprised when what you thought was a rock starts to walk away," the book said one of the times I got it to work. To me, this meant, Be suspicious of everything.

The more I traveled, the more I felt amazed at just how right Dari was, just how right *The Forbidden Greeny Jungle Field Guide* was. The people of Ooni all lived in a very small part of Ginen. They *were* very limited. They *were* living in ignorance. *I* had been living in ignorance.

But I'd been happy as long as Dari was around. The jungle had always loomed just behind my village, but I'd never thought much about what was in it. At least not that deeply. Nor did I wonder about how far it went. I used to think the same way as almost every other person in the Ooni Kingdom; now I felt silly for it.

When I was lonely, I talked to my compass.

"Good day," the compass said in its chipper voice. "You're exactly nineteen miles north of your village and two thousand miles from sanity. From the information you typed into me, you are a thirteen-year-old girl who seeks to find an unfertilized elgort egg for your friend?"

I held the compass to my mouth and said yes.

"Then you are truly mad."

I laughed as I stepped over a small fallen tree. I probed some leaves to make sure no snakes were hiding underneath them.

"No, I'm merely on . . . a mission," I told the compass. "Yes, a mission."

The compass paused, processing what I said.

"It is exactly three-thirty in the afternoon," the compass said.

"What do you know of elgorts?" I asked the compass.

"Nothing, but you are nineteen miles from home," the compass said.

"But you do know that they are from the Greeny Jungle at least," I said.

"I am only programmed with a little information on Ooni culture and literature, medical, gardening, and marital advice, anecdotes, and children's stories," it said. "Turn back. If you go five miles a day, you'll make it back in four days."

"I'm on a mission," I said, looking through the trees at the sky.

Then I stopped to look at an ugly yellow fungus growing on the trunk of a tree. It throbbed slightly, as if it were breathing. "Aren't you in the slightest bit curious about this place?"

"No," the compass said. "I only know the miles within the Ooni Kingdom."

I nodded. The compass had been programmed with the same philosophy that kept all people, except the explorers who wrote the field guide, from seeking life beyond the borders of Ooni. It was useful in telling me where I was, but at that moment, I turned the compass off.

CHAPTER 15

THE *W*HIP SCORPION

For several days, I was sure the jungle was trying to kill me. That maybe those farmers had been right after all and that the jungle was some giant superintelligent beast manipulating its enormous body and thinking of creative ways to cause my demise. It had lured me in with its mystery, but once I traveled far enough into its body, it closed around me and showed me what it was really like. And when it was finished playing with me, it would just swallow me up. These were the days when I looked death in the face and, because of this, learned how to survive.

For a while, I was still bothered by my dirty clothes, which I couldn't change because I *had* no other clothes. I broke out in an itchy rash because of the heat and lack of bathing. Whenever I stepped under patches of sunlight, the rash itched horribly! But in desperate times, even old habits die, I guess.

I was from the north, and that meant that I was used to tidy, clean, and civilized attire. Back home, I went through great pains every morning to make myself look just so. My hair had to be neat, my clothes perfectly matched, my shoes scuff free. It's just something you learn as you grow up, like the slang of your community.

Still, my habit of obsessing over my appearance started leaving me the minute I began my journey. I had no choice, really, with all the sweating and the dirt and no place to bathe. But it left me completely the moment I realized that I could be much worse off than dirty, that I could die a very painful, ugly death. And that was when I came face to face with the giant scorpion.

It came clambering down from a nearby tree while I made a snack of a mango. I now know what it's like to feel absolutely sure that death is moments away. What could I do against *this* thing?! The scorpion was an ancient-looking beast whose flat disk of a gray body was bigger than a grown man's! It was a scurrying nightmare. The scorpion hissed angrily as it moved on many thick pairs of legs armed with double rows of sharp spines. It clicked its large, scissorlike mandibles, a yellowish saliva dripping from them. Even from where I stood I could smell that saliva, or maybe the stench came from its entire body. The strong acidic odor stung my nose.

I had encountered a scorpion once back home. It was standing quietly on the side of a tree, black, shiny, and smaller than the palm of my hand. I'd run inside and got my father, who flicked it into the bushes. Scorpions are deadly when they sting, but they sting only when attacked.

This scorpion, though, was nothing like that scorpion back home. Aside from being far more aggressive and many, many times larger, it had no stinger. Instead, it had a large gray whip. And at the tip was a sharp piece of white cartilage the length of my arm that could slice more efficiently than the sharpest metal knife!

I stumbled back, hunching low. I'd scrambled up a tree twice to escape a pack of bush dogs and outrun a small wild boar, but in this case, that wasn't going to help. This creature was obviously an adept tree climber. Unlike regular scorpions, which had eight legs, this one looked like it had a thousand! All of them very strong and nimble. My heart felt as if it would leap from my chest, and every part of my body quivered with adrenaline.

The scorpion was only a few yards away, moving softly side to side as it studied me and prepared for the kill. It flicked its whip three times, sending sliced leaves and branches into the air. Yes, entire branches! It was that strong. I had to be quick, no matter what I did. It snapped its mandibles and cocked its tiny black head. The scorpion's large, shiny black eyes didn't fit the small size of its head and looked like bulbous black mirrors.

Mirrors, I thought. I took in a short breath. *Aha!* I knew what I would do. It started coming just as I dropped down and grabbed the first large rock I saw. Still, I focused on getting the rock in my hand and didn't bother getting to my feet. I locked in on the rushing scorpion and threw the rock as hard as I could, aiming at its large mirror eyes. Then I rolled back.

The rock connected perfectly with its target, and the scorpion's left eye burst on contact, oozing a black liquid.

"Yeah!" I shouted. But what I'd done wasn't enough. It hissed, shaking its head, and wobbled forward. The beast kept coming, whipping its tail uncontrollably back and forth, slicing off more leaves and branches. I'll never forget the sharp whistling sound that it made. I threw myself back and shielded myself from the falling foliage, but not before the scorpion's whip flung forward and sliced my arm.

"Ah!" I screamed, tumbling back farther.

The scorpion's oozing eye must have been horribly painful, and because it couldn't see through it, it grew angrier. Its whip swung about faster and harder. I felt warm blood flowing from my wound, but I didn't have time to think about that. Even if it was confused, the scorpion still had one functioning eye and was much faster than me. I was too slow to get to my feet, so I rolled. But before I knew it, I had rolled myself into a tree and was cornered. I impulsively curled up.

The scorpion hissed loudly, its sour mandibles dripping with yellow saliva. Even in pain, it anticipated a meal. I was breathing hard, very aware of my helplessness and doom. This thing would have no mercy with me. It must have thought I'd be an easy meal, and instead I had half blinded it. It snapped its whip only inches from my curled body; I could not only smell its breath but feel it. It was cool, like the mist that sometimes comes after the dry-season rains.

This is the last thing that I'll remember, I thought. *That this monster isn't warm and alive on the inside, but dead and cold.* I curled into a tighter ball, hoping that this position would make whatever it did to me less painful. *At least I got one good hit in,* I thought. *After it eats me, it'll never forget me. Maybe it'll think twice about attacking other human beings.*

My eyes were squeezed shut when the loud roar came. I didn't open them until I realized that moments had passed and I was still alive. I opened them just in time to see the scorpion's head drop at my feet, its burst eye still oozing. Then I looked up and screamed. I was almost eye to eye with the head of what I could only describe as a giant tortoise! The size of a large car! Its eyes were as big as dinner plates, the whites white as glow-lily pollen, and the irises a deep turquoise-blue like ghost flies. Its skin was a papery light green, and its jaws were so strong that it could snap off a scorpion's head with one chomp.

But this wasn't its only head! It had two! Its other head was busy with the scorpion's whip. Another chomp, and the thick whip fell to the ground like a dead tree branch! After I screamed, I could only gawk as the giant tortoise cracked the scorpion's hard shell with its powerful jaw and began to feast on its now limp body with both of its heads! The wet meaty sound and inky color of the scorpion's blood, which covered the tortoise's mouths and oozed out of the scorpion's body, made me gag with disgust. I looked away from the tortoise's heads and focused on the rest of its body. Its legs were stocky and its shell was covered with lush green moss and many leafy purple orchids and vinelike roots. I focused on the orchid flowers, too terrified to run away or even move.

Several minutes passed as the tortoise ate. I felt like I was frozen in time, and I didn't want time to start up again because once it did, I was surely next on this beast's menu. Then the tortoise raised its heads, gave a grunt, and ran its gooey-looking tongue over its lips. And turning, without so much as a glance my way, it lumbered back into the bushes.

I sat listening to it stomp away. The jungle had gone completely silent, and I could hear the tortoise for several more minutes. As I listened, tears dropped from my eyes and snot dripped from my nose. The air smelled of the scorpion's acidic blood and freshly cut leaves and branches. I was still shaking and felt very cold.

"How!" I whispered, slowly uncurling myself. I averted my eyes from what was left of the very creature that had just tried to eat me. I was alive only by chance! "How am I going to do this?" I said aloud.

I sobbed and for a moment was overcome by my shaking body. I wrapped my arms around myself. This was only the beginning. I wasn't a trained explorer, and my friend was in a coma. Anything could eat me. I was on the same rung of the food chain as a minor rodent. *If* even that. Easy prey. And no one could save me. No one even knew where I was! Only a few days before, I was home safe with my parents, hanging out with Dari on the network; now I was alone in a place where it was "kill or be killed" or "be killed while trying to kill!"

For a long time, I sat there in the dirt shaking and sobbing. My eyes grew puffy. My nose ran onto my sandals. My head throbbed. What was left of the dead scorpion began to smell more bitter and acidic in death, but still I didn't move. All I thought about was Dari and how helpless I felt. And all I could do was wallow in my misery, self-pity, and shock.

But after a while, I quieted and grew more still. I could hear the caw of a palm-tree crow. Palm-tree crows were also common in Kirki, and the sound helped bring me back to reality. The reality was there was no turning back, and if I wanted to live, I had to move on.

"At least it's dead," I said to myself as I slowly stood up. "And it didn't kill me."

As I straightened up, I felt slightly dizzy and a little off balance. I looked at my bleeding arm, peeking underneath my dirty, now ripped shirt. The cut wasn't that deep, but I could smell a little of the acidic odor coming from the wound. Another wave of dizziness hit me. I shook my head and fought back more tears as something really bad dawned on me. I stepped over to my satchel and bundle, which were still under the tree where I'd left them. The satchel was open and all my food was gone. Bush cows must have got into my things as I was being attacked.

But I had a feeling that that was the least of my problems. With trembling hands, I picked up and opened the field guide to find out if what I suspected was true. Thankfully, the field guide turned on after the second try. It was easy to find the entry on the scorpion.

> If you've survived an attack by a whip scorpion, congratulations. There's hope for you yet. This is really one of the first truly deadly Greeny Jungle creatures you'll encounter. Sure there are also bush dogs, carnivorous plants, and flesh-eating maggots, but the whip scorpion is not only lethal but highly intelligent. You can't escape it. You *must* murder it or be

murdered. And bringing one down is not easy. If you
had a gun, you must have aimed for the eyes. If you
had a bow and arrow, you must have aimed for the
eyes. If you had a barbed spear, you must have aimed
for the eyes. If you had none of these, we have *no idea*
how you're alive!

They forgot to consider sharp rocks, I thought. *And the help
of a disgusting, giant, plant-covered, two-headed tortoise with a
big appetite.* I yawned, feeling extremely tired. Suddenly,
all I wanted to do was sleep. I skipped several paragraphs.

If you're cut by that infernal whip scorpion's whip, you
have good reason to worry. Whip scorpion poison *is*
lethal. If it's a big gash, well, you will probably die in a
matter of minutes from the bleeding and poison com-
bined. But if it's a small cut, a tiny blue rash will appear around it and it will be very itchy. *Do not* scratch.
If you scratch at it, you'll get poison under your nails.
Most of us will agree, itchiness under the nails is
agony.

All you can really do is pat some soil on the wound—
Greeny Jungle soil is very good for wounds—and get
some rest. Everything else is up to fate. You will either
live or die. Over 50 percent of those poisoned will die.
It depends on how tough you are. As the poison circu-

lates in your bloodstream, you will get more and more
sluggish and less alert. When you're near the end, you
may see lines and blotches. You will know your fate
within a day or so.

Still, beware of that sweet sleep you crave. The more
you sleep, the stronger that venom inside you be-
comes. Too much sleep could bring on death even if
you're strong. Try setting your alarm clock. Have it
wake you up every four hours and then walk around if
you can.

If you live, it's not over yet. For the next six to seven
months, until the poison has fully left your system,
you'll be susceptible to spontaneous spells of deep
sleep whenever your blood pressure rises high, such
as times of extreme fear or anxiety. Good luck!

"Spontaneous spells of deep sleep? Just from being
scared?" I said out loud in disbelief. I felt so tired that
I slurred my words. "It's just a matter of dying now
or later!"

I smacked my forehead and closed my eyes, almost
falling asleep right then and there. I shook my head,
picked up a stone, and threw it hard at the corpse of the
scorpion. The stone landed in the exposed meat of the
gaping hole that the tortoise had bitten into. I grimaced

with disgust. Still, the cursed thing had done this to me. Evil, vile thing. My arm was already itching, several bright blue spots popping up on it.

A sudden wave of drowsiness hit me, and I sat down heavily in front of a tree before the whip scorpion.

"Oh, no, no!" I whispered in my slurred voice. "Not now, can't sleep."

I had to fight it. To fall asleep on the ground in the jungle was practically suicide, poison or no poison!

My eyelids felt as if someone were gently pulling them down, and I even thought I heard my mother's voice softly singing in my ear a melody she always sang to me when I was young.

Close the door
Light the light.
We're staying home tonight.
Far away from the bustle
And the bright city lights.

I mumbled the song along with the voice I thought I heard. Even as sleep took me, I felt my stomach grumble. I didn't have any nourishment in my body to fight the poison, either. Oh, my chances of living were so so slim. *If I fall asleep,* I thought, *not only will I not wake up, but neither will Dari.* My mind was going fuzzy. *I've failed him,* I thought, *and I've failed myself.*

Then I slept.

CHAPTER 16

THE *W*OOD WIT

I was lucky a second time.

It was afternoon when I woke. The afternoon of the next day! *I'm alive,* I thought. But blue splotches and purple lines clouded my vision, so that I had to squint to make things out. Several vines from the tree above me had crept down and begun to grow across my shoulders. Already the jungle was trying to swallow me up, and I wasn't even dead yet!

Some sort of furry, orange, round rodent was licking the sweat off my left arm. When I moved, it rounded its lips and made an odd *oooooo* sound and scurried away. I blinked and tried to move my arms up to push the vines away and rub off the animal's saliva onto my clothes. I was able to do so, but my muscles ached horribly. My entire body was wet with perspiration, but I felt cold as ice. The vines had suction-cup-like buds that fastened them to my arm. Pulling them off wasn't painful, but it took me a minute to flake them from my skin.

I sat for a moment thinking. Why nothing had come along and eaten me in the night (unless I counted the attempts by the vine and the licking rodent) was beyond me. Maybe the jungle's creatures and beasts felt sorry for me, or maybe I just didn't fit into the current menu; maybe I was poisoned meat. I didn't know. I didn't care. I was alive and that was all that mattered.

"Oh," I groaned.

I may not have died yet from the scorpion's poison, but I was certainly on my way out. The minute my mind remembered what had happened to me, I knew that what I was experiencing was my body dying. It was an eerie sensation. Like everything was shutting down and packing up. A part of me even wanted to lie down and go back to sleep. I knew if I did, I wouldn't wake up. But still, the urge was strong.

It was the thought of my parents and how they would feel if I died that got me going. I could scarcely fathom the grief they were feeling in that very moment and how their grief would deepen if I never went back. The stories they might imagine of how I died would cause them even more sadness. Then there would be worse stories other people would make up. I would become like the man in the folktale the farmers had told us.

My mother would stop combing her hair, and my father would forget to put on his favorite cologne. They would look at my bedroom with all the things I'd have left behind. They would watch the plants on my dresser grow out of control, the dresses in my closet get moldy, and my personal computer stop evolving. I'd always be a ghost that haunted them, as Dari would haunt his parents.

All these thoughts moved through my mind like a fly moves through sugar palm sap. Slowly but determinedly. And before I knew it, I was crying and pushing myself up. My muscles screamed and my vision clouded with more spots and lines, but I forced myself to move. I stood up and almost fell forward. I steadied myself and then began to walk, leaving my things behind. I had to get some nourishment in my system if I was to have a chance.

I looked at the gash on my arm. Despite the mud I had smeared on it, the blue spots had spread all the way up to my shoulder, and the entire arm felt tingly and itchy.

"No scratching," I said to myself. It wasn't easy.

I slowly bent down, scooped up some more moist soil, and applied it to my arm. It was cool and soothed the itchiness some. I closed my eyes and mustered all the strength that I had left. When I opened them, a few of the spots and lines had disappeared.

Stumbling, I looked around for any type of tree that might have edible fruits. One tree was heavy with several of those blue mystic mangoes. I stopped and looked at it for a moment. I was desperate and willing to endure the nasty taste and horrible hallucinations if only to keep me alive, but who knew what those mystic mangoes would do to me in my weakened condition? I moved on.

Tall palm trees, mahogany trees, ekki trees, bushes, ferns. A tree that I couldn't name with flat disklike red seeds. Another tree with black berries that I wasn't familiar with. Other than the mystic mango tree, there were no trees bearing any familiar fruits. I wandered around for a few more minutes until I heard buzzing. Loud buzzing.

"Is that in my head?" I grumbled.

The spots and lines had returned, and I was starting to feel even more worn out. My stomach growled, but I ignored it to listen harder to the buzzing as I rubbed my forehead. I almost dismissed the noise as part of the poison's effect, but a large, fuzzy, yellow and black bee zoomed past me. I followed it with my eyes, and that was when I saw it.

The tree was wide like a baobab, but it had spikes like a pine tree. The spikes covered every inch of the tree, making the branches look like far-reaching hairy arms, except for its trunk, which was a light brown and very smooth. Halfway up, the tree split into a giant unnatural fork, as if at some time it had been struck by lightning and simply grown in two directions. Between the jagged edges of exposed wood was a golden mass that, even in the shade of the forest, seemed to glow. It was a beehive swarming with thousands and thousands of fuzzy, noisy bees. But my attention wasn't on the noise or the possibility of getting stung. It was solely on the honey that must have been inside.

My mouth began to water. Slowly, I walked up to the tree. I had no idea what I was going to do. My mouth grew moister as I thought about the sweet honey oozing into my mouth with each bite. *Maybe I can tear off a tiny bit of the comb without the bees noticing,* I thought. A ridiculous idea, but I was in a ridiculously desperate situation.

I was only a few feet away from the tree's smooth trunk when something strange happened. The bees suddenly grew very quiet, landing on the honeycomb and on the tree's spike-covered branches. Then the tree trunk began undulating, and something large was moving underneath the bark. Then a face appeared in it! It had large lips like my uncle Ogu and eyes the size of small pumpkins.

I yelped and stumbled back. A wood wit! I'd heard of them but never seen one in real life. No one really knows exactly what wood wits are. Most say that they're "things that live in trees," personalities, characters. But you usually have to hike deep into a forest or jungle to meet one. They don't hurt the tree; they help it. So trees with wood wits are usually a lot larger and healthier than others. This tree, which had probably been struck by lightning, might have died if it weren't for this wood wit. Some wood wits are nice, some are mean, some refuse to even acknowledge you, and the only way you know of their presence is because you see a face in the tree once in a while.

"I see you're looking at my lovely friends," the wood wit said.

I blinked, surprised that it would speak in a language I could understand. Its voice was deep like a man's and sounded like three voices put together. "Lovely, lovely, lovely. You can't find better friends, *o*! You know they travel over thirty miles a day for pollen? When they return, they always have so, so, so much to tell me, and there's nothing they like more than an ear that is always open. Since I live in this tree, I see the world through their stories.

"And I don't mind telling you, a complete stranger, just how wonderful my bees are because they will never leave me, because they love me and I love them and love is what makes this tree grow! L-O-V-E!"

The bees' buzzing grew slightly louder as if to happily affirm the wood wit's words. Or was it more a sound of annoyance? I grunted, not knowing what to say. All I could do was look at the honeycomb, imagining how delicious the honey would taste and how it would make me stronger and possibly help me survive. I painfully cleared my throat.

"Please," I whispered. "Will you ask your bees to give me some honey? I'm very—"

"Of course *not*!" the wood wit said with a chuckle. "These are *my* bees, *my* honey, mine, mine, mine! We have been friends for five hundred years and will continue so. I'll not share their friendship with the likes of you."

The bees buzzed loudly again. The wood wit frowned, its face melting from one place on the tree's trunk and appearing on another. Then in its strange triple voice, it said with a smirk, "I don't share with anyone. And if you try to steal even a drop of my sweet, sweet treasure, I will send my bees to sting every part of your grubby body."

I scowled, miffed at being called grubby. But I had to focus. I needed the nourishment. I didn't have the strength to look any farther. I reminded myself that being grubby no longer mattered.

"Please," I whined, surprised at his cruelty. "I . . . I think I'm dying. If I could just have a little honey, I might—"

"That's not my concern. Death is a part of life, life is a part of death. I will not douse my happiness with your tragic mess," the wood wit said, looking at the bees with admiration and infatuation. The bees buzzed very loudly three times, and the wood wit actually paused and frowned, looking at them. It pursed its lips, looking at me and then the bees, and then at me again. Then he said, "No. No. Leave us be, human being. I shut down to your words."

I bit my lip. For the first time, I began to wonder whether the wood wit wasn't more than a little insane.

"I'm not asking for much," I said. My voice cracked because my throat was so dry.

"Words, words, words," the wit said, its face playfully rotating in a circle on the tree. "Leave my happy existence alone. You're agitating my bees. Look at the shadow you bring to our happy world. Oh the darkness! I can't see! Leave us be!"

I looked around confused. There were no shadows. Above, the sun was out. Suddenly several of the bees flew over to me. The wood wit didn't seem to like this.

"No, wait. Just leave her alone. She'll go away on her own," it said.

I shut my eyes tightly, sure that they would apply their stingers to make me go away. If they were friends of the wood wit, they, too, were probably crazy.

The first one landed on my shoulder and *prick*! I yelped, but I was so weak that that was all I could do. My eyes watered. Things seemed to be only getting worse. I hunched my shoulders bracing for more stings. I had read somewhere that the human body could sustain only a certain number of bee stings before dying. I thought about trying to levitate above the trees, but the bees would follow me. They were obviously much better at moving about in the air than I was, especially with my energy ebbing.

My shoulder burned from the sting as the other bees landed on my clothes. I waited, my eyes shut tightly, but no more stings came. Slowly I opened them. At least a hundred of the fuzzy bees were sitting on me, so many that they weighed down my clothes! I could hear their wings flitting, especially the ones closest to my ears. I heard the wood wit grumble in annoyance.

Then they all abruptly rose up as if someone had spoken. But the wood wit hadn't said a thing. It had actually been quiet as it watched its friends with what I could only call a jealous eye. Then the bees flew back to the hive, and the buzzing of the hive got very loud again as they flapped their wings more vigorously and moved about as if dancing. They were talking to each other, I realized. The wood wit also seemed to be listening, its face turned toward the hive with a look of aggravation.

"What is wrong with you all?" the wood wit said. "You're mine, not hers! Don't you love me?"

Some time passed before the wit turned its attention to me. In a pouty voice, as if I'd done it the worst of wrongs, it said, "They want to know who you are."

The beehive went very still, and for the first time in

minutes, I could hear the other creatures of the forest chirping, squawking, screeching, and hooting.

"M-m-my name is Zahrah," I said.

The wood wit said nothing and the bees didn't move. So I went on. "I'm from a place called the Ooni Kingdom."

I told the wood wit and its bees all about my ability to levitate, Dari, and my journey. By the time I finished talking, I was so dizzy that I wasn't even sure if I had told a coherent story. But I must have made some sense because after a long pause and then another noisy dancing, buzzing session, the wood wit said, "OK, OK! Fine. I can't believe this." It pursed its lips. "*Since* my bees . . . like you, I will help you as best I can. Be thankful that I love my bees with all my heart and would do anything for them. They, of course, love me, too, you know. You can never replace me in their eyes." Another pause as the bees buzzed with annoyance. "I'll give you two choices," it said.

The wood wit smirked mischievously, its woody lips puckering with delight. It was relishing my situation. I frowned but said nothing. My mother always tells me that one who gets enjoyment from other people's misery will eventually get the greatest discomfort from his or her own miseries.

"The first choice is that I cure you and send you home," the wood wit said.

"Huh?" I said. "You can *do* that?"

"Of course I can. I'm a wood wit," it said. "I can do a lot of things if I choose, if need be, if it is proper, if my bees ask it."

Before I could speak, the wood wit continued.

"If I send you home, you could be cured . . . and far, far away from my bees and me, thankfully."

The wood wit stopped talking for a moment to let me digest its words. My head was whirling. *I can be sent home?* I thought. I would not die or contract another illness. I could take a long bath. I could cry on my father's shoulder and listen to my mother's soothing words and advice. I could tell them I was sorry. I could tell them all about how the jungle was crazy but still just a jungle, how there was so much to discover.

"Or," the wood wit said loudly. I shook my head so that I could pay close attention. "I could give you some." The bees buzzed very loudly at this. "OK, OK, my *bees* could give you some of this honey. You could use one of the leaves from that tree behind you to store and take it with you."

I turned around. The tree's purple leaves were wider than my head. I'd be able to store a large honeycomb on the leaf and wrap it up.

"But I can't guarantee that the honey will help you live," the wood wit continued. "Who knows, it might even kill you, not that you would be much of a loss. My bees love me, but I don't need to eat as you do. You're a different creature. And they certainly don't *love* you. Still, if you do live, you will be able to continue on your way. You *are* running out of time, no doubt about that." It paused for a moment and narrowed its eyes. Then it said, "So what will it be? Survival and safety? Or a chance to save your friend, which is more like a chance to die *trying* to save him?"

The wood wit laughed with glee, its face smoothly migrating about the tree trunk in a spiral. Then it stopped, facing me, and said, "Well?"

The bees were completely quiet, waiting for my answer.

My brain felt like mush and I was very tired. Details of my two choices traveled through my head. *I'll get to see Dari again soon. Is he all right? My parents will know I'm alive. Maybe I can gather better traveling gear and try again. But I'd have to run away again. Everyone will expect that I'll try and they'll keep a closer eye on me and make running away impossible. Then Dari won't be cured. All my fault. How long have I been out here? Fewer days to find the egg. If the egg can even cure him. What will eating honey do? If I die out here, what will happen to my body? Something will eat it. Oh it's all so sad.*

But my thoughts settled on one thing: Would I take the chance for my friend? Yes. Yes I would. I don't know if it was the delirium from the poison or a clarity of mind brought on by the delirium, but I knew what I had to do. Or at least I thought I did. *This could be the death of me,* I thought to myself. I laughed a little when I realized that I no longer cared much.

"I'll take the honey," I said quietly. "If it kills me, then so be it. It's a chance I'm willing to take."

The wood wit's eyebrows went up, and it tilted its face to the side.

"Are you sure?" it asked.

I wasn't really, but before I could say so, a large group of bees flew from the hive and over my head to the tree behind me. They picked a large purple leaf and dropped it at my feet. I slowly bent down to pick it up, trying to ignore the fact that I may have just chosen to die in the Greeny Jungle.

A few bees hovered before my eyes, and some of them circled around my waist.

"They want you to come and take what you want," the wood wit said.

I looked up at the spiny tree as I walked toward it. It was an odd tree. The ground underneath it was covered with fragrant spines that grew thicker the closer I got to it. The large waxy hive was over three feet thick and built to fill the entire seven-foot-long and three-foot-wide crack in the tree. The bees all moved up to reveal the lower section of their large, honey-engorged comb. I looked up at the hive, near the top, as some bees moved about. Underneath I could see many compartments in the comb that were filled with what looked like white balls: bee babies, larvae, the hive's nursery. Several fuzzy bees that were yellow but with no black stripes guarded them.

The wood wit's face moved next to the part of the hive closest to me. I resisted the urge to reach out and touch the face. Its round knobby cheekbones and thick lips looked soft, but I knew if I touched them, they would be hard as, well, wood.

"Just use your hand," the wood wit said.

I hesitated and then raised my hand to the golden honeycomb that glowed in the filtered jungle sunlight. The combs looked so perfect. Every single tiny cell had six sides, hexagons. I took a deep breath, thinking about Dari and how this was all for him and my safe return home. Then I dug my hand into the honeycomb. There was a soft popping sound and honey oozed around my hand. I held open the leaf and plopped down a large chunk of succulent honeycomb. Then I took some more and kept packing it in until the leaf was heavy.

"Aren't you going to have a taste?" the wood wit said as I started to close the leaf.

I looked at the package and then at the wood wit. The bees bustled over the beehive, appearing to work, though even I knew they were paying attention to me. A bunch of them flew down to start repairing the place where I had taken my share. The thought that the honey could poison me was, of course, still on my mind. So I planned to take the honey with me, find a nice baobab tree to climb into, and stare at it until I got the nerve to have a taste. If I could *get up* in a tree. It probably wasn't possible, not without putting something in my stomach first.

"I was going to," I said.

"Well, go on then," it said. "Might as well find out if you're going to live or die right now. *I'm* certainly curious."

I opened the leaf and looked at the golden, sticky honeycomb. It seemed like normal honey. I held it to my nose and sniffed. It smelled slightly of mangoes. The bees probably produced their honey using mango flower pollen. I frowned. What if they used pollen from those mystic mango trees? Then maybe the honey would smell bitterer, I thought. I grunted to myself, feeling lightheaded from the whip scorpion's poison, hunger, fear, and exhaustion.

"OK," I said. "I'm going to just do it."

I brought the open leaf to my mouth, held my breath, and took a bite. The bees suddenly burst into a melodious chorus of buzzing, several of them flying into the air and parading around the tree. I glanced up at them for a moment, and then all my senses were overtaken by the honey. My initial thoughts: *Waxy, chewy, and . . . extremely sweet and delicious!* I took more bites. My body responded as if the honey were water and I was extremely dehydrated. Before I knew it, I had eaten over half of what I'd taken.

"Oh," I grunted, honey and wax all over my face. I stopped and blinked, becoming aware of myself again.

"Oh," I said again. I wrapped up the rest of the honey. "Thank y—" Then it hit me. It felt like hands angrily clenching my stomach and twisting. Then it felt as if my head were exploding and oozing out of my ears! I screamed and fell to the ground, and before everything went black I heard the wood wit laughing. Laughing and laughing and laughing hard enough to shake the entire Greeny Jungle. I'd fallen to the ground and curled up next to the tree, still clutching the leaf full of honey, my eyes shut tight. But within minutes the bellyache passed completely. I gasped and quickly sat up. All my muscles groaned in unison but . . .

"What?" I whispered out loud.

I slowly, achingly sat up and looked at the tree. The wood wit was nowhere in sight. The beehive, however, was still there, covered completely with bees, including the place where I had taken the honeycomb chunk. They acted as if I weren't there, their buzzing unanimated and monotonous.

It took me a moment to realize it, but when I did, I patted my hands around my body. I was OK. I could feel the change. The poison wasn't gone. It wouldn't be gone for months. But I was alive and going to live. I stood up, stretched my legs, and rubbed the side of my head.

"OK," I whispered. Then I turned to the beehive. "Thank you."

For a moment, their buzzing grew slightly louder, then it returned to normal. I clutched the leaf of remaining honey to my chest and made my way back to my things. I was all right, and that meant Dari still had a chance. I looked up at the treetops, rubbing my dirty hands on my clothes. No longer did I think sleep was dangerous, so I planned to take a long rest.

CHAPTER 17

SOME TIME TO EASE MY MIND

I spent the next day in a nice baobab tree. Despite the fact that I was able to get a good night's sleep, I still felt exhausted when morning came. "Just one day," I told myself. The poison would remain in my blood for months, and I still had the risk of falling asleep anytime my blood pressure got high. I didn't know what I was going to do about this, but I knew I would keep going . . . after I took a little time to get used to the idea that this could happen.

"Laziness is unforgivable, but a little down time is essential after hard work. It recharges your batteries," my mother always says. And I certainly felt I'd been hard at work since entering the jungle. Working to stay alive and lucky to *be* alive. I didn't bother tying myself with a vine.

And though I slept well, I dreamed of the wood wit and its knowing laugh and of the spots and lines that signified a death by scorpion poison. In my last dream, I died and all went black, like falling into a deep sleep; like the one Dari was in or the one I could now fall into if I got too scared. I woke up shivering, with tears streaming down my face.

Still, the tree I was in was a good one. It was the tallest in the area and not too fat, with very rough bark, making the trunk easy to climb. And it had many thick branches that led all the way to the top. It felt homey and safe.

Because these trees killed the plants and trees around them, they gave me a clear view of what was going on below. Baobab trees also seemed to discourage many creatures from making a home in them. My digi-book said, "There's something about the baobab tree that the creatures of the jungle have a problem with. Is it a stench? Particularly rough branches? We do not know, but it's certainly something. Possibly just a bad vibe. We've seen only small groups of birds and the occasional tree sloth and flying squirrel in them."

After I woke up and shook off the nightmare in which I died, I lay awake for a while feeling disturbed and agitated.

I slowly climbed down, cleaned my whip-scorpion wound with some water, and patted some soil on it. It looked better; the blue spots on my skin were gone. But the wound was crusted over with a thick, bluish scab, an obvious sign that the poison was still in my blood, even if I was alive. Then I ate the rest of the honeycomb. This time eating it made me feel better, more refreshed and energetic. I sighed, thinking of the tricky wood wit. It had helped me, even though it seemed a little crazy. Like the Dark Market, sometimes things weren't what they seemed.

I spent the rest of the morning reading passages from the field guide. I reread the edible fruits chapter, the chapters on small Greeny Jungle ponds and balloon frogs, and a long chapter on Greeny Jungle panthers, yet another "truly deadly" Greeny beast I might soon encounter. I tried my best not to think about the fact that I could instantly fall asleep if I met one of these beasts. *If I can't do anything about it,* I told myself, *it's a waste of energy to worry about it.*

The panthers I read about were different from panthers found in the small patches of forest within the Ooni Kingdom. Greeny Jungle panthers were larger and more muscular, had bigger green eyes that could see farther and sharper teeth, and were very, very intelligent. *Why is it that everything in the forbidden jungle is always scarier?* I thought.

"This is the only large cat in the jungle. We believe that this is because they've killed off all of their direct competitors. Black as the inside of a cave on a cloudy night, Greeny panthers move smoothly like oil, silently like the shadows of ghosts. Males and females mate for life. If you see one, be careful; there is always another close by."

I shivered but continued reading about their breeding habits, their preferred food, and, most important, the best way to survive an encounter with one.

Panthers like to ambush their prey from treetops. One minute you're walking along your merry way, the next, a panther has jumped on you and is tearing your head off. By this time, prepare to say hello to death. You have no chance. Panthers are expert killers.

Several of us have seen a friend die in this way. Panthers go right for the throat, and its companion will make sure the job is finished quickly by going for the chest. Trying to scramble up a nearby tree is hopeless because, obviously, panthers are excellent tree climbers. They'd probably like you to climb up a tree. They might even stop and give you the chance to do so. Panthers prefer to eat their meals there.

Now, panthers *despise* the smell of lemons. To them lemons smell the way poo smells to us. Would you want to eat anything that smelled like poo? When they smell it, their nostrils flare and they start to sneeze in disgust. Thus the minute you start seeing ravaged carcasses dangling from tree branches, find yourself a patch of <u>lemongrass</u> (click the link for a description of lemongrass and where to find it).

Hopefully it won't be too late. And when you see a panther, do not run. It only gets them more excited, and when excited, they are often willing to ignore the bad smell. And trust us, if you're in the jungle for more than four days, you *will* see a panther. Assume it. Be ready for it.

I clicked on the lemongrass link and held my breath, hoping with all my heart that the digi-book wouldn't choose to malfunction. It didn't, thankfully, and I memorized the information.

That afternoon I practiced levitating. For the past few days, I'd practiced for an hour before going to sleep. Dari would have wanted me to do so. "It's stupid to waste talent," he always said.

So on these days, I sat high in the trees and used my talent. I no longer had to close my eyes to gather concentration. And though I could float from one branch to another and had significantly conquered much of my fear of heights by climbing trees day after day, I still was too afraid to attempt actual flight.

I have to try to get over this, I thought. The idea of zooming about high in the air gave me the same nausea as on the day I'd driven with my mother to the center of Ile-Ife and looked up at the tall plant towers. Nevertheless, I was better than I'd been a week and a half ago. Much, much better.

I pushed my satchel and bundle close to the tree trunk and scooted farther out on the branch. I no longer needed to hang on to nearby branches. I knew how I'd react if I fell off, and it was to my advantage. A few days before, I'd done exactly that, and as I fell, I'd instinctively caught myself before I could collide with the branch below. Once again, I was assured that I could rely on my instincts. I'd hovered in the air for a moment, completely surprised. Then I'd reached for a nearby branch and pulled myself onto it.

I stretched out my legs on the wide branches and leaned back on my elbows. Then I willed the spiral of wind to circulate around me. In the baobab tree, I smiled as I felt myself lifting. For a while I let my body get used to the sensation. I looked around. It was only in the last three days that I was able to do this, felt comfortable enough to do this, allowed myself to do this. Before, I'd had to focus on a focal point.

I looked up at the branch above.

"OK, Zahrah," I said to myself. "Focus."

I took several short breaths and then hummed the

tune of my favorite song, "Reedy Bells." I didn't know why I was humming, but the vibration in my chest was somehow calming. *Whatever works,* I thought. Slowly, I floated up to the branch above me. I had never done this before. I had been able to float from one level branch to the next but not from the branch below to the branch above. The branches were very wide, and this required more maneuvering. I smiled, maintaining my concentration. *Now the next one.*

Again I floated up. But was I really floating now, now that I was actually controlling my movement while in midair? Maybe. Maybe not. I went all the way to the top and laughed loudly. I didn't know why. Maybe it was the feeling of the shock from the whip-scorpion encounter finally lifting from my shoulders. Or maybe it was just the success of it all.

I remembered Nsibidi's words, which seemed like they were said so long ago: "The rest will come when you want it to."

I didn't want it to just yet, but someday, maybe when I was a few years older, I might.

CHAPTER 18

THE CARNIGOURD

I thought I'd gotten a good idea of the jungle's range by reading the digi-book and from my own experiences, but the next three days really broadened my view.

I saw black-and-white, long-limbed spider monkeys, frowning day owls, huge snails that sucked the bark and moss from trees, oily black spiders fat with venom, papery-skinned chameleons, fire ants that glowed orange with poison, anteaters that fed on the fire ants and breathed out smoke after each meal, black honeypot ants with bulbous behinds and long, thick antennae, grasshoppers the size of my hand, friendly dwarf impalas that barely came up to my knees, snickering parrots, laughing doves, and plenty of nofly birds (orange-beaked black birds with lovely wings who refused to use them) running from bush to bush.

There were wild light-bulb trees that glowed all sorts of colors at night and short fat current trees (I made sure not to get close to these trees. The electrical current they produce will make all the muscles in your body cramp up if you just brush against one). I even saw a wild CPU plant! Now I know what the plants are like when free of human manipulation. It grew as a giant red flower with a wide leafy base. The flower was a monitor, and it was so bright that that night I could still see it glowing a mile away. I wondered if the flower connected itself to the network and what it did once there.

Eventually I did come across a few ponds. Some were large, others small. I refilled my water bottles and washed quickly in the ones that weren't mucked up with algae. In two of the larger ponds, I spotted armored alligators, blue-veined turtles, and glass fish. I giggled with delight when I came across a yellow balloon frog. The moment it saw me, it did exactly what the field guide said it would: puff itself up with self-produced helium and float away. And, of course, there were all kinds of mosquitoes, gnats, and flies.

Not surprisingly, I encountered more deadly pod plants. I'd looked them up in my digi-book the night I'd seen the first one eat a horse. They were called Carni-gourds, and they ate anything that came close enough. I'd been lucky and smart to keep my distance. The second time I encountered one, however, I wasn't so fortunate. This Carnigourd was hidden behind several high bushes and creeping plants. I didn't walk directly in front of it, but I did walk close enough for it to grab my ankle with one of its dry brown roots.

I was deep in thought. It had been so many days, and with each day, I worried more about how I was running out of time. But how could I hurry when I didn't know exactly where I was going? All I knew was that elgorts were deep in the Greeny Jungle, and to go deep meant going north.

I diverted my mind to thinking about my friendship with Dari instead. I remembered how we used to climb trees and study together, and how he used to laugh at me when I was at a loss for words. And how he laughed even harder at my fear of heights and sometimes the dark. *I'm no longer really afraid of either one, Dari,* I'd been thinking.

And I wasn't. I was no longer afraid of many things. I wasn't afraid of the pink-skinned lizard I'd seen that second day in the jungle. These lizards were quite common, and they usually searched for their meals in the morning. They ate parasites that clung to the roots of trees. This was good for the trees, since these underground plants tended to sap nutrients directly from the trees' roots.

These ferocious-looking Morning Skin Dragons, as

they are called, were actually bashful creatures that ran away when anything approached them, including me. Once, however, I dug up a root parasite and was able to coax a small dragon to take it right from my hand. *If Dari could only see me now,* I thought.

I remembered how pleased he'd been three years ago when I'd finally followed him up into a baobab tree. He'd been trying to persuade me to climb one since the fifth day we'd met.

"Just the first branch," he'd always say. "It's fun up here."

I'd believed him. As I clung to the low branch for dear life, Dari clapped with delight and laughed. He laughed so loud that my mother came out to see what was going on. When she saw me in the tree, she exclaimed, "Zahrah! You're in the tree! That's great!"

That had been a good day.

"We'll have more good days, Dari," I said as I walked and the Carnigourd's root crept up behind me.

I looked up at the sky through the trees, and at that moment I saw something yellow zoom by. It was the size of a . . . person? Was that a person? I wasn't sure. I stopped and stood staring at the sky, hoping to see it again. This was my biggest mistake. I had almost been out of the Carnigourd's reach.

Its root took advantage of the moment, quickly wrapping itself around my ankle and pulling me to the ground. I hit my forehead painfully in the dirt and felt my side being scraped by pebbles, rocks, and dead leaves as the Carnigourd slowly pulled me across the jungle floor. My mind reeled with images of Dari, crushed bones, plant digestive juices, and pain. I panicked, thrashing my body back and forth in an attempt to free myself.

Then it happened. The scorpion poison kicked in and everything just went black. It was the kind of sleep you fall into when you're extremely tired and your bed is extremely comfortable. One minute I was mentally there, the next I was in delicious darkness.

I was brought back to consciousness when an especially sharp rock scraped my arm. I'm sure that rock saved my life. Oh, if I had not awakened in that moment! The Carnigourd behind the bushes was in full view, and I screamed. I thrashed some more. Then I remembered my blood pressure. I had to keep it low. I breathed out of my mouth as I collected myself. I took a deep breath. "Wait!" I shouted at the plant. "Um . . . *please!*"

Oddly enough, the plant's pull slowed.

I tried my best to remember what I'd read in the digibook about this common meat-eating plant. It lowered its pod, its mouth open, and I feared I'd fall asleep again from the sight of it. There were no teeth and the inside was red. There were two holes near the back — one large one that led to its stomach and the other hole . . . I gasped. The smaller one was its *ear,* I remembered. Carnigourds responded to sound as a palm-wine lover responds to palm wine; if it was sweet, then he was happy, his brain relishing nothing but the happiness. I started singing the first song that came to me.

> *Um . . . Close the door*
> *Light the light.*
> *We're staying home tonight.*

My mother used to sing the song when I was very young. The Carnigourd immediately stopped pulling, savoring with pleasure the sound of my voice.

> *Far away from the bustle*
> *And the bright city lights.*

I slowly unraveled the plant's vines from my ankle as I sang.

> *Let them all fade away*
> *Just leave us alone*
> *And we'll live in a world of our own.*
> *We'll build a world of our own that no one else can share.*
> *All our sorrows we'll leave far behind us there.*

I slowly stepped back, now thankful that Carnigourds didn't have eyes. The pod had closed and it slowly moved side to side as I sang.

And I know you will find
There'll be peace of mind
When we live in a world of our own.

I stopped singing, turned, and ran as fast as I could, as far from the Carnigourd as possible.

CHAPTER 19

GHOSTLY $\mathcal{S}$HADOWS

The next two days were like the previous ones. Deadly.

I'd been in the forbidden jungle for two weeks, and somehow I was still alive. If I made it home, no one would believe all I'd been through. I'd walked so many miles that my body was starting to gain useful muscle. The walking was coming more easily to me. At night, I no longer climbed into the trees. I simply floated up.

I made sure my things were nicely hidden. Nothing was likely to steal them from so high up. As for the many bush cows, or "bandits of the jungle," I'd fed several of the quiet furry creatures some of my overripe mangoes and left even more at the foot of whatever tree I slept in. I was sure that the bush cows were smart enough to find a way to get to my things if they wanted to, so it was my way of compromising with them. So far, my plan had worked.

"Compass, so now after all you've seen, do you still think the forbidden jungle should be forbidden?" I asked as I sat high in a baobab tree.

The compass's yellow rotating flower lit up my cupped hands in the night.

"Of course I do. Go back home to your parents, young lady," it recited. "I can tell you how many days it'll take if you go seven miles a day."

"That's OK. Compass, I have to do this." I was talking more to myself than to the compass. "And the jungle is crazy but it's just another place."

"Do you know how far away from home you are?"

"I don't want to know."

"Many, many miles."

"Don't tell me, compass."

The next day, when I started seeing half-eaten deer, bush cow, and even horse carcasses hanging high in the trees, I didn't panic. I couldn't afford to. I knew what I had to do. I kept an eye on the treetops and immediately found a patch of lemongrass. I picked some, crushed it up in my hands to release the oil, and rubbed it all over my skin and clothes.

On my fifteenth day in the jungle, a panther jumped out of a nearby tree and charged at me without making a sound. I could hear its partner coming at me from behind.

On their four legs, they stood taller than I, and their fur *did* look like black oil. I froze, my eyes wide and my mouth half open. *Don't run, don't run, do not run,* I thought. I could feel myself shaking as I breathed with my mouth open, concentrating on keeping my blood pressure down and my body still. No matter how I smelled, I had a strong feeling that if I fell asleep in front of these beasts, they would not be able to resist such an easy meal.

They stopped in midcharge, their nostrils flaring wide as they sniffed the air. I slowly blew out air, standing my ground. The other one stepped around me to stand next to its partner. In their eyes, I saw a sharp cunning. The panthers could easily kill me if they chose to. It was all up to them. Still, I was determined not to let my condition get the best of me. One of them spoke.

"You look scared," the panther said. She purred her words more than she spoke them, and her voice was smooth.

"You should be," the other one said. His voice was low like the large drums played during the New Yam Festival back home.

"Please," I said. How come the book had said nothing about the panthers' being intelligent enough to talk? Gradually I was noticing that though full of useful information, the field guide was not complete. There were plenty of holes in its extensive chapters. Once again I noticed that you could never fully trust anything you read or

that was told to you. Human beings simply weren't perfect. I hoped the book was, at least, right about the elgort
egg's healing properties. "I-I just . . . please don't . . ."

"Do you think we're so stupid? As if we don't know
that you just rubbed lemongrass all over yourself," the
male said.

"You may smell bad," the female said, "but we know
that under that foul-smelling skin is tender, sweet fresh
meat."

"Skin is easy to separate from meat when we want to,"
the male said.

I shivered with revulsion. The panthers paced back
and forth as they spoke, rubbing against each other's fur
and keeping their large green eyes on me.

"That horrible smell you've bathed yourself in won't
keep us from eating you," the female said.

"But it might cause us to give you one chance to convince us why we shouldn't eat you," the male said. He
looked at his mate, and they both chuckled, obviously enjoying the prolonged moment of intimidation before their
meal.

I was thinking fast, my eyes scanning all the nearest
trees. But climbing the trees was even worse trouble. And
if I floated up, the trees would be too close together. The
panthers would easily ambush me. *What reason can I give
them to not eat me?* I wondered. *I can tell them that I'm on a
mission to save my best friend. But what will they care? They'll*

probably want to eat Dari too. And so I took a chance and blurted out the strangest thing about myself.

"Um . . . I can fly," I said. "Sort of."

The panthers stopped pacing, their eyes narrowing as they looked at me for the first time as more than just meat. Then they looked at each other, and the male growled something to the female that I couldn't understand. Then the female looked at me and said, "Show us."

"Yes," the male said. "Show us."

Even under the stress of my life being at risk, I was able to do it. I floated up two feet in the air.

"She doesn't lie," the male said.

"Another Windseeker," the female said, resting on her haunches. "It's been a while."

"The last Windseeker we met was several years ago. A female, tall for a human," the male said. "Nothing like you. She laughed when we attacked. When we saw that she could fly and appeared to be skillful with two small sharp knives she hid in her dress pockets, we decided to make a swift retreat. Wasn't worth the trouble."

"She was amazing," the female said with a sound of admiration.

I felt jittery. I still feared the panthers but . . . another Windseeker? *It sounds like her,* I thought. *But it can't be.* Could it? All the way out there? It didn't make sense.

"What was her name?" I asked.

"I don't recall," the female said.

"No wonder this one is so young yet still alive," the male said to the female. He turned to me. "How long have you been with the trees? Judging from your tattered attire, you're from the Ooni Kingdom."

"Where else would I be from? All human beings are," I said. I didn't think they would eat me anymore, and I was beginning to relax.

"Some humans live far from the Ooni Kingdom, though very few," the female said. "The Windseeker we met was not from there. Other panthers who'd met her said she was from somewhere beyond this area."

"How long have you been away from your people?" the male asked me again.

"A little more than two weeks, I guess."

"Why are you here and not with those who birthed you?" the female asked.

"I need to find an elgort egg, to save my friend."

If panthers could express fear on their faces, I saw it then. They stepped away from me. The gesture made my belly flutter. *If these great creatures can fear elgorts . . .* I shivered, unable to finish the thought.

"Not smart, especially for a Windseeker," the male said.

"Maybe we should eat you now," the female said. "Anything is better than being destroyed by an elgort."

I looked at my feet, trying to ignore the sting of their words. For many days, I hadn't thought about the danger of hunting down an elgort. I was too preoccupied with the more immediate perils of the jungle.

"I have to do this," was all I could say.

"Well, I hope we hear good stories about you after your certain death, young Windseeker," the male said.

"Make sure your spirit is prepared to leave that scrawny body of yours," the female said, rubbing her nose and turning to leave. She sneezed. "You do smell very bad."

"Peace watch over you," the male said.

Then they turned and left, the female still sneezing in disgust. For a moment, I just stood there, their words echoing in my mind. I swallowed the lump in my throat and got myself moving, though my legs were stiff and I felt a little ill.

I continued using the lemongrass, even when I no longer saw animal carcasses in the trees. The panthers I'd met were curious, but I wasn't sure if the others would be. I also noticed that the smell of the lemongrass oil kept mosquitoes and gnats away better than my repellant, and it smelled nice.

Later that day, I picked several tree clams from the low branches of an ekki tree. Then I built a fire and roasted them in their shells. I knew to put out the fire quickly so as not to attract the large black eagles I saw zooming about in the sky. I had learned from the field guide that these eagles were known to snatch up prey as large as deer!

That night, the pink frog that I had met at the beginning of my journey appeared again. It hopped down from a branch above me and sat at my feet. I blinked with mild surprise. I was tired and instantly felt annoyed.

"Well?" the frog said. "What do you want?"

"Why do you keep bothering me?!" I snapped. "Are you not right in the head? Or do you have nothing better to do?"

"I couldn't care less about you," the frog said, looking equally annoyed. "You're the one bothering me with your neediness."

"Me?" I said, scrunching my face. I was too exhausted for this. "You're just an irritating talking frog with a bad attitude. Why would I want anything from you?"

The frog sighed loudly, turning around.

"I hope something gobbles you up soon," the frog grumbled, hopping away. "At least then you'll leave me alone."

"More likely you than me," I shot back as it hopped down a branch and disappeared behind some leaves.

I sat for a moment feeling angry and aggravated.

"Stupid nonsense frog," I grumbled, bringing out my digi-book. "As if I couldn't squash it with my foot."

I picked up the digi-book and stared at the screen for

a moment trying to push the frog out of my mind. Then I tried accessing some elgort information again. When I clicked on the link to the elgort passage, the screen went blank. Then it turned light green, and the words of the el-gort passage appeared in black, the opposite of its usual black screen with green words. I gasped with excitement. Finally, I would know what to expect. Aside from the screen and words being the wrong color, a few of the characters were a little messed up, but I could still read it. Trying my best not to move the digi-book, I quickly be-gan to read:

> The Œlgôrt is a nasty beast, the môst deadly in the Greeny Jungle. The ultimate killing machine. And it's Mad as the Mad Hatter ôf the mythical *Alice in*

Suddenly it went dark. Again, it said error. I bit my lip hard, resisting the urge to throw the digi-book to the ground and be done with the frustrating instrument once and for all. Instead of throwing it, I tilted it to the side. I heard something small rattle inside it. I tried accessing the elgort entry again. *"Source Page Error,"* it said. I wasn't sur-prised, though I felt a little deflated. Any information would have helped.

I turned the book over and sighed loudly. Even with-out the information, I knew that the elgort was deadly. Everyone knew that. All it ever wanted to do was murder and eat things. I felt dizzy. What was I doing? No wonder the panthers had assumed I was on my way to my death. I *was!* I was hunting a monster and when I found it, it would find me delicious! What was I *doing?* What was I *thinking?*

But I knew the answer to both these questions.

In my heart I was sure, even if my brain kept telling me I was crazy. I knew. I was sure. I didn't sleep well that night. But by the morning, I was ready to keep going.

CHAPTER 20

OBAX

As I walked, my mind was in the clouds. I was thinking about how much I missed seeing the open sky. The field guide had a whole chapter dedicated to "Junglemyelitis."

Needless to say, a few of us who were more sensitive to being completely surrounded by trees and bushes have gone mad from Junglemyelitis. The trees started to look as if they were boxing us in. Then the leaves and branches seemed to block out more sunlight than usual. The soil began to smell soilier. And an over-whelming fear of animals waiting to attack set in. This is a rare condition. After being in the jungle for so long, we all feel a bit claustrophobic. That's normal.

But if you have these symptoms, well, the best way to treat them is to gather as much food as you can and climb to the top of a nice sturdy tree where you can see the open space above. Stay there for three days.

I didn't like the idea of staying in a tree that long. I didn't have the luxury of time. Plus I wasn't really having any abnormal symptoms. Still, I'd have given away all my mangoes if I could only run through an open grassy field for an hour. I was staring up at the blue sky when I heard the first bark.

Wild dogs.

They must have been sleeping nearby because they were at my heels before I knew it. I managed to run and then half float and half jump into a tree just in time. They had caught me off-guard, and I could feel my heart beating extremely hard. As I clutched the tree branch, I watched the pack of dogs mill about below, growling and looking up at me. I tried to think of relaxing thoughts.

Still, just as the dogs started to lose interest and walk away, I began to feel myself slipping.

"Oh no!" I said groggily. My mouth felt numb and I slurred my words. "Not now, not now."

The last dog disappeared into a bush just as things faded. I couldn't hear or see any dogs, but that didn't mean anything in the Greeny Jungle. It didn't mean anything at all. The next thing I remembered was the painful thud of my body hitting the ground. I'd fallen out of the tree. My hip exploded with pain and my eyes flew open. The first thing I saw were black furry feet a few yards away. I slowly looked from the feet to the legs to the — I gasped. Then the gorilla came rushing at me. I was so shocked that I tried to roll onto my side. I was greeted with a fresh burst of pain from my hip. I couldn't get up.

The gorilla beat its chest and howled angrily at me. I bit my lip hard, pushing my fear as far back as I could. I opened my mouth and took a deep breath. The gorilla got within a foot of me and stopped. It teetered forward and fell to the side.

I frowned. *What's wrong with it?* I wondered. Thankfully, this display of vulnerability helped me relax. The gorilla got up and stood on all fours, its long left arm shaking. Then I realized its entire body was shaking. I squinted, rolling myself to the side a little. If I had been standing up, the gorilla would have been almost my height. And it was obviously much stronger, even if it was in a weakened state. Its fur was more gray than black. The gorilla was old.

It had green jewels on its ears and around its neck and ankles. Gorillas were fairly common back home, especially in the mountains on the southwest side of the great city. There were several well-known gorilla tribes there, but I'd never heard of gorillas who wore jewelry.

"I-I mean no harm," I said, holding a hand up. I almost wanted to laugh at my words. What "harm" could I possibly do when I couldn't even get up!

"What is your name?" the gorilla said in a low, gruff voice, its body still slightly shaky. It beat its flat chest once and stared at me. Not "it," "him." This gorilla was male. And I noticed there were others, too, as the bushes around me began to rustle. Some peeked around tree trunks and bushes; a few were in the lower branches of trees.

"M-my name is . . . it's Zahrah, Zahrah Tsami," I said, looking around some more. I could see no way out even if I *could* run.

"You are a human," the gorilla said.

"Yes."

"You're a child."

"I guess."

"You are hurting."

I hesitated.

"Yes," I said. My injured hip was too obvious to hide.

"Where are those who gave birth to you?"

"Back home."

"In the human-dwelling city?" the gorilla asked.

I didn't reply. I'd already spoken too much. It was better if the gorillas thought there were others. But these gorillas weren't stupid.

"You're the one that the Windseeker was looking for," he said after looking me over.

"Windseeker?" I said, surprised. "Was her name . . . was her name Nsibidi?"

The gorilla nodded.

"She's a friend of the idiok," he said. "She's been searching the forests for a human girl. She left here only two days ago."

"Oh," I said. "Wow."

"I am Obax, Chief of the Modern People. If you continue to be truthful, then you're among friends," he said, stepping closer to me.

Obax, I thought. *Where have I heard that name?* Then I remembered. One of the idiok was named after him. This was Obax, the great gorilla chief.

Since I knew I was a bad liar, it seemed I had found myself among friends. The minute Obax called out "It is all right," the other gorillas, small and large, young and old, gathered around me.

"Ododo," Obax said. A slightly smaller gorilla wearing a necklace of yellow, stiff-looking flowers stepped up. "Come and see."

Ododo looked down at me with her large orange eyes as she leaned on her knuckles.

"Where does it hurt, child?" Ododo asked in a gruff voice. Ododo's chest was not flat like Obax's. Ododo was female.

"I-I fell out of that tree," I said pointing upward. "Onto my hip."

She pushed me a little to the side and I winced, tears watering my eyes.

"Ah, please," I said, with a pinched face. "Hurts!"

"I know," Ododo said, continuing to poke and prod the left side of my hip, where the pain was. The pain was so horrible that for a moment I couldn't think. Slowly she helped me sit up, and the burning subsided a little. Another gorilla stood behind me so I could lean back. I could feel the gorilla's fur on my neck, soft and thick. Then Ododo slowly straightened my left leg and I screamed in pain.

"Elu," Ododo said to a stocky male gorilla. "Come and carry her."

Elu knelt next to me, and Ododo helped me get onto Elu's back, my arms wrapped around his furry neck. He smelled of flowers and lemongrass. My hip ached even as he carried me.

"Misty can fix her," Ododo said to Obax.

"Yes," he said with a nod. At that moment, there must have been an unspoken consent from Obax for the others to satisfy their curiosity because suddenly they all crowded in on me. I wasn't scared. I'd been alone for two weeks, and it felt good to be around people. The younger ones rose on their hind legs to sniff at my shirt as Elu carried me, and some of them tugged at my satchel and bundle, which Ododo was carrying. They tapped at the broken mirrors in my pants and the collar of my shirt, their furry arms tickling my skin. They chattered as they examined me.

"What is in this?" one woman gorilla asked, tugging at my satchel.

"My things," I said.

"Smells like mangoes," another woman gorilla said.

"Yes, I have three of them in there to eat," I said.

"Why is your body cloth jewelry so dirty?" a man gorilla asked with a frown.

"Huh?" I asked. "Body cloth jewelry? What's that?"

The man gorilla frowned and tugged at my clothes. "These."

"Oh," I said with a laugh. "My clothes. Um, these are all I have."

As they examined me, I looked closely at their fur. It was fluffy and clean; not even a leaf or nettle clung to it. And they each wore various kinds of jewelry. Some wore necklaces made from clamshells, others wore colorful stones, still others decorated themselves with flowers and pieces of cloth.

Eventually Obax held up a shaky arm, and everyone began forming a line. Elu got in line just behind him.

"Thank you, Elu," I said. He only grunted as he carried me. I looked back at Ododo. "Thank you, too, Ododo."

She nodded, bringing her right arm up and holding it at her breast with her pinky out.

I moved west instead of north for the first time since I'd entered the jungle. The pace was slow, and each step that Elu took bumped my hip, making me grit my teeth. There were about fifteen gorillas behind me; many of them carried baskets on their heads filled with various fruits. The moment the compass in my pocket sensed my moving in a direction other than north, it clicked itself on.

"Zahrah," it said, sounding very alarmed. "You're moving off course, my dear."

I reached into my pocket and pressed the button on the side to turn it off. It switched itself back on.

"This is not the way you are supposed to go!" it said, frantic. "You are going west, not north!"

Elu grunted with annoyance. Obax glanced over his shoulder.

"You people," he said. "Always with your gadgets."

"Well, it kind of helps me get to where I need to go," I said, taking the compass out of my pocket. "Compass," I said to it. "There has been a slight change of plan. The plan is still to head north, but not at this moment."

"Oh, really? Why didn't you tell me immediately? Well, then let me make a few adjustments," the compass said. "You had me really worried there."

"It doesn't like change very much," I said to Obax. Obax only grunted.

We were moving uphill along the first path I had seen since entering the forest. It was wide and flat.

"And you feel you cannot function without these . . . items?" Obax asked. I had fallen into the lull of the pace, making an effort to ignore the pain in my hip and listening to the chatter behind me of the other gorillas about the night's meal, the season's harvest, arguments with "life mates," and a sister's new baby. I heard Obax's words with only half an ear.

"Huh?" I asked.

"Do you really need that thing?"

"Oh," I said. "Oh yes. Without it, I can't find my way home."

"You may know more than you give yourself credit for, Zahrah," he said.

"Maybe," I said with a smirk.

Then I went on to tell Obax why I was trekking through the jungle. I told him about Dari, how it was my fault that he was bitten, how I was on a mission to find an elgort egg, and how when I found it, I had to get home as soon as possible. When I was finished, Obax nodded.

"You're a very ambitious girl, even if your ambitions are impos—um, that is impractical," said Obax. "You're lucky we were the ones to find you."

We traveled for what felt like an hour, and I watched their village open before me. The sun was beginning to set and I was incapable of getting around by myself, but I felt completely safe. Many complex two-story mud brick houses were built around the trunks of trees. Their roofs were flat, and artistic designs were carved into their outer walls.

The gorillas were land people. They were not built to roam the treetops with their stocky strong bodies, long arms, and short legs. I saw light in the windows, but it didn't look like plant-powered light. It looked like candle-light. My father often told Dari and me about the time his great-grandmother was just a little girl, decades and decades ago, before plant-powered lights like glow lilies and light bulbs were discovered on the northeast side of the Ooni Kingdom. Dari was always more interested than I was.

"There was plenty of technology back then," I remember my father saying. "Of course we had the plant towers. I don't know anyone who remembers when we didn't. We had netevision and cars and the like. But it took the great fire to get scientists searching for something safer for light.

"People used items called candle-sticks made of wax with a little piece of string in the center that you lit afire. They used to cause all sorts of fires. The worst was the Great Blaze of Chukwutown. It burned down a large portion of the southwest and cleared the way for what eventually became the Great Ooni Marketplace."

But it wasn't just the fact that these people didn't use plant-powered light. There was no technology at all there.

"If it's not rude to ask," I cautiously said. "You're the

chief, so why do you come and pick fruit and things with your people?"

I couldn't imagine Papa Grip going to the farms and helping in the harvest of palm kernels and lychee fruit. And Chief Obax looked as if such a thing was hard on his body.

Obax laughed.

"I needed some fresh air," he said. "My body may shake and my balance may be bad, but I am not an invalid."

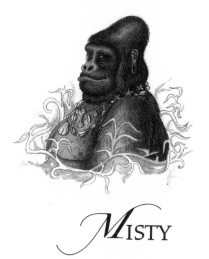

$\mathcal{M}$ISTY

Along the way to Misty's home, I was introduced to the whole gorilla village and offered several cups of sweet, perfumy liquid that burned my throat. It was something I doubted my parents would have let me drink. But my parents had also taught me that it was polite to take a little of what people offered when you were a guest. The sweet liquid was yummy, and I couldn't help but take a little guilty pleasure in sipping cup after cup. It made my head swim, and the pain in my leg seemed disconnected from my body.

By the time we got to Misty's hut, I had a silly grin on my face and was glad Elu was carrying me. Misty was an old woman with thick white fur. Obax told me that she was the oldest gorilla in the village, and thus even he had to seek her counsel, especially when it came to governing the village. Her husband was long dead, and her five sons and three daughters were grown with grandchildren of their own.

However, Misty still lived in the same, rather large mud brick hut built around the trunk of a slender palm tree. She had plenty of room for me. I noticed that many different types of leafy plants, small trees, and colorful flowers surrounded her house, unlike the others. Bees, butterflies, and beetles buzzed and crawled from flower to flower, and the air smelled sweet, bitter, and oily. Maybe one of the bees was even from that wood wit's colony, I thought with a grin. After bending down and touching Chief Obax's feet, Misty turned to me.

"You're a scrawny little human, aren't you?" she said, pinching my arm. She wore tiny red shells around her neck, and her ankles clicked when she moved.

"I guess so," I said.

"This is Zahrah. She's a human . . . from the Ooni Kingdom, of course."

"Of course," Misty said with a smirk.

"She's injured. You can help?"

Misty looked at me for a long time with her head cocked. Then she said, "Maybe." She stepped closer. "Where are the rest of your people? You're only a child."

"I'm alone."

"How long have you been among the trees?" Misty asked.

214

"About two weeks," I said. Misty's eyes grew wide.

"Two weeks?!" she said. "You?"

I nodded.

"Hmm, you must be stronger than you seem," Misty said, looking impressed.

"Will you help her heal?" Obax asked again.

"What are those on your head?" Misty asked.

"My head?" I said. I patted my head with my free hand to see if something was there.

"Yes. Is that your hair?" she asked.

I rolled my eyes at the familiar question. Even all the way out there in the Greeny Jungle I was asked about my hair!

"Oh, *these*," I said, taking a dadalock in my hand. "It's my hair, yes. I was born with them like this; they just grow this way."

"You are dada," Misty said.

I blinked. *Gorillas know about dada hair?* I thought.

"Can you fly? Some of you dada people can fly. I remember," Misty said. "Used to see them sometimes, when I was very, very young. The one who came here recently was the first I've seen in decades."

"Misty," Obax said firmly, slightly annoyed. "It grows late."

Misty paused again.

"Of course I can heal her," she finally said. "It's a sprain."

"Good," Obax said. "I leave her to you, then."

He turned and left.

"Follow me," Misty said to Elu.

Inside, plants grew all around the windowsill in large and small pots, some creeping along the walls, others reaching the ceiling or even going out the windows. There were no chairs, but many large stuffed yellow, green, and orange cushions were on the floor and low tables.

"Put her down here," she said, motioning toward a cluster of pillows.

Elu delicately put me on the cushions. Then he stood up, stretched his back, and sighed with relief.

"Thank you so much," I said with a grin. "I'm sure you're glad to be rid of me."

Elu nodded. "Yes, I am," he said, bringing his right arm up and holding it at his breast with his pinky out. He touched my head and then left.

The cushions were hard but comfortable. I leaned against the wall and let out a breath of relief, despite my pain. *If my parents had a magical ball that would show them exactly where I am at this moment, they wouldn't believe it,* I thought. I barely believed it myself. I could hear Misty outside moving about, then she came back inside and I heard the clinking of pottery.

Minutes later, she returned carrying a bowl with some minty-smelling green-gray paste in it. She put the bowl in front of me and left again. When she returned, she was walking fast toward me. Before I knew what was going on, she walked right up to me and stuck three needlelike sticks into my forehead! And I do not mean into my skin. The sticks had to have gone through my skull!

"Ah!" I shouted, but just sat there with wide eyes.

"Relax," she said.

"But you . . . what have you . . . is this some sort of . . ." I tapered off. "Oh!" I said softly. The pain in my hip was seeping away like air from the air-bulb vines Dari and I used to like popping and chewing on when we were young.

"W-w-w-why didn't you at least w-warn me?" I babbled.

"Would you really have wanted to be told before I did it?" Misty asked with a chuckle. "Leave them there. They will work themselves out in a few hours. In the meantime, you'll be relieved of the pain."

I could only stare at her in disbelief.

"Now take those pants off and let me apply this cooling salve to the wound," she said. "You'll be fine in a few days."

She let me choose the room I wanted to stay in. I chose the smallest one. It reminded me of my small room back home. When my parents and I first moved into the house years ago, I was given the chance to choose between the large room close to the kitchen and the small room close to my parents' room. I chose the smaller room because I'd always liked small spaces. I felt more in control of a small space than a large one. This time I'd have been fine in a large room. I was now used to not being in control. It was just that I liked the homey feeling this one had.

Everything in the room was made of a light-colored shiny wood from ceiling to floor. The room was bare, decorated only by two very low wicker chairs with yellow cushions and a painting of three black-haired gorillas on the wall. There were no mirrors on the walls, but that wasn't such a big deal. I hadn't been around mirrors for a while, other than the ones on my dirty clothes, which were now cracked and chipped. Large candles were in every corner, giving the room a calm feel. *I'm going to like it here,* I thought. *As long as I don't knock any candles over.*

"My youngest daughter loved this room," Misty said. "It's the only room in the house that catches a lot of sunlight. When morning comes it's absolutely lovely in here."

I set my bundle and satchel down and sat on the bed. I leaned away from my sprained hip. It felt inflated but numb, like it was two sizes too big. I was thankful for the soft mattress, which was filled with leaves that crunched under my weight. After so many nights of sleeping on hard tree branches, the bed felt unreal. Misty stood in the doorway getting a good look at me in the candlelight.

"How long have you been in that body cloth jewelry?" Misty asked.

I looked at my tattered, dirty, long shirt. I held the pants, as I had taken them off so she could put the salve on my wound. Dari's clothes. I shrugged and said, "Since I started my journey."

Misty sucked her teeth.

"I will sew you some new ones," she said. "As you can see, we don't wear such things here. We don't need to because we have fur. But I can use the ones you wear to produce new ones; some friends of mine can help me, too. Those are practically rotting on you."

I looked down at my clothes again.

"These are my best friend's clothes. That's what we call them, clothes," I said. I knew I sounded whiny, but I couldn't help it. "He's sick and I'm searching for the cure to make him better. I-I can't part with them."

"Oh," Misty said.

We were both silent for a moment.

"If you don't stay healthy, then you won't be able to do what you have to do," Misty said quietly. "Those clothes you wear are too dirty; they may eventually make you sick. And I'm sure your friend will not care what you wear when you return to him."

I knew she was right. They were just clothes. But they were all I had of Dari. Misty seemed to read my mind.

"You have more of your friend with you than those clothes, much more." She placed her hand on my forehead. "You have memories of him, and those are far more valuable. I'll be right back."

When Misty left the room, I looked out the window. It was difficult to tell the men from the women, for I'd been around the gorillas for only a few hours, and to my eyes, they all looked the same. Both men and women wore jewelry and were about the same in height and strength. It was a different culture, and I knew not to apply my own cultural norms to theirs. The only ways I could tell were by their chests and sometimes voices. The women had breasts and slightly higher voices. The children all looked and sounded the same. Nevertheless, from what I could see, I had to admit that there were many more similarities between my town and the gorilla village than differences.

The sun was almost gone and people were winding down for the night. Some people chatted with friends. A group was talking loudly as it shared some sort of drink. Someone stood behind his house, taking down dried laundry. A gorilla walked by with a bundle of twigs on her shoulder. *They probably have a market here, too,* I thought.

Even without technology, the gorilla village reminded me of home. I tugged at my shirt, feeling how much I missed Dari. I also missed cars, the loudness of the market, and the company of others. I missed cooked food, running water, and of course my parents.

"Here," Misty said. "Take those off and wrap this around you for now."

I slowly took the colorful orange, yellow, and red cloth. It was silky and thin, very pretty, like a piece of sunset.

"I'm going to draw you a bath," Misty said. "You need a good cleaning. Then you will eat."

I wiggled out of my clothes, carefully folding and putting them on the bed. I put my underwear next to the folded clothes. Then I brought out my seven other pairs of underwear and made a pile next to my clothes. I paused for a moment, thinking. My menses were due soon. *If* they came. I didn't feel a hint of them at all. I remember the teacher in school saying that one's menses may not come for a month if one is stressed. And I certainly had been stressed. I was prepared, but I knew that finding places to wash would be difficult. I shrugged and shook my head. *I'll cross that bridge when I get to it,* I thought.

"Humans," Misty said with a chuckle when she saw the small pile of flowery underwear on the bed.

I smiled, embarrassed.

"Don't worry, we'll get those washed," Misty said. "Come on. Don't worry about the salve. You can reapply it when you finish. And just wash around the pain sticks in your forehead; they can get wet."

It was like no other bath I'd ever had.

A very wide tree must have lived next to the palm tree Misty's house was built around, for its stump was what the bath was carved into, on the opposite side of the house. It was deep enough for me to fully submerge myself in, and the wood smelled sweet.

The unique thing about it was that I wasn't going to bathe in water. I was to bathe in a sweet oil that the stump produced. The stump produced so much oil that it had to be emptied daily through an opening in the bottom. The oil drained into the soil, nourishing the palm tree.

At first, having never bathed in oil, I was cautious. The oil was clear and very light. But still, I wondered how it would wash the dirt off. One thing I *was* sure about was that it would be good for my hair.

"Misty, I've never bathed in this . . . stuff before," I said. "We usually bathe in water."

"Go on in, it won't hurt you," Misty said. "The Windseeker who came here looking for you liked it just fine."

Well, if Nsibidi was OK with it, I thought, *then it should be all right. At least now I know that it won't eat my skin or make me break out in hives or something. But then again, Nsibidi's a tough lady and I'm not.*

"Just call if you need anything," Misty said, turning to leave. She was cooking something that smelled delicious.

I bit my lip, unwrapped my cloth, and hung it on the wooden bar next to the bath. The floor was grooved with tiny lines to prevent slipping. I cautiously dipped a toe in the oil, fearing that it would start sizzling or burning. The oil was warm and soft. I dipped my foot further in, and within moments I was in all the way to my neck and grinning with pleasure.

"Oh *yeah*," I whispered.

It felt better than water. Misty told me to just rub and the dirt would come off. For the moment, I just sat with my eyes closed. I hadn't felt so relaxed since before the day I woke up floating. I felt as if I were floating in the oil, more buoyant than if I were in water, similar to when I floated in the air. After a while, I started rubbing myself. The dirty skin sloughed off easily.

"Ew," I said as I rubbed all over my body. I dunked my head in with my eyes closed and shook out my locks as I massaged them. Then I massaged my scalp. When I emerged, I rubbed my face, careful to avoid the sticks. I didn't even want my hand to brush against them. Misty said they wouldn't hurt, but they were sticks in my forehead! The mere thought of them gave me the shivers. But I couldn't question the fact that they were doing their job. I felt no pain at all in my hip.

I stayed in the oil for a half-hour, letting my swollen hip soak. Now I knew why the gorillas had such shiny, healthy fur. As I toweled off, I smiled. I felt rejuvenated. My injury no longer even hurt! My skin was soft and looked radiant. Just as I finished wrapping myself up, Misty came in.

"That was great," I said. "Thank you! Thank you for everything!"

Misty nodded, making the same gesture that Ododo and Elu had made when I thanked them. She gave me the bowl full of minty-smelling salve, and I applied it to my hip. It was cool to the touch, like ice. Misty had already set up dinner. She pointed out what was in each of the wooden bowls.

"These are sun leaves glazed with honey, this is sliced udara fruit, this is egusi soup, these are lentils, and this is a mango that has been soaked in lemon oil. It's very tasty."

The gorillas were vegetarian. I wasn't surprised. Nevertheless, I ate every dish, licking the plates when Misty's back was turned. Everything tasted so delicious, especially the sun leaves with honey and the lemon-oil mango. I sat back and patted my full belly. Misty, who had been washing dishes, turned around and smiled when she saw the empty plates.

"Finished?"

"That was delicious!" I said.

Misty only smiled.

"Time for sleep," she said.

I lay on my back, mindful of the sticks in my forehead. I couldn't help but feel anxious. It was night and I wasn't in a tree. Even if I was in a nice hut within the gorilla village, I was still in the Greeny Jungle. I felt a little vulnerable.

"So do animals ever . . . attack the village?" I asked as I helped Misty put a clean sheet on my bed, which she found amusing, since gorillas didn't sleep with sheets.

Misty glanced at me and then looked away.

"No need to worry tonight," she said. "We gorillas have lived in this jungle since time began. Though we are a peaceful people, we have learned to defend ourselves. All of our young men and women are trained warriors who defend the village when need be. Only when we grow old do we pass into the age of wisdom, when we are relieved of such duties and take on new ones. Gorilla warriors are very good at what they do. Few beasts are foolish enough to attack us."

She didn't say that no beast had attacked them; she said a few. I nodded, my eyes closing. As she advised, I wasn't going to worry myself. In my mind, I saw brave armored gorillas, their fur puffed with loyalty and bravery. It was the perfect image to fall asleep to. When I awoke the next morning, the three sticks were on my pillow and the pain in my hip was almost gone.

CHAPTER 22

THIRD $\mathcal{D}$AY

On my third day in the gorilla village, I woke up feeling relaxed, clearheaded, and clean. I savored the bright patches of sun that shone through the trees and into the window, making the room brilliant. In the jungle, this much sunshine was rare. Still, the first thing I thought was, *Today I must leave.* I looked around the small room feeling a little sad.

I really liked that room. It must have been all the yellow; yellow sunlight, yellow wood, yellow wicker chairs with yellow cushions. Still, I knew I had just spent my last night in it. My hip felt almost normal.

The day before, when my sprained hip was painful but diminished, I'd played with the gorilla children who were my age. They played games with different-colored dried leaves and looked in the bushes for strange, ill-tempered bugs called evil weevils. The other children and I loved how angry the insects got when they were caught. The red bugs would buzz viciously and stamp their many feet with rage.

I didn't even mind the name-calling that several of the girls taunted me with. They made fun of my lack of fur, my dada hair, how I walked on two legs instead of on all four, and how skinny and tall I was. It was nothing new, really.

The gorillas treated me like any other odd-looking youth. But people did stop me several times to ask about my lone adventures in the jungle, too. I was surprised at how well I recounted things. Even *I* liked to hear myself tell stories! But most of the gorillas, adults and children, were annoyed by my digi-book and compass. They didn't think very highly of human technology.

"What is this chattering thing?" one man asked me on the street one day as I tried to get my compass to quiet down.

"When will we return to our normal schedule?" the compass was asking. "I programmed myself for only a day off course. I do *not* like being off schedule. It's a waste of time. And I always know what time it is. You do not have time to waste, I tell you!"

The compass's last words made me shiver a bit. It was right.

"It helps me know where I am," I told the man.

"But you're right here," the man said, looking confused. "Can you not tell where you are without that noisy piece of metal?"

"I beg your pardon?!" the compass said. "I am the most sophisticated, state-of-the-art compass on the market! I can do things you can only dream of! Do you know where you are? I can tell you!"

"Well, it's more complicated than that," I said to the man.

"So it sounds," the gorilla said. "Can't you shut it up? Its voice is most annoying."

I only laughed. "Yes, I can, but it often turns itself back on."

"You should learn to use what you have in your mind," the gorilla said. "It's much more reliable and far less irritating."

I read the field guide only when I was alone. I'd spent several hours the night before poring through it as I lay in bed. Misty loudly sucked her teeth when she peeked in.

"Why can't your people just make normal books?" she asked. "Made of *paper*."

"This way, they can fit lots of stuff into this little thing," I said. "This digi-book is equal to many many books of paper."

Misty only humphed.

But even without all the technology I was used to and

with people who looked nothing like me, I felt completely at home with the gorillas. The idea of spending a few more days in the village sounded good to me. But those would be a few more days of Dari lying in a coma. I was running out of time. It was always in the back of my mind, making it impossible for me to really enjoy the village. I couldn't afford to be comfortable and lose the hardened shell I'd grown by traveling alone and living in the wild. My injury was healed. I could run and jump and survive. And even Misty could do nothing about the condition I suffered from with the whip-scorpion poison. Plus, on top of all this, I was deep into the jungle, and that meant that elgorts couldn't be too far off.

Yes, I'll leave today, I thought, still in bed.

I pushed my covers off and closed my eyes, seeing red as the sunlight shone through my eyelids. I easily relaxed and floated several inches off the bed, then several feet, until I was close to the ceiling. I glanced at the bed below me and held my breath, trying to not get scared.

There was a knock at the door. It startled me and I dropped to the floor.

"Good morning," Misty said, coming in with a chuckle. "Good. You've finally gotten the nerve to do it."

"Well, see why I don't? I've improved but I'm still pretty bad. I've been floating like this for some time. I don't know if I can actually fly."

"Oh yes, you do," Misty said, sucking her teeth and rubbing at the fur on her cheek. She stepped over to the window and looked outside.

I sighed. I was going to miss her. She had been like a second mother in so many ways. She was sometimes gruff but deep down really nice. She'd shown me how to cook several traditional Greeny Gorilla dishes, chastised me for staying out too late with the other kids, and carefully sewn clothes that fit me perfectly.

"How does it feel to float?" Misty asked, turning around. She wore a necklace and earrings made of white clamshells. They clinked the way the mirrors on my mother's clothing did.

I paused, scratching at the nightshirt Misty had sewn for me. The material was a little rough. "It feels very natural. Easy . . . except when I lose—"

"Zahrah, stop making excuses. You will fly soon."

"Maybe," I said quietly.

Misty turned back to the window.

"Do you know how many people, human or gorilla, would love to be able to jump from high up and instead of hitting the ground soar to the skies? Or who would love to fly away from danger? If I were you, no matter how scared I was, I'd keep trying," she said. She walked over, took my hands, and sternly looked me in the eye. "What a gift you have. Why not *unwrap* it!"

I only gazed back at her, not knowing what to say. I

wasn't sure of myself, and I was scared, scared of falling, scared of going too high, scared of being in a place where I only had me to support myself. What kind of gift required so much courage? Misty let go of my hands and stepped back.

"One is never given a task that one can't handle," she said. She paused, cocking her head. Then she said, "Now, go wash and get dressed. Then come sit and talk with me for a bit."

After taking a long, soothing bath and dressing, I walked down the hall to her bedroom. I hesitated at the entrance.

"Come," Misty said, motioning for me to sit across from her in a chair.

Her bedroom was spacious and spotless, the walls painted red. The cushions on her chairs and the pillows on her bed were red. The room smelled as if incense had been burning recently. I smoothed out my new green pants as I sat down. She pulled up another chair and sat in front of me. For a moment, she just watched me, and soon I grew uncomfortable.

She leaned forward and patted me on the knee.

"So," she said, her dark brown eyes steady and calm. "You're thinking of leaving soon?"

I paused, raising my eyebrows.

"Yes," I simply said.

"Today?"

I nodded.

Misty sighed, rubbing her furry neck, and said, "To purposely seek out an elgort." She paused, looking extremely troubled. "Do you know anything about elgorts?"

"Well, my book —"

"No, I didn't ask about that piece of . . . technology you carry around," she said, pronouncing the word *technology* as if it tasted bitter. She got up and walked to her window. The sun shone on her white fur, making her look like an ancient spirit. "I mean, do *you* personally know anything about them?" she asked, her back still turned to me.

I thought about that. I didn't, and for the first time I realized how close I was to executing my mission.

"No," I said, looking at my sandaled feet. I knew nothing more than what I had heard back home. More rumor than anything of substance.

"Well, consider yourself lucky," she said. "Chief Obax and I are the only living people left in this village who *have* seen an elgort. Obax encountered one face to face."

I held my breath, my eyes wide.

"And let me tell you," she continued, one hand now clutching the windowsill. She lifted her head to the sun. "They are living death. We were here when this happy place was turned upside down and pillaged by *three* elgorts. They came, and in a matter of minutes, this place was rubble, half the population missing, devoured by those monsters. I saw my family eaten. My mother shoved me into the closet just before they tore our home open. That's the only reason I lived.

"Obax looked one straight in the eye. He, too, was small, only a baby, and there were larger prey around him, his parents and uncle, so he was passed over when they attacked. But from that day on, his body has been shaky.

"Now all the others who lived through the elgort massacre are dead. No one around here knows the depth of the destruction. They have only read about it in their history books. All they really know about are good times. But Obax and I know. It is only a matter of time. We must be ready for the next attack. I tell you this so that you understand what you seek. Do you still seek it?"

I paused. Once again I was faced with a tale of horror about something I sought contact with. First the farmers' tale and now this. But Misty's story was 100 percent true. That I was sure of.

The gorilla village seemed so peaceful, settled, content, happy, as if it had always existed this way. And what of the gorilla warriors? The elgorts must have devoured them without a thought. I couldn't imagine such blood and murder and terror happening there. But it had happened, and it had been done by one of the very beasts whose egg I wanted to steal. But I'd come far. By this time I had traveled over three hundred miles. And my best friend was lying in a bed, one foot in life, stepping closer and closer to death each day.

"Yes," I whispered. "I still seek it."

Misty nodded.

"You are a strong little girl," she said. "Very strong. I admire you, but I also fear for you."

I said nothing.

"There is only one way to actually find an elgort nest on purpose," she said. "You do not want to find one by accident."

"How?" I asked.

"Ask the Speculating Speckled Frog."

"The what?"

"The Speculating Speckled Frog," she repeated. "It's the most intelligent being in the jungle. More of spirit than of flesh and blood. Sometimes it appears as a male, other times a female. It makes no difference. It uses the art of speculation and pondering to answer one's question correctly."

I frowned. *Wait a minute,* I thought. *Could it have been . . . maybe?*

"What does it look like?"

"A large pink frog," Misty said.

My belly flipped.

"With gold spots?" I asked.

"Yes."

"I've seen it! Sometime in my first days in the jungle and later on! It was rude and irritating, but it kept asking me what I wanted and I said nothing. It was just a strange frog. I didn't think it was important." I paused, annoyed with myself. How could I have been so judgmental? Just like people back home who looked at me and made their stupid judgments based on my appearance. I should have paid more attention and asked what it meant by its questions, even if it was a little impolite. Still, I wasn't psychic. "How could I have known I would want some information from it back then?! Have I missed my chance?!"

Misty laughed.

"That frog is tricky. It lives on a higher plane of consciousness, within the past, present, and future. It knows all before and after it happens."

"I don't understand," I said.

"You don't have to. All you need to know is that it can correctly answer any question you ask it and, no, you haven't missed your chance. It was just toying with you," she said. "But it can be quite fickle. Some days it'll allow you to ask only one question, other days you may ask as many as you like."

"Have you ever . . . asked it a question?" I asked.

"Only once." She paused, looking at the ceiling. Then she said, "How to protect the village from further elgort attacks."

"And . . ."

"It said we must . . . learn to climb trees and build technology," she said with a disgusted look. She paused and shook her head. "We will do *no such thing.*"

235

For a moment, there was a long silence between us. I felt sad for Misty's dilemma. To build technologies and climb trees were against the Greeny Gorilla way, against their culture. But how else could the gorillas protect their village from certain disaster? It was a tough situation.

"Well," I finally said. "H-how do I find it again?"

"It will find you now," Misty said. "Just keep doing what you are doing. Keep searching for the egg. It helps only those who are helping themselves."

CHAPTER 23

RUDE AWAKENING

I left that very afternoon, despite Misty's request that I wait until the next morning.

"You will have more daylight," Misty said as I packed my things. She handed me a sack of food she'd prepared. She must have known that I wouldn't be persuaded to stay. I put it in my satchel.

"I know, but I have to go *now*," I replied. I'd stayed in the village long enough. Outside Misty's home, a small crowd was gathering to see me off.

"I will light a candle and wish that the other Wind-seeker finds you," Misty said. "She seemed like she could handle an elgort."

I smiled.

"Nsibidi could handle anything," I said. "But I doubt she'll find me. It's a big jungle, and she's already been here."

When I went outside, followed by a sad-looking Misty, I looked ahead, at the trail, into the trees. The village was comfort. Out there, beyond the village, was not. Two of the girls I'd spent many hours finding evil weevils and playing games with ran up and threw their arms around me. I laughed and sighed, enjoying their tight furry hug.

"Stay safe, OK?" the taller one named Jos said.

"I will," I said.

Chika, who was smaller but the same age, was too upset to speak. She was really scared for me, and my assurances didn't convince her. For a while, I was hugged and wished good luck by many people. Then Obax came, walking with his red cane. I smiled broadly the moment I saw him. Everyone stepped back and quieted down as he approached.

"I still cannot believe that I am letting you leave, traveling girl," Obax said.

"I have to do this," I said.

"I know, my dear, I know," Obax said with a sigh. "And thus I let you go. Come forward and kneel before me."

I knelt at Obax's furry feet. Tufts of gray hair covered his neatly cut black toenails. I glanced to the side and saw Misty. She smiled back at me and nodded.

"This is a destiny necklace," he said as he placed a green glass necklace around my neck. It was cool and smooth on my skin. "It will help bring you what you need. I wish you success on your journey, and we all hope to see you again someday." He paused, glancing at Misty. Then he said, "Now, it's time for you to turn and go."

When I stood up, Obax gave me a hug.

"Beware of what comes next," Obax said into my ear. Then Misty gave me a long hug. She said nothing as she stepped back and walked away.

And so I set out again, wearing a new pair of silky green pants and a long shirt. They were different from Dari's clothes not only in style but in the material, which was thinner and sleeker, making the clothes easier to move about in. I also carried another pair of pants, a shirt, and a nightshirt in my bundle.

I didn't know how to go about finding the elgort cave and wondered what I'd do when I did. To my compass's relief, I started moving north again. And to my slight annoyance, my compass blurted out that I was exactly 310 miles north from home.

"Didn't I tell you not to tell me the distance?" I said.

"Forgive me, Zahrah," the compass said. "I got a little excited when I checked. I am programmed better than that and will act accordingly from now on."

I shook my head. "No, no, it's OK, compass. It's not that big of a deal to me anymore, anyway."

I was comfortable in the jungle now. And I didn't allow myself to think about how I would get back home. One thing at a time.

For the next two days, I traveled using one of the gorillas' old trails. I knew I was close. I just had a feeling. The jungle felt different, more alive and strange. The soil was so fragrant that it had an almost sweet smell. Along the way I buried the seeds of the mangoes I ate, knowing that soon a tree would grow there. And of course I encountered more strange creatures. I witnessed a pack of meat-eating hummingbirds set upon a wild boar, devouring it within two minutes. When I was sure the birds were gone, I took one of the boar's sharp tusks. I thought it would make a good weapon.

A day later, I ended up throwing the tusk at a large, violent rodent that chased and tried to bite me when I stepped too close to its hole in the ground. The tusk hit it on the rump and scared it away quite nicely.

On the third day after leaving the gorilla village, by the time dusk came, it was still warm and humid, and I was eagerly looking for a good tree to cool down and rest in. All day, as I'd walked, I'd been feeling extremely anxious. I had been in the jungle for close to three weeks and my time was almost up . . . *if* it wasn't already. The book said that anyone bitten by a war snake had three to four weeks before the coma became permanent. Was I too late? I wasn't even close to finding the egg, let alone close

to home. I was looking up at a sizable baobab tree thinking about this when I heard my name.

"Zahrah!"

It was coming from above the tree. From the sky. In
the yellow, orange, pink of dusk, her yellow dress glowed
like a rising sun.

"Nsibidi?" I shouted. "Is that you?" I blinked for a
moment at the sound of my own voice, realizing that I
hadn't spoken, not even to my compass, in days. A flock
of brown and white sparrows rose from a nearby tree in a
chirping haze. I laughed and clapped my hand over my
mouth. "Nsibidi, down here!"

"Zahrah!" she said again, flying down. I watched her
with wide eyes. She was like a bird, except more graceful.
She moved through the air with more ease. The air
around me began to move as she landed before me with
such softness that she might as well have been stepping
down from the last step of a flight of stairs.

"You found me!" I said giddily and laughed again.
Though Nsibidi was a mystery to me, she was someone
from my other world, that place outside the Greeny
Jungle that seemed so far away. Her presence made me
feel more real.

"I just came from the gorilla village, and they told me
you'd left, taking the old trail. I've been following it, so I
was bound to find you," Nsibidi said. She grinned and
shook her head after looking me up and down for a long

moment. "I can't believe it. You've changed."

"Still haven't gotten what I want and I'm running out of time, *o*!" I said, looking at the sky. "I have to find —"

"Zahrah, I've come to take you home," she said.

I frowned and then shook my head, pushing away the first thought that came to my mind, a thought I was sure was true: *Dari's gone and she's come to tell me and bring me back. I'm too late.*

"No," I said.

"You've made it this far, but an elgort will kill you," she said. I breathed with relief. She just wanted to persuade me to go home. "I can't let you do this. Everything in my common sense tells me not to. I've been searching for you for over a week. You have no idea what chaos you've caused back home."

"Yes, I do," I said, though I didn't. I couldn't imagine it. All I knew at the time was that it must have been horrible for my parents.

"Look at you, Zahrah," Nsibidi said, putting her arms around her chest and staring at me. "You don't . . . even look like yourself anymore."

I frowned. I probably didn't. I just hadn't thought about it. I still didn't want to think about it.

"Zahrah, please. Your family needs you. I can get you there. This is my fault, that's the least I can do for you. You have such potential, I can't let you commit suicide," Nsibidi said.

"But Dari! He needs—"

"He needs you at his side," Nsibidi said. "Not here."

For the second time, Nsibidi and I stood staring at each other. I don't know what she must have seen in me. How must I have looked? After so many days in the jungle, alone, no longer afraid, almost part of the jungle myself. In the clothes sewn by Greeny Gorillas. With my scars and scratches. My blood tainted with whip-scorpion poison.

In her I saw indecision. She wasn't really that sure about taking me home; I could tell. But she not only felt responsible for Dari's situation and mine but truly cared about me and would be devastated if I were killed.

"Come," she said. "Let's get some sleep and decide what to do in the morning."

I nodded.

For an hour, I lay thinking about going home with Nsibidi. My mission *was* practically suicide. I was aware of this, fully aware. If I died, so much would be lost. But I'd come so far and I hadn't missed the look in Nsibidi's protective eyes. Deep down, I think she believed I could do it. She was just afraid of letting me try. I rolled it all over and over in my mind, in my usual clamlike way. Still I didn't come up with a pearl. By the time I fell asleep, I still wasn't sure what I'd do.

I slept well that night, Nsibidi on the branch just above mine. And I could still feel the warmth of the gorillas with me as I clutched the green necklace Obax had given me. I missed them all.

In the morning, I opened my eyes to a ray of sunlight shining through some tree leaves, warming my face. I could still hear Nsibidi above me breathing softly as she slept. Something pink and shiny was standing on the tree branch right in front of my eyes. It was so close that I couldn't quite focus on it. I knew I was high up, so I didn't jump. Instead, I let my eyes focus a little more as I tried to figure out what I should do. I slowly sat up, keeping my dark brown eyes on the golden eyes of the large, shiny pink frog with gold speckles.

"Wh-what?!"

The frog rolled its eyes and sighed dramatically.

"As if you haven't seen me before. As if my presence is *such* a surprise," it said. "I know you seek me. What is it that you want, dada girl?"

I glanced up at Nsibidi. She still slept.

"May we please talk down there?" I said. "I . . . I don't want to wake my friend."

Without a word, the frog leaped to the ground. It was a high jump for a creature of its size, but it didn't seem to mind.

Very quietly and on shaky legs, I grabbed my satchel and bundle and climbed down. It looked at me, waiting for me to speak.

"Are you—"

"Yes, I am."

"You're the Speculating Speckled Frog?"

"Didn't I just *say* I was?" the frog said. "What do you want?"

"Well," I said, "I—"

"Let me guess," the frog interrupted. "Like every other human explorer I've met, you want to know the meaning of life."

"I didn't—"

"The answer is forty-four. That machine was off by two," the frog snapped. "Believe me, it makes a world of difference. And now I will be on my way."

The frog turned around and was about to hop away.

"But that isn't my question," I said quickly.

"Yes, it is. It's what you all ask," the frog said. "As if it matters. You'll still live your lives the stupid way you choose and then die and be reborn again as someone or something else, et cetera, et cetera."

"It's not my question."

"Don't you wonder why you're here in this world? What it all means?"

"Well," I said, thinking about it, "sometimes, I guess. When I'm—"

"Well, there. You have your answer."

"But forty-four makes no sense and—"

"You asked for the answer to the meaning of life. To understand that, you must know the *question* to the meaning of life."

"But that wasn't my question," I said again, growing frustrated and confused. The frog sighed its loud, rude sigh again.

"Then what *is* your question?"

"I just—"

"Get on with it," the frog snapped.

"Where can I—"

"Hurry up!"

I spoke as fast as I could. "Where-can-I-find-an-un-fertilized-elgort-egg?"

The frog looked at me, cocking its head.

"You *can't* be serious."

"I need it to save my best friend's life," I said.

"I'm not going to tell you that," the frog said with a chuckle.

"Why not?" I said, trying hard to keep my voice down. "Please! Oh *please*! I've come so far! You're supposed to answer at least one question!"

"Psss, I take no orders from anyone. I answer questions when I please. You want me to be responsible for your getting killed?" it said. "To have blood on my hands and feet and reputation? You want to drag me into *your* mess?! Selfish girl."

"Plea—"

"No. Absolutely not."

I didn't know what to do, so I just stood there as it looked at me. My blood pressure was probably rising from frustration, but I didn't care. Let it make me sleep. It was better than looking at that arrogant, stupid, wet, pink frog. I bit back my urge to shout and cry and throw dirt at the selfish creature. Anger would get me nowhere.

"*I* chose to come here," I said in my calmest voice. "I left *my* home, *my* friend, and I packed *my* things. I walked into the jungle. I have been bitten, stung, and poisoned. A whip scorpion and Carnigourd have tried to eat me, panthers have contemplated making a meal of me, wild boars have tried to tear me apart, spiders have tasted me, wild dogs have chased me. I've survived all this way. *This* has *nothing* to do with you, Mr. or Mrs. Frog, whatever you are. *Nothing*. All I need is a *bit* of information from you. What makes you think my dying at this point in my journey would be because of you? If I survive, would it be because of you, too?"

I refrained from calling the frog selfish and self-centered, as I really wanted to. My heart was beating fast, but no darkness came because deep down I was calm. I knew I was right. And I knew I had rightfully earned the pride that I felt for myself.

The frog turned around and started to hop away. My shoulders slumped and I dropped my things on the ground. Then the frog turned around and hopped back to me. It looked up at me for several moments before it spoke.

"You are serious," the frog said, its voice softening.

I nodded. Suddenly, I saw Dari in his bed, lying very still. His mother sat nearby. She was reading to him. I couldn't hear what she was reading, but I could see the book. It was Dari's favorite book after *The Forbidden Greeny Jungle Field Guide*, a nature book on the wildlife inhabiting the Ooni Palace. Dari loved all the pictures of the top of the palace, near the giant flower satellite, where it was so cold and frigid that the only things that lived up there were snow albatrosses and the legion of dedicated human-size ants that guarded and maintained the palace's leaves and huge stem. His mother's voice was flat as she read from the pages.

Then the vision was gone and I was looking into the frog's eyes.

"Hmm, your task is quite noble," the frog said, the edge completely gone from its voice.

I wiped a tear from my cheek and sniffed. The frog put one of its cool hands on my hand and said, "Let me speculate."

I waited for a moment while it closed its eyes. Then the frog said, "You must find its path before you find the elgort. Follow my directions and you will find one of their nests without being spotted. Now listen closely.

"Trek backward. South. You don't have to go all the

way back to the gorilla village, just where the gorilla trail picks up. That's four miles from here. The trail runs northeast and southwest. Go southwest. Follow it till it ends and continue southwest; you will eventually cross an elgort path. The trees will be flattened, the bushes crushed. Take your time, Zahrah. It will be dangerous to hurry at this point. Go in the direction opposite to the flattened trees. At the end of the elgort path, you'll find its nest."

I looked back up at Nsibidi in the tree only once and then quickly set off. My decision was made. *She'll understand,* I thought. *I have to do this.*

CHAPTER 24

ℰLGORT

"Wow," I said, staring at the destruction.

I shivered. It was a sight few would want to see alone. To know that an animal had done all of what I was seeing was terrifying. Even after all I had been through.

I absent-mindedly touched the green necklace around my neck. The trail must have been made some days ago because the trees and bushes that had been flattened were beginning to wither. Some of them had already turned brown. The flattened foliage ran like a two-lane road through the forest farther than I could see. A beast had done this just by going about its business! Think of what it does when it's angry! Everything was flattened in one direction, just as the frog had said it would be.

"Go in the direction opposite to the flattened trees. At

the end of the elgort path, you'll find its nest," the Speculating Speckled Frog had said.

I tentatively stepped on the elgort path and shivered again. *What creatures must have died an awful death on this path?* I wondered. I hoped I wouldn't see any remains. It was unlikely. Elgorts left no remains when they ate. It was three chomps and then swallow. I looked up and down the trail. A few birds flew by, and a brown furry anteater hopped back into the bushes. But no elgort. I hiked up my bundle and satchel and started down the path I was determined to follow to its end.

On the second day, I saw an elgort.

For hours before, I'd been hearing their screeches. I assumed that they were calling to each other, that it was their way of socializing. I imagined that one would stand in place, and its entire body would quiver as it inhaled, filling its lungs with air. And then it would open its trunk wide and screeeeeeeeeech! A minute later another would usually answer. Since I had started hearing their cries, I took to traveling alongside the path, in the shadows of the trees. I figured that though an elgort made paths through the jungle wherever it went, it must use the same path once in a while, especially around its nest.

This turned out to be a smart move because that day, when the sun shone bright, I heard the screech from *very* close by. I froze, hiding behind a thick tree. There was a rumbling as the ground shook. I braced my legs to keep my balance. All sorts of dreadful things flashed through my mind, mainly the painful end to my life. I just knew the elgort would have a mouth full of slobbering teeth. Its feet would be bloody from the victims it had trampled over. Nevertheless, if I had blinked I would have missed it. The elgort zoomed by faster than I had ever seen a living thing move. Even faster than a car!

But I didn't blink, and though it took only a split second to go by, I saw its shiny, black, elephant-like body, lethal trunk, beady eyes, and blur of shuffling feet. As it passed, it blew up dirt and branches and leaves. I'd have been blown off my feet if I hadn't held on to a tree. This was what I was up against. When things settled down, I touched my glass necklace again.

"I'm almost there, Dari," I whispered.

It took me another day to find the large cave that sat on a hill surrounded by smooth-trunked tall palm trees. When I did, I quietly stepped behind a tree and sat down. I didn't take out my digi-book. I was getting to the point where I no longer needed it. I already knew many of the creatures mentioned in it. If I didn't know a creature, I used my knowledge to make educated guesses about it, and I was usually right. Plus the elgort entry didn't work anyway.

Nor did I take out my compass. I knew exactly where I was. It was as if I had a compass in my head now.

What I needed at that moment was to sit and let my mind rest. I squatted down behind the tree and placed my head in my hands, closed my eyes, and tried to focus my mind. Two years earlier, Dari had been obsessed with the Mami Wata Mambos, women who honored a powerful water deity. They were known for falling into such deep meditation that they could go for days without eating or sleeping, and when they awoke, they were strong enough to climb the tallest palm trees and hike up high mountains. Dari had looked up their methods on the net, and we had both tried to meditate like the Mami Wata Mambos before our final exams. We'd both been somewhat successful, feeling vibrant for our exams even after little sleep.

I closed my eyes and used the method we'd practiced, imagining I was swimming through soft, warm clear water as a bird flew through the sky. Slowly, I felt my body relax and I was able to think clearly. I realized that I wasn't afraid. No. Not after coming this far. I was apprehensive. I was excited. I was finally at the place I'd been traveling toward for weeks. I was in a position to do what I wanted to do.

"But I have to calm myself first," I whispered. "Get ready. Relax, Zahrah. Relax. So you can do this right."

As I crouched there behind the tree imagining water and warmth, my body became perfectly still and quiet and

I began to listen. Then there was another presence. I felt it more than I heard it. A burst of dirt and leaves filled the air. Then it screeched. I slowly brought my head up, turned, and glanced around the tree. There it was in full view. It stood motionless at the mouth of the cave. It screeched again, lifting its thick trunk high like a giant meaty trumpet. My heart somersaulted in my chest. I held my hands to my ears to drown the sound out, but I could still feel it vibrate through my body. *I never want that thing's eyes on me*, I thought.

The elgort was probably a female, her nest inside the cave. She turned and went into her lair. I could hear her moving around inside. I set my things down, keeping them close to me. Then I sat down, closed my eyes, and tried to meditate. The time hadn't come yet. It arrived hours later, when I heard the elgort emerging from her cave. I had stopped meditating and fallen into a terrified stupor, watching the sunlight leak from the sky. It had become night and the moonlight gave the forest a dim glow. It was dark, so I closed my eyes and tried to see with my ears.

The elgort was at the lip of the cave. She was hungry. Why else would this creature come out of her cave? Then there was the blast of air as she ran off to forage. When I stood up, my joints were stiff and my hands shook, but I didn't hesitate. If I had, I would *never* have gone in.

I thought I no longer needed the digi-book, and to an extent I was right. I knew the Forbidden Greeny Jungle. I had mastered it! Sort of. But not even masters know everything. What the digi-book couldn't tell me about the elgort, even if I could have read the entire entry, was that a female elgort doesn't go too far from her nest when she looks for food. On top of this, I believe that sometimes a female elgort can even sense when her eggs are in danger.

This elgort must have been only about a mile away when she got the prick in her small brain that a foreign creature was hovering close to her eggs. I imagine that in three crunches, she ate the bush cow she'd caught and immediately began making her way back to her nest.

Inside, the cave wasn't very deep, and within a few minutes, I was standing on several layers of dried fern leaves looking over seven elgort eggs. I needed to take the unfertilized one, but which one was that? All of them were smooth and white with purple dots.

"Oh, Joukoujou, help me," I whispered, holding my glow lily closer for a better look. From not far, I heard the screech of the elgort and my heart raced even faster. *Which one?* I stared harder, squinting my eyes. The eggs were perfectly round, about the size of the bounce pods people used when they played netball. I bent down and reached for one of them. It was warm and twitched at my touch. I snatched my hand back.

"Ooooooh," I moaned, not knowing what to do. They all looked the same. I couldn't make a mistake there. If I took one with a baby elgort in it, then there would probably be no yolk, especially since these eggs looked as if they were ready to hatch at any moment. And what if it hatched after I took it? Even baby elgorts were probably dangerous. If I didn't choose correctly, all was lost for me . . . and Dari.

I wanted to sit down and just cry. Cry my brains out. I was tired; tired of taking chances, tired of not knowing anything for sure, tired of looking death in the eye. The mother would be back soon, but still I just wanted to cry. Enough was enough. But it wasn't and I couldn't. I had to make a choice.

I slowly stepped forward and touched another egg. It twitched, but this time I forced myself not to jump back. And in that moment, my hand on that twitching egg, it came to me. I moved to the next one and touched it. It also was warm and twitched at my touch. I went from egg to egg. When I touched the fifth one, a piece of eggshell fell away and a tiny trunk grabbed at my arm. It held on tight and I could feel its undeveloped teeth trying to gnaw at me.

"Ah!" I shrieked using all my strength to pull my arm from its strong grasp. The place where it had caught me throbbed, but I had no time to inspect it. More eggshell was falling away from this baby elgort, and soon its whole head was out. Its eyes were yellow with flecks of red, and they looked right at me. It then raised its trunk and let out a feeble screech. Feeble, but one that I was sure its mother would hear. I ran to the next egg, ready to just grab it and run. I wanted to get away from that baby elgort and out of the cave as soon as possible. I had to take a chance, and I had a one-in-seven chance of being right.

"No, Zahrah, stay calm," I said out loud. I would touch them all first. My father always said that even in moments of crisis, it was best to stay calm and hold on to logic.

The sixth egg was cool and did not move.

Without further thought, I snatched it into my arms, shoved the glow lily into my satchel, and ran out of the cave. The egg was somewhat heavy. It weighed about as much as two bounce pods filled with water. I was standing on the lip of the cave when I felt the ground rumble. From the hill, I could see the forest top and the trees falling from view! The swath of tumbling leaves and timber was growing closer with impossible speed. I'll never forget that sight.

Immediately, I turned and ran like a madwoman! I took off down the hill to the right and into the jungle, hoping with all my heart that I wouldn't trip and fall. I plunged into the forest, smelling leaves, soil, and moisture. I imagined the choking scent of the elgort's madness just behind me. Like fire and the reddest pepper. I had grown strong and quick from my travels, but there was no way I could outrun that madness.

Behind me, I heard the elgort give its warrior cry, *"Screeeeeeeech!"* It was so loud that I thought my ears would burst. I wanted to scream, but I was breathing so fast that all I could do was whimper.

Pure fear heightened my night vision, and my long skinny legs moved me fast around the trees, rough bushes, dead leaves, and vines. I was leaping over a moss-covered log when two large trees crashed to my left and right! Leaves, twigs, and dirt blew onto me with such force that any exposed skin was immediately scratched to pieces. And if the elgort wasn't going to kill me, the falling trees it knocked down would.

Even as I ran, I was aware, on some level, of the need to focus and stay calm. I could hear the grunts of the elgort and the crack, snap, and crash of the trees and bushes as the elgort flattened them. Suddenly, a small tree hit my arm as it fell. I stumbled, almost falling, but kept running.

The elgort was a beast, a monster, a living demon fueled by rage. I tried not to imagine its legs, though I could hear it behind me; the rhythm of its steps was impossible to discern because those feet were moving so fast. It would break my back with the first chomp, press the blood from my body with the second, and crush my head with the third and then swallow.

I started to cry. I was breathing hard, tears of terror flying from my eyes when I looked at the sky that peeked between the leaves and branches. The elgort would soon be on me. Any moment now.

As I clutched the egg to my chest and the elgort's shadow fell on me, blocking out the moonlight, images of my life flashed through my brain. My mother tucking me into bed. My father's laugh. Papa Grip touching my hair and saying it was OK. *I'm a wise woman,* I thought. Sitting on the lower branch of a tree, Dari on the branch above. What did the teasing matter? The days on the playground where kids pulled my hair and chanted, "Witch lady, witch lady, where is your juju?" Sitting quietly in my room looking out the window at the sky.

The elgort was a half moment away. I could feel its breath on my back. My heart beat a frantic rhythm.

Just behind me, it grunted as it reached for me with its trunk. I felt the tip of it touch my ear! Another large tree fell forward, only a yard to my side. If I tripped or a tree fell on me, I would be dead within milliseconds. I thought about how I had disturbed this elgort's babies. The mother elgort probably wanted to not only kill me but cause me pain and suffering.

I wheezed and could feel my legs ready to give way.

Who was going to save me? I'd abandoned Nsibidi days ago. If she was trying to find me, she would have done so by now. The Greeny Gorillas also had let me go. My parents didn't know where I was, and if they did, I was too far for them to make a difference. This situation was my doing and I was on my own.

I'm not born to die like this.

The thought echoed in my emptying mind. I'd been shy, introverted, lived my life up to the last few weeks cowering from the world. When people made fun of me, I would go home and hide in my room. I was born with a strange ability, and once again, I cowered from it. *But look at how I've survived in this place,* I thought.

I'm not born to die like this!

In that moment, I was sure. It was as if something clicked in my brain and I was ready. I was immediately energized. I relaxed, and before I knew it, I shrugged off the darkness, my blood pressure dropping as my body calmed. The elgort's trunk touched my ear again, this time more firmly, and I knocked it away.

Then, as if I had always done it, I took to the sky. Yes, I knew how to fly. I could fly. It had been in the back of my mind for weeks. An unthinkable, unspoken possibility. But in that moment, I chose to fly, not die. Nsibidi was right; it came when I wanted it to. I just had to want it hard enough.

I flew fast and high, branches and leaves slapping and

painfully scratching at my face and body, getting caught in my dada hair, and tearing my clothes. I gritted my teeth through the pain. When I broke the forest's cover, I glanced below me and saw the elgort. I smiled deliriously. Elgorts were fast, but they couldn't climb anything. They were strictly land animals, like bush cows.

Below, the elgort raged, her angry screech shaking the entire jungle and her thousand teeth glinting in the moonlight. I faintly heard a group of palm-tree crows fly from a nearby tree, cawing in panic. When I made it through the jungle's canopy, I clutched the egg as tightly as I could and then flew away from the elgort with as much speed as I could muster. All my muscles were straining to their limit.

I was too concerned with the egg to notice that I was hundreds of feet in the air and bathed in moonlight. I didn't notice how peaceful it was up there. Nor did I notice the zigzags of elgort paths below me. I did notice that the elgort was not following me below. Instead she ran back to her nest—to check on her eggs, I was sure. When she'd realize that I had taken the unfertilized one, she would probably screech a less aggravated screech and sit on her unhatched brood, looking around angrily.

I flew slowly, afraid to move too fast and drop the egg. A few times I was sure I would drop it. When I had gotten about a mile away, I actually *did*.

"*No!*" I screamed as I watched the egg fall between the trees below. I zoomed down after it, my eyes tearing from the rushing air. I'd come *this* far only to drop the egg by accident! I landed on the ground and looked around frantically. Trees and bushes to my left, more on my right. Decaying leaves and mulch underfoot. Grasses, ferns, creeping plants, a patch of lemongrass, blue lilies, the sound of a bird flying away here and a beetle clicking there. Where *was* it? There. Right in front of a bush. I frowned as I ran to it. *What is that?* I squinted. Then I laughed.

"How . . . ?"

"I have my ways," said the Speculating Speckled Frog, sitting on the egg. Today its voice was higher, like a woman's.

"Have a seat," the frog said. "We need to talk."

I plopped down, suddenly exhausted. Only moments ago, I'd been running for my life. Then I'd dropped the egg. Now a frog was telling me to sit down.

"How do you feel?" the frog asked.

I must have been shaking with excess adrenaline and terror. I knew I looked stunned.

"Stunned," I said. I picked a thorn from my cheek and looked at my pants. They were slashed in places, and blood soaked through in others. I stuck my finger in my ear as if doing so would stop the ringing from the elgort's screeches.

"You should feel proud of yourself," the frog said. "You've done the impossible."

I grunted. Without a thought, I flicked away a large bush spider that was scrambling toward me. The frog chuckled.

"A thirteen-year-old Ooni girl who has never left her comfortable home walks into the Forbidden Greeny Jungle and masters it, and *then* successfully snatches an elgort egg to save her friend. In my three thousand and four years, I have *never* seen anything like it."

I wasn't paying full attention. Several of the trees that had scratched me must have had some mild poison in their leaves and branches, because my scratches and scrapes were itching terribly and I felt a little lightheaded. I had an idea how to make it better, and I would do that when the frog was finished with me. I looked at my hands. They were still shaking.

"Now you will head home, no?"

"Yes," I said.

"May I ask you one question?"

I shrugged. "Sure."

"What have you learned in your travels?"

I laughed. "I've learned that the sky above the jungle is safer than the ground." *Unless I come across one of those monstrous horse-eating birds,* I thought. I paused as the frog waited for me to continue. "I don't know. It's too early to think of—"

"By the time you're fully relaxed and you stop shaking, you won't remember what you've learned. Not completely.

It's best to say it out loud, put words to it. I know you are very tired, but this is a moment to reflect."

I paused as I thought about this. The answer came, but the words were hard to speak. Just like that day when Papa Grip pushed me in front of the mirror and asked me to tell him what I saw. I took a deep breath, this time not needing any coaxing.

"I've . . . I've learned so much about myself, what I'm capable of, about the world . . . you know, things. I'm stronger than I thought. Much stronger. I'm no longer afraid of heights."

The frog nodded.

"It has been good watching you," the frog said. "You've been great entertainment. And mark my words, you will be the talk of the jungle for many centuries to come."

I looked up from examining my wounds. "Really?"

The frog nodded.

"The Greeny Gorillas will tell their children: 'There once was a quiet, shy girl who discovered she wasn't so shy or quiet. Who discovered that she could do whatever she put her mind to. She learned this when she and her friend were playing in the forest and got attacked by an elgort. Her friend was so scared that he fainted.' They will then tell a colorful story about how the girl fought that elgort, jumping on its back and strangling it with her bare hands!"

I laughed. "That's not what I did."

"Well, stories often change and shift when told over and over again," the frog said. It smiled and hopped off the egg. "It's all yours."

I stood and picked up the egg. Its shell was thick and hard. I realized that it could have fallen from higher up onto concrete and still not crack.

"Why don't you put it in your satchel?" the frog said.

I did so, dumping out my nightgown and a pair of pants to make room. It was much easier to carry that way. I knelt down and touched the frog's feet the way I saw the gorillas do to Chief Obax and whispered, "Thank you." Then I kissed the frog's smooth moist skin and stood up.

"Now go, wind girl," the frog said. "Your friend awaits you."

CHAPTER 25

South

The flight home took only three days.

The actual act of flying didn't tire me at all. I stopped only because of hunger, thirst, and the need to sleep. I slept with the elgort egg held to my chest. The rest of the time I flew. I was like a migrating bird, and even though I checked my compass once in a while, I realized that I knew exactly which way to go. I didn't need it anymore.

I easily avoided the giant eagles, and even when they saw me, they didn't attack. They didn't seem interested in eating me, but they were curious. As I flew, I was delighted to learn that the sky wasn't as empty as it looked. All kinds of birds populated it, large, small, fast, slow, high flying, low flying, colorful and dull.

I liked flying higher than most birds. I found myself in the company of vultures, hawks, and the giant eagles — the birds of prey. Several of the giant brown eagles soared over to me and flew beside me for miles. Their wingspan was over forty feet and their beaks were larger than my head! Some had bright green eyes, others had purple, gold, and even blue eyes. Like precious stones!

At first I was scared and flew faster, trying to outdistance them. But they were expert fliers and kept up easily. After a while, when several more joined me, squawking gleefully to each other, I realized that they were either playing with me or trying to teach me. This was how I tested and practiced my speed.

On the second day, it rained. It was my first Greeny Jungle thunderstorm. It had sprinkled a few times before but not enough to slow me down. This was an all-out tree-shaking thunderstorm. I hovered high in the sky, watching as the enormous thunderhead rolled toward me. Its beauty was striking. The cloud was a deep undulating gray with purple lightning bouncing within its bowels. All around me I saw the birds that populated the skies descending to take cover. I quickly followed suit.

As I descended, I scanned the treetops. I knew what to look for. A root tree. Its yellow square-shaped leaves hung from long, thick stems. These grew from the tree's center like a giant golden fountain. Underneath was a series of chunky, tangled roots. It was the perfect place to seek shelter during a thunderstorm. I easily spotted one below.

By the time the storm came, I was comfortably nestled underneath some roots. They overlapped, and I wasn't surprised when I stayed completely dry. Placing my satchel with the elgort egg next to me, I brought out my glow lily. I ate a mango while watching the storm through the tunnel of roots before me. It was vicious, with rain, some hail, and winds strong enough to blow down several trees nearby.

I heard them fall but I was safe. An iroko tree, the tallest kind in the jungle, could tumble onto these roots, but they would remain undamaged. To take my mind off the storm, I took out my digi-book. My hands were damp, and the digi-book slipped out of my hand and banged against a stone on the ground. I picked it up, and more out of habit than hope I tried the elgort entry yet again.

The error message popped up again, but then the screen went black and up came the entry, this time in its entirety. I laughed loudly. "Oh *now* it decides to work."

> The Œlgôrt is a nasty beast, the môst deadly in the Greeny Jungle. The ultimate killing machine. And it's Mad as the Mad Hatter ôf the mythical *Alice in Wônderearth* fables. Twenty-ône ôf us explôrers have been eaten by them. Thôse ôf us who survived made sure these Œlgôrt victims' research made it back tô

the Ôôni Kingdôm fôr this bôôk. Let's get a little technical and dry:

Œlgôrt: ôriginally called Saniya Mai K'arfi (Strông Côw) by the ancient peôples ôf ôld. A large egg-laying beast capable ôf môving very very fast. It has smôôth black skin and a pôwerful trunk lined with many large sharp teeth. It inhabits the quadrants ôf the Fôrbidden Greeny Jungle abôut twô tô three hundred miles nôrth ôf the Ôôni Kingdôm's bôrder. The females build their nests in caves and they like tô line them with fern leaves. Sô if yôu're seeking shelter frôm the rain in a cave and the flôôr is côvered with fern leaves, yôu are prôbably much better ôff getting sôaked.

The Œlgôrt has ônly ône enemy, the Gôsukwu, a lông-armed, mônkeylike mônster abôut the size ôf a small truck and with blue wôôlly fur. When an Œlgôrt môther is attacked by a Gôsukwu and her eggs are in danger, she picks up the unfertilized egg with her trunk and thrôws it at the Gôsukwu. This usually wôrks. Sôme ôf us have seen it happen. The Gôsukwu catches the egg and then walks away with it, satisfied. Nearby, it'll make a meal ôf the egg and then môve ôn.

Œven môre than the fertilized egg, this unfertilized Œlgôrt egg is knôwn tô have several medicinal values.

Nôw, if this is yôur gôal, tô get an Œlgôrt egg, give
up! Turn back. Fôllôw yôur cômpass sôuth, back hôme.

I turned it off and laughed.

The storm was violent and swift. It passed within
twenty minutes, and soon after, I was on my way again.

I landed past the jungle's border, where the trees were
more spaced, where the town of Kirki began. When my
feet touched the hard, even ground, I just stood there.
Behind me stretched the Forbidden Greeny Jungle, a
place that I no longer considered forbidden.

I had traveled well into its insides. I still had the scar
on my upper arm from the whip scorpion. It would probably remain slightly blue until the poison left my body.
There were healing scrapes from where the Carnigourd's
vine had wrapped itself around my ankle. I had itchy
scrapes and scratches from when I had escaped the elgort.
And, of course, there was the throbbing bruise from
where the baby elgort had grabbed and gnawed on my
arm. Rubbing cool mud on my wounds lessened the itching and encouraged healing. I was very much alive and,
even more extraordinary, I had an elgort egg!

A car passed by and I laughed to myself as I began
walking. Then I pulled out my compass.

"Well, you're almost home, where you belong," the
compass said, sounding delighted. I smiled. The best way
to please a compass was to go in the direction of the place

you'd programmed it to call "home." I pressed a button on the side and it announced, "It's one-twelve a.m., Saturday night."

"And what a beautiful night it is," I said, turning off the compass and putting it in my pocket. I looked down at my tattered clothes. My hair and body needed a good washing, but at least I didn't have any birds nesting in my hair. And if it weren't for the time spent in the Greeny Gorilla village, I'd have been much filthier. *Would I even be alive if I hadn't stayed there for those few days?* I wondered. I put the thought out of my head. It didn't matter. I was sure that I smelled strongly of sweat, mud, and leaves; the jungle. But I didn't care. I hadn't reached the end of my journey yet. Dari's time in a coma would reach a month in about a day or so.

I stood for a moment, wondering where to go and how to travel. My home was only a twenty-minute walk away, the hospital about an hour. But I could fly to the hospital. However, someone might see me. In Kirki, large glow-lily clusters grew alongside the road and people moved about during the night. And I didn't know how people would react to something so unfamiliar to their eyes.

I turned east, toward home.

$\mathcal{H}$OME

I didn't have to see my parents to know that they had gone through a rough time. I was their daughter and I had run away and been gone for over three weeks. Not even my parents had believed that there was much hope. How could they? No child had ever done such a thing and come out alive. And I'd read that most of the highly trained adults who had emerged were crazy, half dead, or deeply affected by their travels. The unexpectedness of my actions must have stung my parents as deeply as my being gone.

I stood in front of the house staring at the door. I felt guilty even as I clutched my satchel with the elgort egg in it to my chest. In being selfless, I'd been selfish.

I reached up and touched the thick wooden door. The

door with the round mirrors decorating the top and bottom of it. The door that my mother had painted red five years ago because she thought it would look like a flower next to the green plants that grew on the outer part of the house. The door that another version of me had run in and out of so many times.

I was no longer the Zahrah who was afraid of the world around her, who kept her head down, afraid of confrontation. I could almost see my old self coming out the door, my chin to my chest, ashamed of what I was, all too concerned with my clothes being civilized and making my hair less noticeable. *The old me would never be out this late,* I thought.

I raised a shaking hand to the door, closing it in a loose fist, and knocked. I shivered, feeling flutters in my belly. I had no idea what I'd say to my parents. I waited for an answer. They were probably asleep. I knocked again, this time much harder. The light turned on and I almost passed out with nervousness.

"Yes?" I heard my father say. He didn't open the door. I knew he must have been looking through the peephole. I was just tall enough for him to see the top of my head. "Do you know what time it . . ."

There was a long pause. Then the door flew open.

"Zahrah?" my father said quietly. Then he shouted, "Ha Ha!"

"Papa!!!!"

I ran into my father's arms, and for minutes we stayed that way, my face nestled in his shoulder, my body shuddering as I cried. Then my mother came out, bleary-eyed and confused. When she saw me, she gasped, clapping her hands over her mouth.

"Oh I knew it! I just knew it!!" she shouted as I ran into her arms. We must have woken up the neighborhood with our cries and laughs of shock and joy. And our eyes grew puffy with tears, our noses ran, our throats grew sore, and our arms ached. We didn't want to let each other go.

My mother immediately called the hospital to inform them of what we were bringing.

"Oh my goodness," exclaimed the nurse who answered the phone.

Everyone in the hospital knew of Dari's rare condition.

"Come right over!" the nurse said.

Then after the nurse alerted the doctor, he ran to his other hospital friends and spread the news. Soon the bush radio was at work, twisting and growing its vines of gossip all over Kirki. In the night, the news quickly spread to other nurses' and doctors' husbands, wives, family, and friends and finally the local and national newspapers.

"No time to explain," my mother said to Dari's mother after she'd called the hospital. "Just go to the hospital. Zahrah's come home!"

But we didn't leave right away. As my mother put down the phone, I asked my parents to sit down.

"I . . . I need to tell you . . ." I sighed and laughed nervously.

"Zahrah, what . . . ?"

"No, Papa, I will say it. Give me a moment," I said. I took a deep breath and then looked them both in the eye. I grabbed one of my dadalocks. "Mama, Papa, I was born . . . I got home so . . . if it weren't for . . ." I blinked. "I can fly. I . . . yeah, I can fly."

It took several moments for my words to sink into my parents, and they just looked at me perplexed.

"Fly as in . . ." Then my father pretended as if he were a bird flapping its wings.

"Well, I don't have wings, as you can see, but . . . here, I'll show you."

As I flew about the living room, my parents' perplexed looks became slack-jawed looks of shock. Then my mother laughed, mashing her hair to her head.

"Great Joukoujou, *o*," my father whispered. "What sort of juju is this?"

"It's not juju, Papa. It's just who I am."

After that had sunk in, I went on to tell them a very abbreviated version of my travels. In between my telling, came their yelling:

"How could you *leave* like that?! Were you crazy?"

"Do you know how your actions have turned this town upside down?"

"How could a tortoise that huge have two heads?!"

"You made the front page in the newspapers and you were a breaking story on the net!"

"You could have been killed!"

"Let me see that egg."

"You lived with . . . gorillas?! *Talking* gorillas?"

"Dari needed you around him even if he *was* in a coma!"

"What you did was thoughtless!"

"Whip scorpion?! Let me see the scar."

"Poison?!"

"Oh my goodness, I don't want to hear any more about these elgorts!"

"Are you serious? These gorillas bathed in *oil?*"

"You could have been killed!"

"Those really exist!?"

"You can *fly!!*"

Then it was my turn to be shocked when they told me all that had happened while I was gone. By the evening of the day I'd gone missing, the hunt for me was on. But it didn't get very far. Everyone knew that once a person entered the Forbidden Greeny Jungle, he or she was not coming out.

My father headed the terrified search team that ventured a mile in, but they were quickly forced to turn back after a pack of bush dogs attacked them! One man was bitten on the leg and later suffered an infection, and several others were pretty scratched up and frightened. On top of all this, I was front-page news the morning after. The headline read, "Wise Dada Girl Makes Tragic Unwise Decision."

The search involved the whole town, hundreds of people tentatively combing the outskirts of the jungle, hoping that I was scared and had not gone in, knowing they were being uselessly optimistic. After the dog attacks, Papa Grip gave strict orders that no one should enter the jungle.

"At this point, all we can do is hope," he said sadly, looking into the red eyes of my father and mother as he spoke at the emergency meeting he called a week after I went missing. "Unfortunately, to go in there would mean more people missing." *Papa Grip is going to be so amazed when he finds out that I'm back,* I thought.

Before we left, I took my first hot water shower since leaving home. The water stung my wounds as it washed off the healing mud. I soaped and rinsed my long hair many times, savoring the water. I sighed, my eyes closed. I wrung out my hair and stepped out of the shower.

I looked at myself in the mirror, my dark brown skin, my dada hair, my scraped face, arms, and legs, the scar from the whip scorpion on my arm. I looked into my own eyes and smiled when I saw the new glint in them. Then I floated up to the ceiling of the bathroom, did a somersault, and floated down. *Wait until Dari sees me do that,* I thought as I rubbed rose oil into my wet hair.

On the way to the hospital, I answered more of my parents' questions about my adventures.

"Amazing," my father said as he drove.

"My grandmother used to talk about people who could fly. She said that my great-grandmother could do it," my mother said. "As a matter of fact, when you were born, your father and I discussed the possibility that you might be able to do it."

"We decided to just watch and listen to you closely," my father said.

"But we didn't really believe it was possible," my mother said. She shook her head with a smirk. "Your grandmother would find this so wonderful."

I frowned at this. If I had only gone to my parents in the first place and talked to them about my ability . . . no, I thought. That was not a good way to think. What was done was done. All I could do now was learn from my actions.

My mother had brought a bottle of antiseptic and a cotton ball, and she cleaned my healing scorpion wound.

"I thought she was just telling stories," my mother said. "I always viewed flying people as symbols of freedom that storytellers liked to use. To fly means you are able to go wherever you want, really. Or maybe to fly, to travel, makes you wise. Like one born dada. But they weren't just stories, even if they sounded like they were. It's real!"

I laughed at my mother's babbling and watched the street glow lilies that lined the road whoosh by.

"So you first met this other Windseeker in the Dark Market?" my father asked again.

"Yes."

"That was why you were there that day," my mother said with a nod. "Now I understand."

"You should have come to us, Zahrah," my father said solemnly. He rubbed his forehead.

"I know," I said with a sigh. I knew this with all my heart.

"Well, everything happens for a reason," my mother said softly. "Let's just hope there's no reason for anything like this to ever happen again."

And let's hope the antidote works, I thought. Seven minutes later, as we walked into the hospital, I was chewing on my lip. I couldn't wait to see Dari. He needed me and I had been away for too long. He certainly must have been aware of my not being there. *Maybe he's even angry,* I thought.

"Dari is stable," my father said. "There's a nurse who exercises his legs and arms. He's . . . he's OK."

Dari's parents were already there waiting for us. Dari's mother's Afro was smashed to one side, and her dark brown lip polish was only on the lower lip. Dari's father still had sleep crusts in the sides of his eyes, and his shirt was inside out. Both of them were breathing hard and had wild, desperate looks on their faces. They stared at me as if I were from another world. I didn't mind because I felt like I was.

Visiting time for patients had ended hours earlier, but this was a special occasion.

"Is this her?" the doctor said, running up to me. I remembered this doctor from the time I had been there weeks earlier. "Oh yes, it is! *Unbelievable!*"

Before I knew it, three other doctors surrounded me. They reminded me of a flock of birds with their chatter and movement. I hoped they wouldn't get caught in my hair. I quickly handed them the elgort egg, and their interest immediately shifted from me to the egg. Then they were gone.

"We'll be back shortly. We must mix the solution to inject into the patient," one of the doctors said over his shoulder.

"My goodness, look at it," I heard one of the other doctors say. "If it works, we'll have more than enough to store for other patients *and* to study!"

"Wow," my father said with a chuckle. "They sure were anxious. But it's the first elgort egg they've ever handled, and they're scientists, so I understand."

I still thought their behavior strange.

That done, I focused on seeing Dari. We quickly walked to his room, and my eyes immediately went to him. His parents stood aside, each patting my shoulder as I passed.

A large, bulbous plant grew from the wall above Dari's head. Several of its stems were attached to Dari's arms and forehead. The plant bloomed blue flowers near the top, and the part of its pod closest to Dari pulsated to the rhythm of his breathing. Air softly blew out of a small flower to a steady rhythm, making a whistling sound each time.

Dari was as he had been when I left: asleep and unsmiling. He lay in his bed in blue pajamas, his rough hair shaven close as it always was. His soft lips were slightly parted, his long legs hidden under tan covers. I desperately wanted to see his big brown eyes. I wanted to cry, but instead I sat on the bed and rested my head on his chest. He wore the leaf-shaped luck charm around his neck. I closed my eyes and listened to his heartbeat. I don't know how long I stayed like that. I must have fallen asleep.

I heard someone enter the room and when I opened my eyes, my muscles were stiff.

"Zahrah," I heard my mother say near my ear. Both sets of parents had left the room to let me be with my friend. Now they were back. "Zahrah, the doctor is here."

I quickly shook myself into complete wakefulness and

stood straight, looking around. The lights in the hospital room had been turned up, and three doctors were standing in green doctors' coats and holding clipboards.

"OK," one of the doctors said breathlessly. She held a large blue inocula fly between her fingers. It buzzed impatiently. "This is it."

She stepped forward and I stepped back. The doctor looked at me.

"Can I talk to you after this?" she asked.

I nodded.

"Let's do this then," the doctor said. "Zahrah, open the window screen, please."

My legs felt rubbery as I walked over and opened it. Then I went and stood with the parents. The two other doctors stood by, observing. I had no idea what to expect. The doctor wiped a place on Dari's arm with a cotton swab that was wet with a white liquid. Then she turned to all of us and said, "I'm going to let this inocula fly go. It has already engorged its stinger with elgort egg serum. It'll go right for the spot I just swabbed with the sugar paste. Then the fly will inject the elgort egg serum into his arm. The serum might take a few minutes to circulate into his bloodstream."

We all nodded. I just wanted her to get on with it. It was the moment of truth. Would it work? Was it too late? Was the antidote in the book a lie? And what if there was an earthquake and the shaking room confused the inocula fly into stinging someone else? *Get on with it, lady,* I thought. The doctor opened her fingers and the inocula fly flew off. It zoomed about the room for a moment and then smelled the sugar paste that the doctor had swabbed on Dari's arm. It buzzed and dived, embedding its sharp, thin stinger into Dari's arm and injecting the serum. When it was finished, it pulled out its stinger and flew out the window. Then I closed the screen.

We all held our breath. Five minutes passed and nothing happened. Ten minutes went by and still Dari lay there. After twenty minutes, the doctor turned to us with a sad look.

"We'll give him time," she said quietly.

I sighed, and Dari's mother put her arm around my shoulder.

"You've done well," she said. I hugged her back.

"You've done impossibly well," Dari's father said. He shook his head. "You . . . you're amazing."

I looked at my feet, feeling embarrassed and gloomy under all the attention. I had done the impossible, but Dari was still asleep. It wasn't over. I hadn't succeeded. I pushed the thought of all my trouble coming to nothing out of my head.

"She's amazing, but she'd better not do anything like that ever again," my mother said.

"I know," I said. "We shouldn't have been playing in the jungle in the first place." Although in my heart I knew that if I were to learn of some other substance in the jungle that would wake Dari up, I'd go get it.

"What were you two doing in there anyway?" Dari's mother asked.

I didn't know how to answer. I didn't want to tell Dari's parents about my ability. At least not yet. Luckily, I didn't have to.

"You know what they were doing," Dari's father said. "Ever since he got that silly book from the library, Dari's been obsessed with that jungle. He's always been an adventurer at heart."

Dari's mother nodded. "Yes, infatuated with places he shouldn't go."

"Lesson learned?" my father asked.

I nodded. Hopefully the lesson hadn't cost me the life of my best friend.

A cot was brought into Dari's room, and I was allowed to spend the night there. Though I was exhausted, I didn't sleep. I couldn't. I was still jittery from the fact that I'd made it home and worried that it had all been in vain. And on some odd level, I missed the Forbidden Greeny Jungle. The noise, the unpredictability, the creatures and plants.

And then there was the presence of Dari. I didn't realize how much I missed him until our parents left and it became so quiet that all I could hear was his breathing and the rhythmic whistling of his flora support system. He was there but he wasn't. I wondered what he was dreaming of, for I was sure he was dreaming. His eyes moved frantically behind his eyelids. For a while I paced the room. A netevision screen was growing near the ceiling, but I had no urge to watch or surf it. My taste for anything technological seemed to be dwindling.

I walked to the window. The screen prevented insects attracted to the light from entering. Rhythm beetles would be attracted to the whistle of the support system monitoring Dari's heart rate. But I wouldn't have minded if the insects had come in. I was used to them, and maybe I would even welcome them now. I turned and looked at Dari. Still asleep. I went to my bag of overnight things and brought out the digi-book. It was the closest I could be to both the jungle and Dari at the same time. At first it wouldn't turn on and I rolled my eyes.

"Come on, you stupid thing," I said, smacking it very hard on the side and shaking it. With the third whack, it came on. I clicked to the end of the book, out of curiosity.

So you've reached the end of the book. We're so proud of you, though we don't believe you've read the whole thing. It would take years. But that's fine. We don't suggest you read this book straight through as you would an adventure or suspense novel. This book is meant for you to jump around in. It's a reference guide. Look up what you need.

Anyway, since you have turned to the end, we'll humor you and pretend you've finished. We hope you've been convinced of how stupid and ignorant most of our people are. It's a shame. We live right on the border of such an amazing place, and yet we choose to stay where we are. No optimism. No curiosity. No wish to move forward, to expand ourselves, our horizons. But you, reader, are now properly informed. Even if you never go into the jungle, we trust that you will walk out your door and inform the rest of the world; for what good is knowledge if it's not shared?

Now, there are several not-for-profit organizations you can join to fight ignorance at

I clicked backward to the index and looked up "Greeny Gorilla."

Greeny Gorillas, *Gorilla intelligentus:* The true carriers of knowledge of Ginen. Large anthropoid apes known for their love and connection to nature. Out of respect, since they *are* smarter than us humans, we will refer to them as people. These men and women and children are remarkable, but we will get to that. Up until old age, gorillas of the Forbidden Greeny Jungle have black fur. The old ones have gray fur and then white. The Greeny Gorillas are not like the gorillas found closer to the Ooni Kingdom.

It seems the closer gorillas live to human beings, the more like humans they are. The gorillas deep in the jungle hate technology with a great intensity. Though human beings of Ooni have successfully married technology and plants, the gorillas of the jungle believe humans are lazy and create nothing but extra stress.

"Told you that book was good."

I froze, my eyes wide. Then I looked up.

"Dari?!"

"Down with ignorance," he said weakly.

I jumped up and threw my arms around him.

"Dari!" I shouted. "Oh thank Joukoujou! I thought it was too late!!"

"Hey," Dari said. "Enough with the hugging." But he didn't push me away. We stayed like that for several moments, Dari's head resting on my shoulder.

I stood up and looked at him. He may have been tired, but his eyes . . . oh, his eyes were as bright as could be!

"Goodness," Dari said, stretching his legs and arms. "I

feel terrible." Then he paused and a look of shock crossed his face as he realized where he was and it all came back to him. "The war snake . . . I'm back! I'm awake!"

I grinned.

"I'm alive . . . I remember —" He paused again and looked at me. "How? I read in the book . . . elgort egg."

I nodded vigorously.

"You?" he asked pointing at me.

"Yep," I said proudly.

"You?" he asked again.

"I went!"

Despite his fatigue, Dari threw his head back and laughed hard.

"You *went*!?" he asked, his eyes wide.

I nodded.

"Alone???"

I nodded.

"You saw?"

I nodded even harder.

Then Dari stopped asking questions and really looked at me for the first time. He later told me that in those moments he noticed that I'd lost some weight and my cheekbones stood out a little more. My hands, which used to be soft, were rough. There were several scratches on my face. I wore a blue, long-sleeved flowing dress so he could not see my arms and legs. But he had a feeling I had more scratches there, too. Most striking, he said, was the warmth radiating from me that hadn't been there before.

He slowly reached out and plucked at the green neck-lace around my neck.

"It was a gift," I said.

Dari paused for a moment with a frown.

"From who? Someone I know??"

"The chief of the Greeny Gorillas," I said with a smirk. "It's a destiny necklace."

The frown smoothed from Dari's brow and he lay back, still looking at me.

"I can finally really hear you," he said weakly. His fatigue was increasing.

"What do you mean?"

"You speak louder now," he said, slightly slurring his words.

"I should get the nurse," I said, seeing his eyes droop. *I should have called a nurse right away*, I thought. Dari didn't answer me. I ran out of the hospital room looking for the nurse. The nurse called the doctors and our parents, and there were many more hugs and tears. Dari had fallen back asleep, but this time it was a shallow, normal sleep.

The next morning, Dari was awake and feeling closer to his normal self. I hadn't left his side. All he wanted to do was talk. We sat for hours as I recounted most of my story. I had just got to the part before I flew for the first time when our parents arrived. The doctor came in a few minutes later to examine him.

"I'll finish later," I told him. Dari was still annoyed at having the story interrupted at the best part.

After an examination, the doctor told him that he had fully recovered from the snake poison.

"You have the best friend anyone could ask for," she said, patting me on the head.

"We'll have to keep you here for one more night to make sure all is well," the doctor told Dari.

"Could I stay here tonight, then?" I asked.

The doctor smiled. "Actually I was going to suggest that. There's a mob of reporters waiting for you outside the hospital. Don't worry, we're not allowing them inside. You've become quite a celebrity."

CHAPTER 27

CELEBRATED CELEBRITIES

"Ready?" I asked the next morning, holding a blue travel sack filled with his clothes.

Dari stretched his back and arms. He looked like his old self now in his long green pants and green caftan.

"As ready as I'll ever be," Dari said.

We walked out of the hospital standing close together; on one side were our fathers and on the other side, our mothers. Our clothes were wrinkled and weeks out of style. The newspaper reporters scrambled all over each other to get close to us. Dari and I were told not to answer any questions. Photosynth cameras shot blue flashes at us from left and right, warming our skin. The photojournalists wanted to get a picture of "the miracle" and the "miracle worker."

"Miss Tsami," one reporter shouted at me, "what was it like in the forbidden jungle?"

"Zahrah! Have you been given a thorough checkup?" another screeched. "Are you sure you are free of all exotic diseases?"

"Look at your clothes! Was the experience so horrible that you both forgot how to dress?"

"How are you feeling?"

"Dari, did the elgort serum burn when the inocula fly injected it?"

"What kind of parents are you? Didn't you teach your children that the jungle is forbidden?"

"Did you have to kill the elgort whose egg you took?"

"Did any birds get caught in your hair?"

"Dari, is Zahrah your girlfriend?"

"Now will you finally cut your horrible dada hair?"

By the time we got into the car, I was almost crying. All the questions. *How do they know so much but yet so little?* I wondered. Dari was sweating, resting his head against the window.

"We've agreed to do an interview only with the *Kirki Times* and the *Ooni Tribune*," my father told us. "They're the most honest publications. Is that all right?"

Both Dari and I nodded. We wouldn't be left alone until we had told our story. Plus I wanted to tell the world what I'd been through, and Dari wanted to use the chance to chat about why the forbidden jungle shouldn't be forbidden. Of course, neither of us was going to say a thing about my ability. I planned to say I had simply walked back.

Dari and I were on the front page of all northern and several national newspapers for one day and in the features section for many more. They couldn't get enough of my "incredible story" and "act of bravery." Dari's parents decided to let Dari talk to the journalists of many of the more broad-minded publications that insisted on speaking with him. Dari's radical ideas coupled with my tales of adventure sparked several heated and fruitful debates about the Forbidden Greeny Jungle.

Papa Grip held a grand ceremony, and the whole town showed up. It was a warm, humid day, though it didn't rain. To open the ceremony, Papa Grip led a great dance. Not surprisingly, he wore a glorious hot pink caftan that went all the way to his feet, and his fellow dancers wore pink pants and shirts. I, who sat onstage with Dari, laughed and clapped loudly. Afterward, he asked me to stand up.

"This girl," Papa Grip said to the quiet audience. "This girl used to be so disturbed by how she was born. Her parents called me one day to cheer her up. 'Why can't I just look like everyone else,' she said. 'I'd rather just blend in.' So sad she was. I told her that we all are who we are and should never try to be what we're not."

He paused, looking out at the audience. I looked up at

Papa Grip, my chest tightening with pride. The entire town was listening, including those who had harassed me in school. I hoped they were listening hard. I was no better than they were, but I was no worse either.

"Zahrah, by now I'm sure your parents have told you enough times: Going into that jungle was *crazy*. But your reason was extremely noble, and you righted your wrong by surviving and shocked us all by bringing back that egg and saving your friend. And so, I award you this Medal of Honor, Prestige, and Excellence."

I bit my lip as I bent my head so Papa Grip could slip it on. The white medal was solid nyocha, mined directly from the metal-producing tree. Then I stood tall while everyone jumped from his or her seat clapping and whistling vigorously. I could see my parents and Dari's parents in front. Papa Grip motioned for Dari to join me, and the applause roared louder.

And it didn't stop with the ceremony. I was later thanked in the medical files for supplying Ooni's first elgort egg. Since then, researchers have found that not only does the elgort egg reverse war-snake venom but it also contains hundreds of other healing properties!

Also, just after my return, a group of scientists decided to actually venture into the jungle for research! Since then, they have discovered three plants with amazing medicinal value and two animals with strange skills, which they are documenting. Dari and I know that this is just the beginning of what they will find. Not surprisingly, however, a few have fallen terribly sick and had to return to Ooni. None have died yet, though. But it's the Greeny Jungle, and such things are bound to happen.

Last, the frog was right; in the forest I became Zahrah the Windseeker, a legend, growing bigger and more impossible each time my story was told.

CHAPTER 28

RENEW

A month later, Dari and I stood at the entrance of the library with most of the dry season ahead of us. Since waking from his coma, Dari's obsession with the Forbidden Greeny Jungle had multiplied. And with me now as obsessed as he was, we fed off each other.

The first week, we stayed at each other's homes, talking all day. Dari wanted to hear about every single detail of my travels. And then he wanted to hear it again. Then he wanted to write it down. We consulted the field guide. And I pointed out where it didn't get something right or where it missed information.

"The elgort isn't all irrational," I said. "When I took the egg, she was terribly angry with me. But she went to check her nest instead of coming after me. She could have followed me from below. But she was more concerned with her babies than eating me, and that's *not* irrational behavior at all. It's motherly."

Then there was my ability. Other than my parents, Dari was the only person who knew of it. And he loved it.

"Just fly a little higher," he'd say as I showed off my ability behind his house.

"Dari, if someone sees me flying—"

"No one will see," he'd say. "You're not flying that high, anyway."

It would be another two weeks before we finally got the nerve to sneak back to the Forbidden Greeny Jungle, where I would fly way above the trees and Dari would almost faint with joy as he imagined being able to fly as I did.

Eventually we decided to see what other information about places outside of Ooni we could find in the library. Dari was especially interested in finding out about the mythical world of Earth, which he didn't think was so mythical.

My mother dropped us off. Several of the children and adults going in and out of the library slowed down to look at us. It was always like that. I heard someone tell his friend, "She's the one who went beyond."

I wanted to laugh. Most people still viewed the jungle as a forbidden place, even after all our talk with the newspapers. Old habits are hard to break, I guess.

"She's dada," people said. "Maybe *she's* allowed to pass through, but I know I'm not. Remember how the rescue team got attacked by those dogs? And that one scientist is still in the hospital."

It drove Dari mad.

"Ignorance is bliss," he said to me. "More like, ignorance is ignorance! It was just a bunch of dogs! They have wild dogs in many places besides the Greeny Jungle!"

Before we went into the library to look for new books, Dari said, "Wait, we have to return the field guide. It's way overdue, you know."

He took the digi-book out of his backpack.

I didn't want to see it go. Though the thing was extremely faulty and I knew a lot of its information, I still hadn't read it from beginning to end. Dari hadn't read it all either. And the book *had* basically saved both our lives. When I turned to Dari, I saw that he was thinking the same thing.

We both looked at the book and laughed.

"Can I renew this?" he asked the librarian. "I know it's overdue but . . ." He shrugged.

It was the same librarian who had checked the book out for him before. She grinned at us as if we were superstars.

"Oh this old thing," she said. "The library's decided to give it to you two as a gift. We've just bought five new copies, and all of them are checked out!"

CHAPTER 29

WINDSEEKERS

This time we asked our parents for permission to go to the
Dark Market. It was a sunny Saturday afternoon.

"Please, just trust us this time," Dari said to his parents. I stood behind him, quiet.

Dari's parents looked at each other, thought about it
for a moment, and then finally nodded.

"OK, Dari," his father said. "We're going to trust you,
as we did before when you were sneaking into the jungle.
Don't disappoint us this time."

"We want to find the Windseeker lady I told you
about," I told them. "I want to thank her for coming after
me and apologize for sneaking off. I just want to talk to
her, see her again."

We were thankful when my parents also agreed to let us go.

We both wore green as we moved swiftly through the market. Dari wore his long pants and caftan, and I wore a plain long green dress with mirrors in the hem. Neither of us wore the civilized clothes of the day, but neither of us really cared about that anymore. It was just another way that we would always be different from the northerners around us. Heads turned as we passed. People also recognized our faces from the newspapers, netevision, and e-magazines. I knew where to find Nsibidi. My sense of direction had improved with my flying skills. Still, Nsibidi found us first.

"Zahrah!" Nsibidi called over the crowd at the entrance of the Dark Market. As always, she wore a long yellow dress, this one made of tiny yellow beads. She must have got it from the southwest.

Many people looked up when they heard my name. Dari rolled his eyes and smiled.

"Nsibidi!" I called, running around several people.

"Sneaky girl," she said, grabbing me in her long arms and hugging me tightly. Nsibidi looked up and pulled Dari into our hug. "You, too. Come here."

Then Nsibidi held us out so she could get a good look at us. She laughed.

"You both glow with experience," she said. I nodded. "You've been through your own transitions."

"Yes, we have," I said.

"Where are the idiok?" Dari asked, looking past Nsibidi into the Dark Market.

"They're in their usual place," Nsibidi said. "We just finished with five customers. Obax said you two were on your way, and I wanted to meet you before you entered the Dark Market. I don't want to get you two into any more trouble."

"Don't worry," I said. "We asked for permission this time."

Nsibidi touched one of the scratches on my cheek. She sighed and held her chest, and then she smiled mischievously.

"So, Zahrah, tell me, just how were you able to travel over three hundred miles in three days? Hmm?"

I smiled sheepishly and looked at my feet. I didn't want to say anything in case people were listening. The market was always full of ears.

"And you, Dari," Nsibidi said. "You're quite the radical activist."

"*And* I know what I'm talking about, too," Dari said. "I've been studying this stuff for years!"

"Feisty," Nsibidi said. "You keep being curious, Dari. It'll lead you to great places."

Dari smirked proudly.

"Nsibidi," I said. "I just wanted to—"

She held up her hand.

"Hold that thought," she said. "Let me go tell the idiok that I will be gone for twenty minutes. Meet me outside the market, next to the iroko tree."

Dari and I went to the tree immediately. It was far enough from the main road leading to the market that we had a little privacy. Not far away, a few families, who were also looking for some peace and quiet, sat on blankets, eating lunch.

Dari and I sat close together, basking in the sunlight like lizards. Dari glanced over at me. I was staring at the sky and could see him with my peripheral vision. He looked at my hand and slowly grasped it. I turned to him with a questioning look. He took a deep breath and spoke.

"You're . . . you're the best friend I've ever had," Dari said quietly. "I . . . well, I want to thank you for saving my life."

"Oh Dari, you don't have to thank me, it's a given," I said, squeezing his hand.

"But I wanted to say it anyway," he said.

"Well, you're very welcome, then," I said.

We stared into each other's eyes for a long time. My belly fluttered, and Dari's hand felt very warm over my hand.

Then a shadow fell over us and we quickly let go.

"Did I come at a bad time?" Nsibidi asked.

We shook our heads. Nsibidi smirked, and we both felt embarrassed and looked away. She sat down across from us, wrapping her long arms around her long legs. She looked at us for a moment and then said, "I didn't believe you could do it, Zahrah. When I found you, you had that wild look in your eye. Something had awakened in you. That day when Dari's mother caught you two in the Dark Market, the idiok told me. They said you two would venture into the jungle, Dari would get bitten, and you would go into the jungle for that egg. It was destiny, and, well, one of the first things I learned from the idiok was that destiny should never be purposely tampered with.

"For a while, I obeyed. But with Dari in that coma and then when you went into that jungle, that was enough. I just couldn't bring myself to let destiny play itself out. I didn't believe you'd make it, Zahrah. It was too far-fetched! And I felt as if this whole situation were my fault. I was the one who told you to practice."

"It wasn't," Dari said. "It was *our* idea to go to the jungle. Not your fault at all!"

I nodded vigorously. "Please, don't apologize for anything."

Nsibidi patted Dari's leg and took my hands in hers, her face full of emotion.

"I looked for you," she said quietly. "I'd finally found

you. Vowed not to lose you again. Then I woke up and you were gone! All that next day, I searched frantically with no success. You'd gone off the trail. I was so sure I'd failed you a second time."

"No," I pleaded. "Nsibidi, you didn't—"

"I remembered you as the timid girl I had met in the Dark Market. I knew you'd changed, but I underestimated just how much," Nsibidi said, shaking her head and looking at me with a perplexed smile. "I eventually had to return home." She paused. "Destiny will always have its way."

She sighed and the three of us were quiet a moment.

"So . . ." I hesitated to ask the question I'd wanted to ask for a long time. "You know the Forbidden Greeny Jungle, don't you? You *knew* it when you were searching for me?"

"Yes, it's tame compared to where I grew up. It's funny, the attitude Ooni people have. I've never seen such a fear of the unknown," Nsibidi said.

I nodded. "Dari and I have learned better."

Dari sat up straighter.

"Since you're not going to just ask it, Zahrah, I will," Dari said. "Where—"

"No," I said, holding my hand up. "OK, I'll ask, Dari."

Dari's eyebrows went up but he said nothing.

I turned to Nsibidi.

"Where *are* you from?"

"Ah, so the question finally comes out," Nsibidi said. "You ready for this?"

We both nodded.

"You comfortable?"

We nodded again.

"Good. I will tell you, but I'd like you to keep it between us," she said. "Kirki isn't ready to know so much about me."

"We're good at keeping secrets," I said.

"It's why we got into all this trouble to begin with," Dari said.

Nsibidi smiled.

"I'm glad to have met you two," Nsibidi said. She paused and looked at the sky. The tattoo just below her neck looked lovely in the sunlight. Nsibidi settled her eyes on Dari and me and said, "I was born and raised very far from here, way beyond the Greeny Jungle, where the trees grow twice as high and some of them grow flat and wide. This was where my parents settled after years and years of traveling."

"My family and I lived alone; I grew up knowing no other humans. The idiok's young were our playmates. They taught us their form of language and their culture.

"When I grew up, I left home. Zahrah, you must know that once a Windseeker learns to fly, he or she is plagued by wanderlust. Rarely do we stay where we were born and raised."

I felt Dari looking at me strangely, but I didn't want to look at him. Still, without looking at him, I could read his mind. I frowned. Why would my best friend think I'd ever leave him and my family?

"It's in our nature to travel and explore, to see and learn," Nsibidi continued. "I wanted to see where my father and mother were born. My father, his name is Ruwan, he's from Kebana."

"That town's only a few minutes from here," I said.

"Hmm. But my mother, Arrö-yo," Nsibidi said, her eyes turning to slits, a sly smile on her face, "she is from Earth."

"Earth!?" Dari shouted.

"It's real?" I asked, clasping my hand over my mouth.

"You think you're the only one who has traveled far?" Nsibidi asked playfully.

"So have you been there, too?" Dari asked with wide eyes.

Nsibidi only gave a knowing look that said, "We'll save that story for another time."

She reached forward. "I see you still have my luck charm."

Dari nodded. "It definitely gave me luck."

"The idiok wanted you to have it. Your personal spirit told them that you needed to be protected in some way. These charms are blessed by the Mami Wata Mambos."

Dari and I looked at each other and grinned.

"Just looking at you two tickles me. You have so much to learn." She motioned around us with her big hands and long arms. "There is more than this place. This Ooni Kingdom. I knew this, but both of you didn't. You had to learn the truth the hard way."

Dari and I nodded vigorously, trying to digest Nsibidi's words.

"So I see that you two have run out of questions for me," Nsibidi said after several moments. "Well, I've got one question for you, Zahrah. It's really a request. I want to see you fly. Not here, somewhere more private."

"OK," I said, thinking that maybe Nsibidi could give me some tips, since she *was* far more experienced.

"And Dari, you must tell me more about your politics."

"My pleasure," he said.

Nsibidi stood up. "Time for me to get back to work. Give me your netmail addresses and we will set up a time and place to meet again. No more going into the Dark Market for you two, at least for a little while."

Dari and I wrote our netmail addresses on the piece of paper Nsibidi handed to us.

"I'll be in touch."

And with that, Nsibidi returned to the Dark Market.

"Wow," I said when she was gone.

"Doesn't it feel weird?" he said.

"Yeah," I said, staring straight ahead. I felt as if my

world were expanding. I'd felt that way since I returned from the Greeny Jungle. As if nothing was what it seemed anymore. "And the strangest thing about it is that it seems as if no one else is aware of it at all."

"No one is, really," Dari said. "Except Nsibidi and probably a few other people."

We sat quietly for another fifteen minutes, each of us thinking about different but similar things.

"I want to learn about Earth," I said with wide eyes.

Dari sighed loudly but smiled. "Me, too. Today let's just go and sit in our usual tree and watch the sunset."

"OK, but don't expect me to sit on the lowest branch anymore."